PENGUIN BOOKS

Cumbria
County
Libraries, bo

D0784966

SEATON

05

Also in the Assassin's Creed® series

Assassin's Creed®
ORIGINS
Desert Oath

OLIVER BOWDEN

UBISOFT®   PENGUIN BOOKS

PENGUIN BOOKS

UK | USA | Canada | Ireland | Australia
India | New Zealand | South Africa

Penguin Books is part of the Penguin Random House group of companies
whose addresses can be found at global.penguinrandomhouse.com.

First published 2017
001

Set in 12.5/14.75 pt Garamond MT Std
Typeset by Jouve (UK), Milton Keynes
Printed in Great Britain by Clays Ltd, St Ives plc

A CIP catalogue record for this book is available from the British Library

B FORMAT PAPERBACK: 978–1–405–93506–7
A FORMAT PAPERBACK: 978–1–405–93507–4
ROYAL FORMAT PAPERBACK: 978–1–405–93535–7

www.greenpenguin.co.uk

PART I

I

The desert was empty but for a dilapidated flat-roofed huntsman's shelter that interrupted the horizon like a single rotting tooth. *That will do*, thought Emsaf. He tethered his horse in the shade of the shelter, then stepped into the cool interior, grateful for thick mud walls that deflected the worst of the heat.

Inside, he uncovered his head and took stock of his surroundings. Not a place in which he'd care to spend much time, of course – it was bare and dank-smelling – but even so, it was ideal for what he had in mind.

And what he had in mind was death.

He laid his bow down, placed an arrow from the quiver beside it and then turned his attention to a small window looking out on to the plain beyond. He squinted for a moment or so, studying various angles, before kneeling, trying out different lines of sight, and then reaching for the bow, notching an arrow and rehearsing his aim.

Satisfied, he placed the weapon on the ground and then ate the last of the melon he'd bought at the market in Ipou before settling to wait for his prey to appear.

And as he waited, Emsaf's thoughts went back to the family he had left behind in Hebenou, a separation occasioned by a letter he had received from Djerty. Its contents had proved so disturbing to Emsaf that he'd begun to pack at once.

'There is something I must do,' was all he would tell his wife and son, 'something that cannot wait. I will return as soon as I am able. I promise.'

He told Merti he'd be away for several weeks, months even, and that she was to take care of the planting and trampling while he was gone. He'd tasked Ebe, who was just seven years old, with looking after the geese and ducks, making the boy promise to help his mother with the cattle and pigs, and he had every confidence Ebe would do just that, because he was a good boy, devoted to his parents and diligent in the execution of his chores.

Tears had shone in their eyes and Emsaf found it a struggle to maintain his own composure, his heart weighing heavy in his chest as he mounted his horse. 'You'll look after your mother, boy,' he told Ebe, pretending to flick dust from his eye.

'I will, Papa,' replied Ebe, a tremor in his bottom lip. Emsaf and Merti exchanged a heartbreaking smile. They had all known this day might arrive but, even so, it came as a shock.

'Say a prayer to the gods for me. Ask them to keep us safe until my return,' said Emsaf, and with that he turned his horse and headed south-west, glancing behind him just once to see his family watch him leave, the act of departure like a knife in his heart.

He had estimated it to be a twelve-day journey from north of Hebenou to his destination. With him he took the bare essentials and he rode by night, using the moon and stars to navigate. In the daytime he rested his mount and slept, staying out of the treacherous burning sun in the shade of a leafy terebinth or in shacks.

One early evening, he had risen when the sun was still up and scanned the horizon with a practised eye. There in the distance, almost invisible, was a slight disruption in the heat haze that lay like silt across the horizon line. He made a mental note but thought little more of it. The next day, however, he made sure to rise at the same time and there in the band of light on the horizon, in the same place as the day before, was a pockmark. No doubt about it, he was being followed. What's more, whoever was tracking him knew their business. He was obviously keeping the distance between them constant.

Testing his theory risked alerting his pursuer, but he had to do it. He slowed his pace. The heat signature remained constant. He travelled during the day, braving the searing sun. The follower must have done the same. One night he galloped, pushing his horse as hard as he dared. The one who was tracking him saw, anticipated and did likewise.

There was only one thing for it. He had to abandon his mission, at least temporarily, until he could do something about whoever was stalking him. When had his pursuer picked up his trail? An experienced scout himself, Emsaf had been cautious.

Right, he thought. *Let's think about this.* He had spotted his ghost on the fifth day of his travels, which was encouraging, because it meant that Merti and Ebe were safe. As long as whoever it was stayed well away from his home, that was good. What he needed to do now was try to flush out his stalker.

Not far outside Ipou, Emsaf came upon a settlement. Traders had set up stalls and were selling oils, cloth, lentils and beans in tall jars. Many were passing through, and he managed to find one going in the direction of Thebes, offering him coin to deliver a message, with the assurance of more when the job was done. Emsaf bought provisions but didn't linger long. Passing farmers and oxen made him think of Merti and Ebe with a pang of homesickness. He found a crossing and traversed the Nile to the Western Desert, drawing his pursuer, planning his next move.

Two nights later he had come across the huntsman's shelter on the plain, and decided it was the ideal spot to lie in wait.

And sure enough, now his target came into view – a lone figure on horseback in the distance, emerging from the heat haze. Emsaf thanked the gods the sun was at his back and notched the arrow, sighting the rider. He noted the same, now-familiar shape of the cape, the colouring of his horse.

It was time.

Emsaf took a long breath, keeping his quarry sighted, holding his aim for what felt like a long time. The bow needed to be loosed before his muscles shook and his aim was spoiled. He needed to end this now.

He opened the fingers of his right hand.

His arrow found its mark. In the distance the rider tumbled from his mount with a puff of dust and sand as he hit the ground. Emsaf notched another arrow and took aim, ready to fire a second time if needs be, watching the body for signs of life.

None came.

2

Two Weeks Earlier

The killer awoke at dawn, just before the rising sun streamed through the screens and put the white fire in his eyes. In a short while his house would be warm, but as he dressed and then pulled the shawl from his bed and wrapped it around himself, he noted that a crisp chill inhabited the silence.

In another room he prepared the last of his bread and fruit and ate slowly, deep in contemplation, clearing his mind for the task ahead. It had been a long time, but his mind and body were prepared – his blades were sharp.

When the meal was finished he made final preparations, consulting maps. A criss-cross of scars on the side of his face showed in the bronze mirror he used to apply kohl beneath his eyes to prevent the glare of the sun.

Would Iset, Horus and Anubis smile upon him, he wondered.

Time would tell.

Three days and nights he travelled before he came to the farmstead at Hebenou, a collection of buildings in the sand with fences for livestock and a line of washing that gleamed white. Confident he was hidden by the contours of the land, he stopped at a cluster of palm trees and tethered his mount in the shade of a tree. There he took a waterskin from his pack, checked the position of the sun and made sure to keep it at his back as he made his way forward, found a suitable dip in the desert and then dug himself in. He covered himself with the shawl and settled in to wait.

There. At the farmhouse. Movement. A figure was making his, no, *her* way to the sakia well. She carried a large bucket, and the killer's eyes narrowed as he saw how she walked, her motions economical, controlled. As he watched, she filled the vessel, rested it on the lip of the well and then stood with her hands on her hips for a while. Moments later she cupped her hands to her mouth, calling a name that carried on a light breeze.

Ebe!

His target's name was Emsaf, who was either elsewhere – in the town, tending to crops out of sight – or not at home at all. At the farmhouse a boy appeared. This was Ebe, no doubt. The killer watched as the two of them went to work, lifting another bucket from the lip of the well and then carrying them back to the farmhouse. They used smaller buckets to fill troughs for the animals. Goats bent their heads to drink. Out on the plain their watcher followed suit.

He remained in the dip until he was satisfied Emsaf was absent, just the woman and the boy inside the house, and then he scrambled to his haunches and set off at a sprint. He arrived at the farmhouse breathing hard, standing with his back to the mudbrick. Through a rear-facing window he heard the sounds of mother and child eating. He caught the word 'father'. In the mother's reply came the words 'soon be back'.

Now the killer closed his eyes to contemplate. This was a drawback – a minor one, but a drawback all the same. Had Emsaf been warned?

No. Not of his coming. If that were the case Emsaf would have stayed to protect his family. But given notice of something. Made haste in order to warn others, or set to a task maybe? He would find out when he caught up, he decided, dismissing the matter for now.

Time, now. Time was the thing. Time was his enemy.

He slipped off his sandals, the sand hot beneath his feet as he crept around the farmhouse, ducking low beneath windows until he came to the front entrance. There he took up position beside the door, flat to the wall, listening hard to judge the position of the boy to his mother. He took his knife from his belt and looped the leather thong that hung from its handle around his wrist.

Waiting. Counting the sound of footsteps.

Now.

He pushed aside the screen, stepped smartly inside, grabbed the woman from behind and held the knife to her throat, a short scuffle that was over in seconds.

On the other side of the room Ebe heard, turned

and saw a man with a scarred face holding a knife to his mother. The boy was scruffy-haired, his eyes wide with surprise and fear. He had a plate in one hand, a knife upon it, and his gaze skittered across the room.

'Nobody need be hurt,' said the killer. A lie. The woman's breathing hitched. 'Boy, put down the plate, get to your belly.'

'Don't do it, Ebe,' said the woman, her voice strained, determined.

'I'm not playing games,' he warned, and dug his blade into her flesh to make his point. Blood leaked from her wound and on to the killer's wrist.

'Put down the plate,' he repeated.

'Remember what Papa said,' gasped the woman. 'Run, Ebe. Take the window. You can outrun him. He'll have a horse. Find it and go.' Her hands rose to grasp at his arm, to steady herself.

The killer shook his head. 'Take a step and I'll open her throat. Now do as I've asked.'

What happened next was fast: Ebe's wrist flicking, the plate hurtling away to break on the stone. In his other hand bloomed the knife, blade between forefinger and thumb. A flick of the wrist and the knife spun towards the killer at the same time as the boy's mother made her move, twisting and sinking her teeth into her attacker's arm.

It was a good knife-throw but the killer jinked and the blade went nearly entirely clear, leaving barely a scratch on his shoulder The boy's mother jabbed him in the ribs with her elbow, once, twice. Solid, knowing hits. She had training as well. Now he had no choice but to deal with them both. He chose quickly, slitting her throat as she tried to hit him a third time, and then in the same back-and-forth motion tossed his dagger at the boy who was lunging forward, clearly intent on helping his mother fight him.

The boy was close. The killer's aim was true. Young Ebe clutched at his neck where the knife was embedded, blood spilling and then gushing from the wound as he sank to his knees, then lurched to the side. Mother and son died within feet of each other on the flagstones.

The killer tilted his head and stared at the blood as it inched into a pool between his two victims, mingling, slowly soaking into the dirt floor. His lips quirked, a brief, downward motion of annoyance. He'd meant to keep them alive long enough to question them. In choosing to fight, they had denied him this. In death they had won Emsaf time, perhaps even a chance at escape.

Bion sighed, frowning slightly. How contrary of them.

He picked up the trail, following Emsaf on the road to Ipou.

His quarry was skilled, no doubt about that. When caravans or merchants travelled through he followed in their footsteps; struck out in the wilderness when the only trail on the road would be his. But although he suspected he was being followed, it took him too long to confirm his suspicions and the killer had already anticipated his plan by the time he made it.

When, in the distance, he saw the huntsman's shelter but no sign of Emsaf, the killer knew a trap was being laid. It was the kind of trap he'd lay. That knowledge meant that Emsaf's fate was close to being sealed.

Close to fields, some distance from the river, he came upon a traveller riding a donkey laden down with vases. Far off in the distance he could guess at the silhouette of field workers, too far away to see what would happen next.

'Hello,' the traveller called cheerfully as the killer dismounted and approached, knife out of sight beneath his shawl. The traveller raised a hand to shade his eyes. 'And what can I do for y—' he began to say, a cordial, cheerful greeting that he never completed.

The killer led the donkey, unnerved by the smell of blood, still bearing the body of its dead owner back towards the shelter. In shade out of sight he transferred the corpse on to his own horse, using rope and clever knotwork that would release in the right conditions and the onset of death's stiffness to seat the man upright, finally casting his shawl over the cadaver and standing back to admire his handiwork.

Off they went, horse and dead rider, while the killer began a wide, outswinging journey around and behind the shelter. He watched from a distance as the corpse tumbled from the horse, Emsaf's arrow in its neck.

The trap was sprung.

A while later, Emsaf ducked out of the shelter and the killer, having approached from the back, was there waiting for him. He used his knife to sever his spinal column at the base of Emsaf's neck, leaving him able only to see and speak, and then crouched to address him.

'Where is the last of your kind?' he asked.

Emsaf stared up at him with knowing, grieving eyes and the killer felt irritation once more. The family was all cut from the same cloth, and he knew he was wasting his time. He slid the dagger into Emsaf's eye and then wiped it clean on his clothing. On the plain, vultures had begun to settle on the body of the traveller. He watched them idly, taking the moment to rest a bit before going on his way. Soon the birds would find Emsaf as well. Death and rebirth. A never-ending cycle.

Later, the killer found the medallion in Emsaf's belongings, and put it in his own pack.

The mission was done, for now.

Bion stretched and took a deep breath. He'd clean his weapons, get some rest and then report in. There he would get his next orders, a new kill to find, and the game would be afoot once more.

3

That day – the day our lives changed – we were sitting in our favourite spot, our backs against the warm stone of the outside of the Siwa fortress wall. I'd seen the lone rider shimmering on the horizon, but to be honest, I'd given him little thought. After all, he was little more than a speck in the distance, just another part of the day, like the water lapping the banks of the oasis beneath, or the people moving among the green of the plantations.

Besides, I was sitting with Aya and she was talking about Alexandria, as she often did, of how she would like to return there one day. As I listened I watched the horseman reach the shores of the oasis about to make his way into the village below.

'You should see it, Bayek,' she was saying, and I pictured it as she spoke. 'Alexandria is where the whole world meets, where every language under the sun is spoken on its streets, where Greeks and Egyptians walk together, where the Jews have their own temples even – and scholars from around the world come to study at the great Museum and Library. Will you go one day, do you think?'

I shrugged. 'Possibly. But my destiny lies here.'

There was a pause.

'I know,' she said sadly.

'You know what else Alexander did,' I said, to try and lighten the mood, 'besides creating his great city, I mean? He came here, to Siwa. He came to visit the Oracle at the Temple of Amun.'

In Siwa we had two temples. One was abandoned, but the other was like a small town-within-a-town: the Temple of Amun.

'How did he get here?' said Aya.

'Well,' I said, 'the story I prefer is that Alexander and his companions were in the desert, almost dying of thirst, when two serpents appeared to them and guided them out of the desert to Siwa.'

Aya chuckled. 'Or perhaps he just came here on a pilgrimage.'

'I prefer my version.'

'Ever the romantic. So, what happened while he was here?'

'He visited the Oracle. Now, nobody knows exactly what the Oracle said to Alexander, but he came away from the meeting convinced that he was the son of Amun, and he went on to be crowned Pharaoh at Memphis, as well as conquering many lands.'

'You think our Oracle was responsible for all that?'

'I like to believe so,' I said. 'The point is that our Oracle at Siwa is considered infallible, our Temple of Amun is known throughout the land . . .'

'And?'

'And it needs protecting.'

Her head dropped and dark hair fell in braids as she grinned. 'And so we get back to your destiny. Tell me something, Bayek, are you really *sure* you want to follow in your father's footsteps? Do you know it? Truly? Deep in your heart.'

Which was a good question.

'Of course,' I said.

We sat for a while in silence. 'I wish I could be more like you,' she said. 'More . . . *content*.'

'Don't you wish it were the other way round?' I said, testing. 'That I were more like you?'

The question hung. And that was how we sat for some moments more – until our friend Hepzefa came running along the path towards us.

'Bayek! Bayek!' he called, 'A messenger from Zawty has arrived.'

'What of it?' said Aya. She sat up, our afternoon well and truly disrupted.

'He came for Sabu,' said Hepzefa breathlessly.

'What do you mean?' I heard myself say.

'Sabu is about to depart,' huffed Hepzefa. 'Your father is leaving Siwa.'

In moments, the three of us had scrambled down from the fortress wall and made our way into the village, where residents appeared from within their homes, shielding their eyes and craning their necks to see up the lane.

They were looking in the direction of my home.

As we came on to the lane a woman saw me and whispered to her companion, who also looked in my direction and then quickly away again. Children ran past on their way up the hill, wanting to know what all the fuss was about. About to join the pilgrimage, I caught sight of a horseman riding against the tide and it hit me that the man I'd seen skirting the oasis was the messenger from Zawty. He was preoccupied, tucking what looked like a purse of coins into a leather satchel slung across his chest, so that when I burst forward and grabbed his horse he was almost unseated with the surprise. He cursed and rubbed at his chin.

'You leave my horse be,' he warned, fixing me with a pair of eyes the colour of lapis.

'You came with a message for my father, the township's protector. What did the message say?'

'If he's your father then I'm sure he'll tell you.'

I shook my head in frustration, trying another approach. 'Answer me this instead: who sent the message?'

The messenger pulled his horse from my grasp. 'You'll have to ask him that yourself also,' he said, and with that, he left.

Still the townsfolk made their way towards my house. From ahead a call went up for Rabiah and I knew why: she and my father were confidants, often to be found conversing in low voices away from eavesdropping ears. At town meetings the two of them always seemed to speak with one voice.

'Come on,' Hepzefa was saying, starting up the hill.

But even though he and Aya were about to make their way up, I hung back, sure my life was soon to change and wanting to delay that moment.

Aya turned and saw. She told Hepzefa to carry on and then came back to me, the last of the day's sun lighting her up so that she seemed to glow as she strode the few paces between us.

'Bayek,' she said gently, putting her arms to my shoulders, finding my eyes with hers. 'What is it?'

'I'm . . .' I started. 'I don't know.'

She nodded, understanding. 'Well, you never will unless you come and find out. Come on.'

She leaned forward, brushing my lips with hers. 'Be strong,' she whispered, and took my hand, as much to offer comfort as to lead me up the path and towards the home my father was preparing to quit.

4

The next morning I awoke to a feeling of melancholy that seemed to permeate the air in my room. And for a moment or so, fuzzily trying to navigate that period when the real world and the world of sleep are inseparably tangled, I lay wondering what was wrong, what in my world was so strange and different all of a sudden. Until . . .

I remembered.

It all came back.

I remembered my mother, standing with her arms folded in the dusk, her lips thinned so hard they were almost white, and her eyes afire. In the street outside our house, tethered, was my father's horse, his bags already slung over it, and just seeing them there had brought the news closer to home, the realization hitting me like a low punch.

When I looked at Aya she returned my gaze, eyes flecked with worry. Then my father had appeared, only to be brought up short by the sight of the townsfolk assembled there, shaking his head, continuing with his preparations. 'Ahmose,' he said, appealing to my mother. But if he was hoping for understanding there he received none.

Rabiah had arrived. She and my father had exchanged whispered words, none of which seemed to satisfy Rabiah, judging by the expression she wore. She and my mother were clearly of one mind. She was shaking her head, trying to impress something on my father, but whatever it was, he paid her no heed, refusing to speak to her in the privacy of our home, insisting he needed to leave at once.

Then he was ready. He kissed my mother and then took me in a fierce embrace, knocking the air out of me as he thumped my back goodbye.

He mounted his horse. The crowd quietened.

'You took an oath, Sabu,' said Rabiah, but there was a calmness about her, as though accepting the turn of events.

'I have taken many oaths, Rabiah,' he said.

'Who will protect Siwa now?' called a voice from the crowd.

'Without me here, you'll need a lot less protection,' he called back, and with that he drew his horse around and set off, choosing a path through the townsfolk and heading towards the oasis and away from Siwa.

I remembered the sound of his horse's hooves as he made his way down the path towards the plantations, townsfolk lining the route to watch him go, some of them trying to puzzle out what he'd said; I remembered trying to make sense of my feelings as he became a dot in the distance, but I couldn't do it then. As I lifted my head from the headrest and gazed around my room as though it were an unfamiliar place, I found I could not do it now, either.

Mother was already up. She'd taken a beaker of water to the back of our house, where young fig trees grew along the walls, their upper branches providing a canopy through which morning sun dappled the small courtyard. She sat with her legs drawn up, linen stretched across her knees, beaker held so loosely it looked in danger of dropping from her fingers. And though she smiled up at me as I arrived and took a seat beside her, her smile was a little wan, and I wondered how much sleep she'd had.

'He'll be back,' she said. 'Don't you worry about that.'

'And what about us?'

She gave a short dry laugh. 'Oh, life goes on. You just wait, we'll just be getting accustomed to life without him and he'll turn up again and throw us all into disarray.'

'Why did he leave, though?'

'I don't know,' she sighed. 'He wouldn't tell me. I saw worry in his eyes.'

'Was it something to do with Menna?'

Her gaze hardened with memory. She sank into her thoughts and I kept her company, letting her reflect. Finally, she shook her head.

'What difference if it was?'

'It would make sense, at least.'

'I see,' she said, and raised the beaker to her lips, then placed it to the step. 'Well, in that case you should probably go and see Rabiah.'

5

My father was the man who had defeated the tomb-robber Menna. Only the gods knew how much I'd had that particular fact drummed into me. By everyone in the village. Constantly.

Who was Menna? Good question. Some said that there was no such man; that 'Menna' was in fact several people, or simply the name of a highly organized gang of men who maintained the illusion of a sinister figure-head in order to spread fear.

Others said that Menna was indeed a living, breathing, flesh-and-blood person, but not in fact an active member of his own gang. They said he was a man grown fat and rich from the work of his minions and that he controlled his operation without once leaving the courtyards of his palatial home in Alexandria.

The most persistent rumour, and the one we talked of most on the streets of Siwa growing up, was that Menna *was* real, and that he ruled over his gang with a potent mix of fear and the promise of great riches in store. They said his teeth were taken from his victims, wired together, painted black and sharpened, and that they admirably performed their job of inspiring fear in all who set eyes upon him; that he was cruel and ruthless and worshipped no god but money. They said he would kill those he could not bribe and anyone who defied him – he would kill them and he would kill their families and hang their entrails in trees and their skinned corpses in public squares as a warning to those who defied him.

They said he was a demon, sent by the gods to punish the wicked, torment the innocent.

That's how evil he was.

Whatever the truth, Menna and his gang had stayed several steps ahead of the soldiers who were constantly in pursuit. Every now and then one of his men would be captured, tortured and burned alive in retribution, so that his body would be denied the journey into the afterlife, desecrated, just as he himself had desecrated so many burial grounds.

Not that it stopped them. The one unbribable official who had attempted to do so had failed, and then soon mysteriously died. No amount of intervention suppressed Menna's activities, and despite the torture visited upon his cohorts, none had ever revealed his identity or whereabouts. Everyone feared him.

I was much smaller, perhaps just ten years old, when Menna and his men were most active. When I first became aware of them they were little more than a story, a fable. They existed purely as a topic of conversation between my mother and father, and thus in my imagination late at night, when I lay in bed trying to sleep.

What I learned was that the gang had been moving throughout the north. They had been raiding pyramids, of course, but also casting their net wider. It was thanks to tomb-robbers like Menna that the pharaohs' architects had begun to add more traps and dead ends to their burial sites, which were like a burning beacon to those who made a living stealing possessions that the dead planned to take to the afterlife. Even the rich who were now buried in huge secret vaults, tombs built into rock, were not safe from his depredations. But his favourite targets were those less wealthy yet not poor, who would begin their passage to the next life in a necropolis, a burial ground situated close to a settlement. It was upon these that Menna preyed.

He had a method. Posing as traders, his gang would set up camp within striking distance of his target, but not too close. From there they would go to work infiltrating the local community and bribing officials, as well as surveying tombs, taking note of their tunnels and working on ways to avoid any traps that had been set.

His methods would change depending on the nature of the burial ground, but he was in the habit of breaking into tombs and simply taking everything away. That way, the thieves could just disappear quickly, and sort out the gold from the gimcrack later, in the safety of their lairs.

All of which, of course, had brought him to the attention of my father, who, as Siwa's protector – the town *mekety* – had made it his business to know when Menna and his gang were close.

And at that particular time, they were very close.

6

Rabiah wasn't home. I took a seat at the front of her house and settled down to wait, resenting every passing second, until at last I caught sight of her, ambling slowly up the path towards home with a basket of fruit from the market.

'I wondered if I might see you today,' she said, moving past with little in the way of warmth or greeting. I followed her inside without being asked, waiting as she cast off her cloak and set down her basket, and then submitting to her as she stood with her arms folded, appraising me for an uncomfortably long time.

A little older than my mother, Rabiah was nevertheless similar in temperament: neither was the type to mince their words ('I'm *direct*, and there's nothing wrong in that,' my mother used to say whenever my father chided her for plain-speaking) and they both had a habit of making you feel as though they could see right through you.

And right now, that was exactly how I felt.

'I see determination,' she said, when at last the inspection was over. 'That's good. That's what we like to see from the blood of the Siwa protector. Perhaps you hope to take up the mantle presently, do you, now that your father's gone?'

'Perhaps,' I said carefully, wondering what she was leading to.

'How close were you to doing so, do you think?' she asked. Her face was unreadable, eyes slightly hooded.

'I have learned a great deal from him – about the art of survival and combat.'

'Survival,' she said. 'Didn't you learn that from the Nubian?'

The Nubians had been camped on the outskirts of the township when I was younger. I'd been friends with a girl, Khensa, who, despite being younger than me, had taught me much about hunting and trapping. Later I discovered that Khensa had taught me these things at the behest of my mother, who considered the Nubians to be the very best in such matters.

'Yes,' I told Rabiah now. 'But when the Nubians left was when my father took over my training himself. Only he could tutor me in the ways of combat and protectorship.'

'Of course,' agreed Rabiah. 'And how has your training progressed?'

She fixed her gaze on me, and I felt as if she were able to see inside my head and read my thoughts, because it was true that for some reason my training had proceeded slowly, my father seemingly reluctant at every turn. Rabiah and my mother pushed and pushed for him to train me, yet each step was preceded by some variation of 'You're not ready yet, Bayek.'

Yes, I was aware that my training would take years – 'a lifetime, Bayek' was something else I heard a great deal – but even so: it felt to me as though from the age of six, when my training began, until now, at fifteen, I had made barely any progress at all.

And now it seemed Rabiah thought the same. 'Tell me,' she said, 'do *you* think that your training should have progressed further than it has?'

My head dropped. 'Yes,' I admitted.

'Quite,' she said, smiling. 'And why do you suppose your father hasn't taken you the full way? Why is your training so far from completion?'

'I would dearly like to know,' I told her. 'Is it something to do with my friendship with Aya?'

'*Friendship*,' she chuckled, 'that's a good one. Friendship. I've seen the two of you together, like limpets on the hull of a boat. What chance enlightenment in the ways of custodianship when it has young love to contend with, eh?'

I felt myself colour and Rabiah grinned, which only increased my discomfort. 'If he made you think it was about your friendship with Aya, he was trying to hide the real reason. I *know* this. There was something else, I am sure. Some other reason. Tell me, what do you remember of the night Menna struck?'

'So it *is* something to do with Menna?'

'My question first. What do you remember of that night?'

I looked at her. I had been only around six years old, but I still remembered every moment.

*

The night of the intrusion was still. A quiet night. I'd been lying in bed straining to overhear my parents talk. My father had been informed of unfamiliar faces appearing in town. Merchants, they said they were, but they traded precious little. He believed that these new faces were affiliated to the tomb-robbers, and that they'd set up camp somewhere in the desert outside the township, as was Menna's usual practice.

To me, such information was priceless. With the rumours of Menna's coming I was suddenly in great demand, my friends Hepzefa and Sennefer (but not Aya, who had yet to enter my life) badgering me for information on a daily basis: was it true that Menna planned to march on Siwa with an army of tomb robbers? Was it true that the points of his sharpened teeth were tipped with poison? I enjoyed the attention. Being the protector's son certainly had its advantages.

Even so, mine was a fitful sleep. In my dream I stood before rocks, looking into a cave, and inside I saw eyes gleaming, a flash of white teeth in the oppressive dark. A rat. And then another. And another. As I watched, the cave seemed to fill with a heaving, writhing oily mass of bodies. They crawled on top of one another, each one trying to rise to the top of the pile, the shape of them shifting and bulging, more and more eyes appearing in the darkness. The noise of them, that scratching, scuffling sound, seeming to increase in intensity until . . .

I was waking. Only the noise of the rats did not

disappear along with my dream. The noise was in the room with me.

It came from the window.

Now I jerked upright in bed. There was something out there, and at first I thought it might be a rat or . . . no, too big for a rat. Maybe a dog.

Then again, no. A dog didn't sound this way. A dog wasn't *stealthy*.

There was somebody out there. My eyes went to the screen at my bedroom window, and at first I thought it was moving in a breeze, but then I saw fingers. Knuckles. A hand carefully feeling its way inside.

Now I saw the face and upper body of a man as he eased himself through the aperture and into my room. His eyes gleamed evilly and between his teeth was a curved knife.

I scrambled out of bed as he drew himself up, and though my instinct was to run, and my brain was screaming at my legs to move, I couldn't make it happen, couldn't do anything – move, scream, shout, *anything* – and what prevented me from doing anything was fear.

The intruder had one crooked eye, wore a dark, dirty tunic and a striped cloak that reached down almost to the ground, flapping slightly in the breeze from the window. When he took the knife from between his teeth, he was grinning, but instead of the sharpened black wooden teeth I expected to see, his were normal – broken and dirty, but nothing like the deadly weapons my friends and I talked of in the streets of Siwa.

He put a finger to his lips to hush me, and still I wanted to run but my feet wouldn't move, and I stood rooted to the spot as he took a step into the room towards me, light dancing on the blade he held, the knife moving toward me, entrancing and hypnotizing me just as though it were a swaying, hooded cobra.

I opened my mouth. Or, to be more precise, I felt my mouth open, and knew I had taken a first important step, my mind telling me that if I could do that then surely I could force a scream.

If I could just overcome my fear.

He took another step closer. Finger still at his lips. From outside I heard the whispers and muffled foot-falls of more men arriving and I thought of my mother and father asleep in the other rooms and I knew the danger they were in.

And now, at last, I felt the scream bubbling up reach-ing my mouth, about to escape from my lips, when from behind me came my father's shout as he entered my room. 'I see!' he bellowed, 'So your master sought to silence me.'

The effect was instantaneous. The intruder reared back, the grin slipping from his face as he shouted, 'Strike!' and darted forward at the same time.

I turned and saw a second man appear in the doorway behind my father. 'Papa!' I called, and my father swung, meeting the new intruder with his sword, drawing first blood, a twist of the wrist proving fatal for his attacker. He dropped to one knee and span back to face front, blade arcing to parry an attack from the first intruder. Still rooted to the spot, I felt warm droplets of blood spatter my face.

My father was too quick for the crooked-eyed intruder, who took two quick steps back, the element of surprise lost, his knife a pathetic weapon against my father's sword. At the same time my father reached for me, grabbing me by the upper arm and yanking me towards the door, where I stumbled and fell over the body of the second attacker.

From the house behind me my mother yelled, 'Sabu!' and my father turned, hauling me to my feet and pulling me into the house with him.

There, among the cushions and stools, was Mother, a blood-dripping bread knife in her hand, a dark, dangerous look in her eye and a body at her feet.

In the room was another man. A fourth was bustling through the door, armed, his teeth bared for attack. My mother called for me and I ran to her at the same time as Father surged forward to meet the two intruders – 'Ahmose, get Bayek to safety,' he cried, his sword swinging underhand.

In the next second one of the pair screamed and fell, his insides already spilling from his open stomach; the other yelled a curse and there was a ring of steel as their swords met. As my mother dragged me towards the bedroom, I saw my father duck and whirl, his sword held two-handed to meet two more invaders as they crowded into our house. The blade slashed, droplets of airborne blood in its wake. He wore an expression of almost serene concentration and, for a moment, even though we were besieged by killers, I had never felt safer or more protected.

The feeling evaporated. As Mother and I burst into the bedroom we found another intruder pulling himself to his feet, having climbed through the window. 'Easy pickings,' he said, grinning and bringing his blade to bear, but they were his last words, because my mother had taken two decisive steps forward and rammed the bread knife into his sternum before he had even brought his own blade to bear.

'He was right,' she said as he fell, and then pointed to the sleeping mat. 'Stay there,' she commanded, before raising her knife and flattening her back to the wall beside the window, twisting her neck to check outside. Satisfied nobody was there, she moved swiftly to the door, a contrast of bloodstained knife and elegant skirts that swished the floor.

There came a movement, a shifting shadow, and she raised the knife ready to defend herself again, only to relax at the sight of my father. His shoulders were heaving and he was bloody and drawn from battle, but he was alive. Outside in the dim light of our front room, I could see irregular shapes on the floor: the bodies of men who had fallen under my father's sword.

'Are you all right?' said Mother, going to him, pawing at his tunic to peer beneath the bloodstained fabric for wounds.

'I'm fine,' he said. 'And you? Bayek?' He looked meaningfully over her shoulder, at the corpse sprawled in their bedroom.

'We're fine,' she told him.

He nodded. 'Then I'm sorry, but I've got to go,' he said. 'They will be striking at the temple hoping for relics, gold, offerings – whatever they can get their filthy hands on. They fear no gods; they don't care if they offend the Oracle. It's up to me to stop them.'

'Will there be many?' she asked.

'Labourers mostly, the craftsmen he uses. The soldiers were sent here to deal with me. They expect me to be dead by now.'

With a warning to be on our guard, he left, and in the sudden quiet of our house – a house now seemingly littered with bodies – my mother sank against the wall and lowered her head. She rubbed her hands together as though washing, and I realized that she was trembling in the aftermath of combat, but aware that more men might come; that she might have to fight again.

I thought of her stepping to the intruder and stabbing him – unhesitating, unwavering. For the first time that night I'd seen my parents spill blood. But while there was a sense that I'd been watching Father do his job and do it well – that keen sense of being protected I'd felt would stay with me – my mother seemed changed by it, as though ever aware of what lengths she would go to, to protect herself and her family. Over the years I would often see her studying her own hands, pensive yet oddly serene, and wonder if she was thinking back to that night.

Right then, though, I went to sit beside her. And in the moments before she roused herself and went to tell others what was happening, we comforted one another on the floor.

I ended my story, numb with the memory of it.

'Your father foiled the assassination and saved the temple,' said Rabiah. She had been peeling and pitting a date, and now she popped it into her mouth. 'I was not there, of course, but from what he told me the gang had indeed begun its assault and many of those who worked at the temple were already dead. They would have stripped that holy place of its valuables, might even have killed the Oracle, were it not for your father's interception.'

'Was Menna there?'

'Your father never told you?'

'No, he never did.'

'Menna was there, yes, but made his escape.' Now Rabiah looked thoughtful as though considering before she next spoke. 'That night changed everything for your father,' she said at last. 'He saw that night of violence through the eyes of his loved ones and began to question not only his own path but the one you yourself are destined to follow. He feared for you and became unwilling to train you for your role as protector; he began talking about wanting to shield you from violence. He would say you weren't ready, that was his excuse – any excuse would do to not train you, we told him, Ahmose and I – but that was what he said.'

'I was always ready. I wanted nothing more than to follow him.'

Rabiah raised an eyebrow, serious. She studied me for a moment, evaluating, with yet another of those piercing, all-knowing looks she managed so well.

'Really? And how did you show that desire? What action were you planning to take to reconcile these two lives of yours: this "friendship" with Aya and your future as Siwa's protector? What of her desire to return to Alexandria? What steps have you taken to assure your father that you are the right person to follow him into protectorship? That you would stay in Siwa, no matter what?'

'I hoped . . .'

'You hoped!' She gave a full-throated laugh. 'Not enough. What else?'

I shifted my weight, recognizing a battle that did not involve fist or weapon.

'I have been a devoted son.'

She rolled her eyes and sniffed at me. That answer did not pass muster.

'Not good enough. What else?'

I shook my head. 'I might ask, what has *he* done to see that I'm right for Siwa?'

'He's full of doubts, Bayek,' she said, stern and remote. 'Doubts about you, about himself, about the way of the blade and the life supposedly mapped out for you. He needs convincing. After all, are you *sure* you want to follow in his footsteps?'

I rolled my eyes.

'What?' She said, sharply.

'Aya said the same thing to me earlier.'

Rabiah's expression flickered briefly, but I saw the approval there. I wondered what she thought of Aya's dream, and mine, and how they might collide some day.

'What was your reply?'

'I said that I did.'

'Ah, but that was then, when your father remained in Siwa. What about now?'

What if Aya leaves for Alexandria? remained yet unsaid.

'I mean it now as I did then.'

My voice was certain, my back straight and my gaze steady. It was no longer a child's dream. I could think of nothing else to do with my life.

'He needed to see that. Perhaps then he could have changed his mind.' She shook her head in exasperation and said something I'd heard my mother say before as well: 'Perhaps what you both needed was your heads knocking together.'

I put a fist to my chest. 'Then he failed to see what was in here.'

'Perhaps he saw too much,' said Rabiah simply.

That was not the answer I'd been expecting, and I was thrown off balance. Had it been combat, the victory would have been Rabiah's right then and there.

But I was used to discussing with Aya, arguing history and philosophy when she shared her studies with me. 'What do you mean?'

'*Doubts, doubts,*' she repeated, evading. 'Perhaps what he saw was too important to him. Perhaps that's the reason he could not see the lionheart inside.'

I looked at her sharply. 'But you can?'

She nodded. 'Indeed. In you I see the beginnings of a protector.'

'Then why couldn't he?'

'Perhaps he just saw his son. And could see nothing else.'

'Why did he leave?' I asked her, changing the topic. Maybe an ambush would work, now. 'Did it have something to do with Menna?'

She considered, her mouth moving slightly as though trying to dislodge bits of date from her teeth. 'The truth is, I don't know.'

'But I saw him speak to you. He whispered to you. He told you the message, didn't he?'

She shook her head, her frustration gleaming through. 'He did not. He merely said it was too dangerous for me to know.'

I put my hands to my head. 'Then what am I doing standing here? I must leave after the messenger at once.'

'The messenger?'

'He's the only one who can tell us the content of the message.'

She held up a hand, smiling broadly all of a sudden,

in spite of the worry lurking in her eyes 'Wait. This river is not so easily forded. You think I'm going to be left to face your mother?'

She and mother were often allies, but when they disagreed . . . stories were told, in hushed whispers, of those epic verbal duels.

'Besides,' she continued, 'there is more you should know. That night –'

'No, no more. I must go. You can smooth things over with my mother, can't you?'

Rabiah looked at me, eyebrow raised and a wry expression on her face.

'Let's hope so.'

7

'No, he's not leaving.'

My mother's hands were at her hips, her face reddening as she looked from me to Rabiah and then back again. She and Rabiah had always been friends but for the moment that fact counted for very little.

'Sabu has trained him; he learned his survival from the Nubians,' insisted Rabiah. She stood with her hands clasped behind her back, trying to remain a calming presence.

'But his training was not complete. Wasn't that what Sabu said?'

'It could be the making of him, Ahmose.'

My mother rounded on her. 'Are you up to something?'

'No,' insisted Rabiah, although I saw her blink. 'I want what's best for your family and for Siwa.'

Mother frowned. 'Hm, but maybe not in that order.' It was not a reproach so much as simple acknowledgement – knowing and acceptance. 'What have you told him? Come on, tell me exactly what you told Bayek about last night.'

'I told him what Sabu said. That it was too dangerous for us to know why he was being called away.'

'There was more. He must have told you more.'

Rabiah's shoulders squared. I saw her hands clench behind her back. 'I'm not lying to you, Ahmose,' she said tightly.

I could tell my mother realized she had pushed a feather too hard. I stepped in, wanting to give them both a reason to retreat. 'It's all right,' I told them. 'Mother, Rabiah. It doesn't matter why he left. I've made my decision.'

They turned their gaze on me: Rabiah poised, my mother shaking her head sadly – both of them knowing what was to come.

'I'm going,' I told them.

'Just wait,' said my mother quickly. 'Wait. I don't think this is what your father would want.'

'Perhaps Sabu isn't the best judge in this instance,' said Rabiah with a wry expression.

My mother bit back whatever she had been about to say, and then nodded slowly to herself. Whatever Rabiah had meant, my mother had understood even if I hadn't. 'Rabiah, perhaps you should just go home and let me talk this out with Bayek,' she said calmly.

Rabiah raised no objection, knowing my mother had reached a decision. They traded looks, the two of them conveying several competing emotions, then Rabiah fixed me with a meaningful stare and left.

'You're not ready,' muttered my mother without much conviction. It was odd to hear those words from her when they usually always came from my father. She and Rabiah had always supported my desire to train as *mekety*, in spite of my father's ire.

'I'll never be ready, at this rate,' I told her, frustrated. 'I want to go.'

'This isn't exactly what I had in mind when I helped with your training.' She sighed, shaking her head.

'I don't think anyone had this in mind.' I was annoyed, though not at my mother, nor Rabiah. At my father, certainly, for leaving in such a high-handed way. At fate, for bringing this into our lives.

She smiled crookedly. 'Look, give it some thought, that's all I ask. Take the night to think it over, and if by morning you still want to go then I won't stand in your way.'

Later that night I was lying on my mat, trying and failing to get to sleep, listening to the night, when she appeared at my door.

'They can hear you sighing all the way to the temple,' she said quietly. 'You haven't changed your mind, have you.' A statement, rather than a question.

I nodded.

'Then you should go now,' she sighed, 'while it's cool and Siwa sleeps – and before I can change mine.'

She handed me a travel satchel, the contents of which I could guess: a waterskin and food, enough to give me a solid head start on my travels before I had to begin hunting for my survival.

'It wouldn't do any good, even if you did. My own mind is made up.'

'I know, I know. You're as headstrong as he is.'

She rolled her eyes and I resisted the fond impulse to remind her that my father was far from the only one I'd inherited stubbornness from.

'Should I tell Aya?' asked my mother.

'Do you think she'll understand?'

'I know that she will.' She smiled faintly, and even though she was clearly worried at my departure, I could see approval for Aya there, as well.

'And will you find it difficult to say goodbye?'

'Impossible.'

'It's your decision,' she said, and left the room, leaving me to collect my things, buckling belts at my torso and hanging a pouch at my waist, dropping into it a purse of coins, my savings accrued from a lifetime of errands and village chores, every coin I had ever earned – enough, I hoped, to see me clear on my travels.

I said my farewells. Mother hugged me tight, then let me go, shooing me out of the door and turning away with tears in her eyes, and I found myself on the deserted and silent street, lit by a moon that hung over the oasis and watched me impassively as I shouldered my pack and then made my way to the stable at the side of our home where my horse was waiting.

As I rode out of the town my route took me past where Aya lived with her aunt Herit. Many was the evening I'd come to her window, whispered her name and thrilled to the sight of her climbing out so that we could talk, hold hands and exchange kisses beneath the stars. For a moment I wondered if I could bear to leave Aya, whom I'd loved from the moment I set eyes on her: me the little Siwan boy, son of the town's protector and full of myself; she the girl from Alexandria, ready to put me in my place.

She'd understand. She and I were two people waiting: me for my destiny to begin and her to be called back to Alexandria to study with her parents. She'd know I was leaving because I had to follow my path. But leaving without telling her? I did that for myself. I couldn't face the alternative.

'I'm sorry,' I whispered, and my words dropped like stones in the chill night.

8

The journey to Zawty took me across the desert of the Red Lands. At night I made camp, sure to keep myself warm, piling rocks to make windbreaks, and there I discovered that there is no lonelier place than on the plains at night, with only the sound of the vultures for company. I yearned for Aya. I told myself that I would prove myself to her just as I would to my father, my mother and Rabiah, and, looking back, it was that thought that kept me going.

For water, I made stills by digging a hole in the ground and covering it with a sheet to let the sun create condensation on the underside. I sucked water out of what plant stalks I found, and made sure to preserve my own fluids by keeping my pace steady, breathing through my nose. This was what I'd been taught by Khensa, and then my father. Growing up, Aya and I would take trips, build shelters, hunt and forage, and to her I passed on the advice given to me: 'You need to hunt against the wind or across it. The ideal time to hunt is at first light, that's when the animals are abroad . . .'

Thanks to my tutors, I knew what tracks and signs to look out for. I knew which droppings indicated which animals, and how to skin them when the flesh is still warm, removing the glands that create scent and spoil the meat; I knew where to make my cuts, careful not to rupture the stomach and digestive organs.

I cooked my kills on fires made from desert scrub: rabbits, rodents, wild sheep and goats, wild pigs. ('You can't skin a wild pig, Bayek. Gut it first, then burn off the hair.') I remembered being told that liver needs less cooking and that the kidneys are a good source of nourishment but require boiling. Roast the heart. Boil the intestines. Spoon the jelly from the feet, boil the tongue and bones, save the brain to cure hides. I used entrails to re-bait the traps. I drank the blood for nourishment and sucked the eyeballs for fluids.

My first weapon was a slingshot, but the weapon in which I took the most pride was my bow. I made it when I was over the most arduous part of the journey and closer to the river, where the land was more fertile. There I found a yew tree and cut from it a supple wand for the bowstave.

'Here, hold the tip of the bowstave like this. That's your reach. That's how long your bow should be,' my father had told me.

He'd shown me how to strip the bark, taper the stave, notch the ends for the bowstring and whittle it into shape before rubbing it with the animal fat from my kills. I used rawhide for my string and then wound the stems of nettles at the tips of the stave to strengthen my knots and keep the bow tensed.

I made arrows, fashioning them from straight pieces

of sycamore. I'd collected feathers whenever I saw them, storing them in my pouch, and used them for fletching.

Alone on the plain, making my bow, I thought of them all – Khensa, my father, my mother and Rabiah, Hepzefa . . . Aya – and I wondered when I would see them again. *If* I would see them again.

9

Eventually I found myself travelling in the green splendour of the Nile's shores. Where once all I could see was arid desert in every direction, now there were farms, trees in abundance, plantations and wildlife. No longer was I alone. Everywhere I looked were other travellers, merchants, labourers, farmers, even a procession of priests at one point.

And then there was the river itself: the great Nile, whose fluctuations decided the fortunes of those who lived by its shores. When the snows in the high lands melted during the middle months of the year, thick mud was sent torrenting along the river, and this was the *akhet* – the inundation – when people would thank the god Hapi for blessing the land with fertile soil to produce food for themselves and their families. It was their life, their source. They used it for water, food and transportation; they relied on its floods to sustain crops.

These were all things I already knew, of course (things, I realized with a pang, that had been told to me by Aya). There were countless pictures of the river in the temples at home, meaning that I'd already formed a mental picture of it, and I had always imagined it to be grand. Even so, nothing could have prepared me for the sight of it. It was vast, a huge mass of water that twisted, turned and, though busy with boats, flowed in a slow and stately fashion, as though its only response to the thick humidity was languor.

I could hardly take my eyes from it as I passed through fields green with the fruit of the inundation. In the water I saw islands of reeds and palms, and everywhere boats: some large and sumptuous, with huge silk sails that flapped in the breeze with a sound like the beating of a drum; others tiny one-man vessels, not made of wood but woven from reeds. Fishermen propelled themselves using long poles, tossing nets on the river surface. I saw water birds and heard their call, and for the first time in my life I saw the ibis, the great wading birds with their down-curved beaks, long necks and legs. They stood in the shallows and appeared to tolerate the human beings in their boats, the children paddling on the shore, the oxen in the fields.

Another first: a hippopotamus, this great beast which inspired so much fear and respect, a reminder of the goddess Tawaret. I watched as its snout broke the surface of the water as it, too, watched the day go past.

I eventually found myself on the outskirts of Zawty, where I set my mind to the task at hand. What a difference it made to be among people again. Alone in the desert, I'd felt small and vulnerable, and even at times afraid. But now the hustle and bustle of the town gave me a kind of strength, a different kind of security to the one I felt in Siwa, where everybody knew me as the protector's son. Here, I was anonymous. And that made me bold.

I found a place to stable my horse, paying a boy with coin from my purse before taking my leave in order to drink in the sights of the city. Trying not to gawp I wandered among stalls, weaving my way through townspeople, stopping to admire wares every now and then.

The streets were narrower than I was used to in Siwa. Here they had shops with shutters and colourful awnings. Everywhere I looked streets became other streets, forking left and right, branching first one way and then another . . . To slow down invaders, Aya had once told me.

Oh!

I came to a halt. This was the best way to get lost, I realized. Stable your mount, go exploring. The next thing you know you've forgotten where your horse is.

As I cast about to find a useful landmark, I glimpsed a sudden movement behind me. I couldn't be sure, but it looked like a small child – a child who was anxious not to be seen.

With a better idea of my bearings, I moved on, stopping to admire the wares at a stall further along the street. This particular one boasted a selection of knives, all of them more fit for combat than the one I'd taken from home.

One in particular caught my eye. I pulled out my purse to pay for it but before I tucked my new purchase into my belt, I pretended to inspect it one last time, using it to watch over my shoulder, and once again saw movement between the legs of fellow shoppers. A street kid with designs on my purse, perhaps?

At the next stall was a selection of jewellery. I picked up a polished collar, angling it once more to see the street behind. What I saw, of course, was my own face, heavily stubbled, thick with the dirt and dust of the desert, and then . . .

There!

In the reflection I saw him. A boy, younger than me. He wore a tunic not dissimilar to my own, but without the leather belts that crisscrossed my chest.

The question was, why was he following me? What did he want?

Time to find out.

IO

I kept going, drawing the boy with me until I found a square. Stone benches lined the walls and weeping almond trees provided shade for customers who milled around stalls selling food and alabaster jars. I bought a honey cake covered in seeds and then took a seat at a mosaic table to wait.

Right, I thought, *show yourself, little rat.*

In time he sidled into the square. Though it was far less populated than the other streets in the city he was still able to use much taller people as cover. I watched him as covertly as I could. I saw his eyes go to the honey cake and there was no mistaking the hunger there.

I looked over and gestured to him. A look of indecision immediately flitted across a face that was almost as grubby as my own and he went to turn away.

'Hey,' I called over. 'Are you hungry? There's a honey cake here that I'm happy to share.'

That brought him up short. He turned and slunk along the wall towards where I sat, coming close and appraising me with world-weary eyes before he spoke. 'You think you're the big man, do you?' he said, and reached for the honey cake.

'If you're going to be rude then . . .' I scooped up the cake and held it away.

'All right, all right, just that I ain't used to somebody barely older than I am talking to me like they was a military commander.'

I frowned. 'How old are you, then? What's your name?'

'Name's Tuta. I'm ten. What's *your* name? How old are you? And when are you going to give me that honey cake, or are you planning on making me beg, "Oh, please, sir, please, sir, can I have a bite of your honey cake? Do you a dance if you like, sing you a little song if it would please you, sir"?'

True, my arm was still up, honey cake and all. I brought it down, indicated for him to sit. 'Help yourself. My name's Bayek. I'm fifteen summers, and I want to know why you've made yourself my shadow.'

He sniffed. 'I'm hungry, and I live on the streets. I'm always on the lookout for something to eat.'

'I might believe that – but for the fact that I had no food when you first began following me. Why do I have the feeling that it's not cake you're interested in so much as this?' And with that I plopped my purse on to the mosaic table.

Lips dusted with seeds, cheeks full of honey cake, he rolled his eyes. 'All right, all right,' he said, spraying crumbs. 'I got a friend at the stables. He's good enough to put me on to anybody new in town who might have some spare drachme . . .'

'To steal it?'

He shook his head furiously. 'No, just be generous enough to help a boy out.'

There was a pause.

'Do you think you might do that, then?' he said hopefully. 'Help me out, I mean? A little loan. Maybe a gift if I show you the sights?'

'Well, that's a possibility, I might well be able to do that . . .'

'*Really?*'

'Yes, really. First, though, I'd like to know more about who it is I'm helping. What's your story, Tuta?' I indicated for him to take more cake.

He spoke around mouthfuls of cake. 'I came to Zawty from Thebes when I was very young. My mother and father brought me and my little sister, and for a while things were good, as far as I can remember. But there was a fire – a terrible fire, sir, one that claimed the life of my mother and sister.'

'I'm sorry,' I said.

'Thank you sir, it was a couple of years ago now, and there's plenty in my situation.'

'What about your father?'

'Well, that's a tale that's almost as tragic. For losing my mother and sister in the fire meant I also lost my father, who took to drinking and may well have drunk himself to death by now, for all I know.'

'I'm sorry,' I repeated. 'Where do you live?'

'Well, I've lived in this very square more than a few

times.' He grinned. 'Matter of fact, there's hardly a street in this whole city that hasn't been my home at one time or another. It gets a bit cold at night but I make the best of it, and it's not like I'm the only one out here.'

'Where did you get that?' I pointed at a bruise on his neck.

'I said it wasn't all that bad.' His look darkened, 'But I'm not saying it's all that good either.'

'Right,' I said. 'Well, maybe we can help each other, *if* – big if – you can help me in return. Being a visitor, I don't know the place as well as you, but I'm here in search of a messenger who paid a visit to Siwa, recently. This man had striking blue eyes, and he wore a brown leather satchel across himself, a bit like this,' I indicated the belt across my own shoulder, 'but with the bag down here . . .'

'Don't narrow it down much,' said Tuta doubtfully.

I tried to think. 'All right, the last time I saw this particular gentleman, he was pushing a purse of what looked very much like coins into that satchel of his. I wonder if he might have been spending his earnings, perhaps attracting a little attention to himself in the process.'

'I take it back then, sir,' said Tuta, 'there might be something I can do. In fact, I know just the person to ask. A trader of my acquaintance, a man who deals in all sorts of wares. I could start there if you like.'

'You think you can find the man I seek?'

Tuta winked, already looking better nourished thanks to the cake. 'To be honest, there isn't anybody in this town I couldn't set eyes on. You just happen to have hired yourself the right man for the job. Wait here.'

I did as I was asked, blissfully unaware of the terrible mistake I was making.

11

Sabu had ridden for over twenty days by the time he reached his destination. It had taken him longer than anticipated because he'd been very cautious. He had to be certain he wasn't being led into a trap. The safe place – 'Mother' – was used in the message, so he could be reasonably certain the source of the missive was genuine, but even so . . . there was no such thing as being too careful.

He reached the Mother location, a small oasis in the Eastern Desert, where he waited for a day or so until in the distance he saw the familiar shape of a cart, trundling slowly towards him. On the plank seat was The Elder's ward, a boy of about fifteen, his eyes shining white with blindness.

Sabestet, for that was his name, was considered by many to have almost supernatural abilities. But the truth was, his hearing was his secret weapon, even as his sight was not so poor as he allowed people to believe. It was on the advice of The Elder: 'Find your advantage and use it. Keep your friends guessing as you do your enemies, you never know when their loyalties might change.'

The Elder, Hemon, was usually to be found sitting

beside Sabestet on the cart. Though not today, it seemed.

The two greeted one another and Sabu stood to one side, knowing better than to offer Sabestet a hand to climb down from the cart. Shortly, the two of them sat with their backs against a tree trunk, sharing the last of Sabu's flask.

'Hemon thanks you for responding to our message and attending so quickly. We were confident you would,' said Sabestet when he had rinsed the dust from his mouth.

Sabu swatted at a fly. 'How is he?'

'Our master is in good health and as mentally robust as ever, though now reliant on a staff to walk. He would have come with me but he has travelled much lately. Thus we felt it was better that he stayed at home in Djerty on this occasion. Our master hopes you are not at all offended by his absence and thanks you for coming.'

'And this travelling he's been doing?'

'Yes. The travelling he's been doing. This is why he summoned you. He thanks you for coming.'

Sabu sighed, thinking of Ahmose and Bayek back home, the town he'd left. 'He thanks me for coming, Sabestet, I understand that. How about the reason why? The travel? What does this all concern?'

'Our master sent word to Emsaf. He requested they meet regarding a serious issue. Emsaf did not arrive at the meeting place. Instead he sent a communication from Ipou requesting that we go to an alternative location. Why would Emsaf do that, do you think?'

Sabu stood, put his hands to the small of his back and stretched out his shoulders as he tried to put himself in Emsaf's position. He thought back to the days and nights he had just spent traversing the desert.

'He'd reached Ipou, then,' he said, gazing down at Sabestet. 'All the way from his home at Hebenou. He must have thought himself followed.'

Sabestet nodded. He was in the habit of closing his eyes so that when he nodded he looked as though he were in deep thought. 'This is the conclusion our master reached. He requests that you investigate so that the fate of our friend and comrade Emsaf might be recorded with certainty. He will be pleased to receive you at Djerty to learn your findings.'

That was something to look forward to, thought Sabu bitterly. 'Our master believes the old enemy is behind it, I presume,' he said.

Sabestet nodded again. 'This is what our master fears and believes.'

12

It was dusk and the courtyard traders had packed up and gone home by the time Tuta returned. He sidled back into the square, took a seat at the table and regarded me from beneath dark, scruffy hair. 'I think I might have found your man, sir,' he said, and showed me an empty open palm.

I looked at the grubby hand, grinning at his impudence and liking him despite myself. 'Oh no, no coin yet. Not until I'm sure of the merchandise. Where do I find my messenger?'

'You drive a hard bargain,' said Tuta, but he withdrew the hand without protest. 'You need to make sure you've got your man and I of all people understand that. Follow me.'

He led us along narrow, winding streets, and I was heartened to remember landmarks from earlier in the day, thinking I could probably find my way back to my horse when the time came. More to the point, I felt the first rumblings of an excitement, a growing confidence. *I can do this.*

At the end of a street, Tuta pulled me to one side. 'Careful,' he hissed, 'the one you seek is up here a-ways.'

Along the lane sat men beneath awnings, eating or drinking with friends. There were still people around, but through the pedestrians I could make out the man Tuta indicated and just as described. His eyes were an intense blue, and at first glance might well have been the rider I'd last seen back home. Even so . . .

'I can't be sure,' I told Tuta, having spent several moments studying the man. 'There's no satchel?'

'He has it with him, no doubt, sir,' said Tuta, 'perhaps under the table by his feet. Besides, that's the man my contact says has been spending so much lately. According to my friend, who is a very well-connected gentleman indeed, your man with the sudden supply of coin has only recently returned to the city, having been away close to a month.'

I gave it thought. 'That makes it a lot more likely, I'll grant you. If I could hear him speaking, perhaps.'

'Well, let's go down the road, shall we, sir?' said Tuta. 'Before you get too serious a case of the frights and I lose out on my reward altogether.'

I grabbed at his shoulder as he was about to make off. 'No, he might recognize me.'

Tuta gave me a shrewd look up and down. 'Was that your appearance the last time he saw you?'

'No. Maybe you're right.'

'Come on, come with me, even if he does notice you pass by, he'll only take you to be my older brother. Come on, I haven't got all night.'

My heart was hammering as the two of us slunk past where Blue Eyes was sitting with a number of others. However, he seemed happy to listen to their conversation, and, while closer up I was pretty sure it was the right person, I still wanted to hear him speak.

Tuta responded to the warning glance I flashed him, moving over to the seated group. 'Can you spare a drachma, sir?' he asked the man.

'Get out of it, street rat,' he replied, and in that instant I knew he was the messenger I sought.

'Well?' said Tuta when our promenade was complete. 'That was him.'

'Then that concludes our business, does it not, sir? I'll take my coin and be on my way if it's all the same to you.' He palmed the silver I gave him. 'What will you do now then? What's your plan of action?'

Good question. And it struck me that during the whole of my journey and all of my time in Zawty so far, I'd never got as far as planning what I might say to the messenger if I ever saw him again.

'Strikes me you could do with an intermediary,' said Tuta, as though reading my mind. 'I might be able to arrange a meeting.'

That made sense. If he recognized me and ran off into that labyrinth of alleyways I might never find him again. The messenger would not be so wary of a boy, and less likely to slip away in the open. 'Go on,' I said.

'I'll tell him I have a friend in need of his services. Wait in the theatre. I'll bring him to you and leave you to do the rest, how does that sound?'

It sounded good, I thought, and so Tuta disappeared once more and I found myself alone in the Zawty city theatre later that evening, another coin poorer and wondering if my new friend would ever return.

The place seemed almost unnaturally quiet, and when I coughed the sound echoed around tiers of seating recently vacated by the audience of a production of *The Myrmidons*. Earlier they would have spread himations on stone seats, chatting away, eating nuts and dates and cake before the players entertained them with verse. Aya would have loved it. She liked to tell me about the fire effects they used in *The Furies*, the sword fights, the way the theatre company could make it seem to rain, even how they used some sort of crane to create the effect of the gods.

Then, of course, the amphitheatre would be abuzz with the sound of laughter and chatter and the players delivering their lines. Not now. None of the torches or braziers were lit and it was getting dark. I heard birds moving around in the seating above my head, a rustling that might have been rodents, and swallowed a sudden sharp stabbing of fear, a feeling that I was out of my depth.

No, Bayek, you're not. You must do this. Feeling exposed in the area just under the stage, I took a seat to wait, and sat with my hand surreptitiously on the handle of my new knife. I hadn't had a chance to sharpen it (working left to right with quartz sandstone, just as my father had taught me) so there were still some burrs on the blade, but it would do the job if needs be.

What job?

I chased away the thought. There was no reason to suspect anything sinister was afoot.

Was there?

From an entrance tunnel close to where I sat came a noise, and the birds heard it too, because it was accompanied by a sudden flapping in the rafters. Appearing from the shadows was the messenger. He looked around himself curiously, then saw me as I stood to greet him, his eyes narrowing.

'You're the man I'm supposed to meet, are you?' Fortunately there wasn't the faintest sign of recognition on his face. Evidently my travels had changed my appearance.

'We've met before, you and I,' I said.

'Have we?'

'Oh yes,' I said, and was about to continue when a sound from the seating above stopped me. I looked up, wondering if it was just a trick of the light that seemed to make the shadows move. 'In Siwa,' I went on.

At last recognition dawned and his face changed. 'Yes, yes, I remember you. The impudent one. Of course. All right, how about you tell me just what the hell you're playing at, dragging me here? An offer of work, I was told, a little extra in my purse. But I doubt very much that someone such as you has anything I could possibly want.'

'Oh but I have,' I said, 'I have plenty of money, and what I require in return is much less strenuous than what you're used to. I want to know about the message you delivered to the protector in Siwa. Who sent it, and what did it say?'

His eyebrows shot up. 'You couldn't just ask your father?'

'It's complicated.'

'He left straight away, did he?'

'That doesn't surprise you?'

The messenger shook his head. 'Not at all. He said as much when I passed on what I had been told to say.'

'Which was?'

'Don't get ahead of yourself, protector's son. Show me the shape of your money and then we'll talk further . . . maybe.'

As I reached into my tunic for the coins there was a movement, a sound, the scrape of sandal upon stone, and I swung about to see a figure emerge from the tunnel. Into the area in front of the stage came a man with a weathered, hangdog face, tattered clothing and a rusting short sword that he held by his thigh. Something about him was familiar – something I couldn't quite put my finger on. But if I'd thought that he was a friend of the messenger then I was soon disabused of that notion. The messenger's brow darkened and he looked quickly from the new arrival to me and then back again.

'What is this?' he barked. His hands went straight to his satchel, clutching at the bag. 'What's going on here?' He fixed me with a glare. 'Is this a set-up?'

'No, no,' I said quickly, terrified that the opportunity would slip through my fingers and suddenly feeling very alone.

'Oh, I wouldn't say that,' smirked the new arrival. 'In fact, I'd say it's been a perfect set-up.'

13

The man with the short sword lifted his head to call into the tiered seats above, and what he said hit me like a slap. 'Tuta,' he called, 'how about you show your face, boy?'

My heart sank as, sure enough, Tuta emerged from hiding, materializing in the shadows above and making his way slowly down between the seats. Shamefaced, round-shouldered and unable to meet my gaze, he came to stand beside the man who was surely his father, a fresh bruise below one eye. I felt hollowed out – as though I were being punished for my hubris and stupidity, but also like it was no more than I deserved. *Serves you right.*

'You did well, son,' said Tuta's father. 'You brought them together just as you said you would. Now, if you don't mind, gentle souls, we shall take our money.'

The sword was raised in threat.

'Tuta, why?' I blurted. 'Why are you doing this? I would have paid – you know I would. I thought we were . . .'

'*Friends,*' smirked Tuta's father. From him came a reek of beer fumes. 'No, my old mate, you ain't friends. He does *what* I say, *when* I say, and he's friends with *who* I say. And it ain't either of you.' He gestured with the blade, the point of it wavering between me and the messenger. 'Now, hand those purses, both of you.'

'You know these people,' spat the messenger to me. 'You set us up.'

'I didn't,' I said quickly. 'I swear I had nothing to do with this. I just want information.' I turned to Tuta. 'Do you think this is what your mother would have wanted? Reduced to robbing strangers.'

'What d'you mean, *would* have wanted?' smirked the father. 'What's he been telling you?'

I rounded on Tuta. 'That was a lie, too, was it? All part of making a fool of me,' I said.

Tuta swallowed, looked away, his bottom lip trembling.

'Come on, spit it out,' insisted Tuta's father, 'I'm dying to know what he told you.'

'That your wife and daughter died in a fire. That you've taken to the bottle.'

Tuta's father threw back his head and roared with laughter. 'And you fell for that one, did you? More fool you, my friend.'

An extra helping of beer fumes came my way. 'At least part of it was true,' I said. 'And looking at the bruises I can see what Tuta left out.'

'Well, aren't you the hero?' jeered the father. 'Tuta said you were. A minnow trying to swim with the big fish. He said you'd be easily caught.'

I cast a look at Tuta whose eyes dropped with shame. At the same time his father moved closer and raised the sword until the point of it was under my chin. His rheumy eyes fixed on mine, his lips parted from broken teeth and the stink on him brought back a sudden overpowering memory of the man who came into my window the night of Menna's attack.

Not choked by fear now, though. Not a child any more to it.

With his other hand Tuta's father reached, took my knife from my belt and dropped it with a dull clunk to the ground. From the corner of my eye I saw the messenger's gaze go to it and found myself willing him not to make his move. *Don't risk it*, I wanted to call. *Not when I've come so far.* But the blade at my chin was insistent and sharp – no burrs on this one – and I felt something warm tickle at my throat and realized it was blood as my assailant's other hand went to my pouch.

He couldn't do it. Couldn't open the pouch one-handed.

'Tuta, take his money,' he said with irritation.

Without looking at me, Tuta came and unbuckled the pouch, drew out the purse and handed it to his father. A feather fluttered to the ground.

The messenger had moved a couple of steps closer to my knife.

Don't do it.

'Tuta,' I pleaded, the movement of my mouth pressing my flesh further into the sword so that a fresh trickle of blood made its way down my throat, 'at least tell the messenger I had nothing to do with it. Just tell him that.'

'He had nothing to do with it, sir,' said Tuta firmly, suddenly looking the messenger square in the eye. 'This was all down to me and my father and our wicked ways. This man here just wants to find his kin; he just needs answers. He's a good man, I can vouch for that, for what it's worth, and if you have a heart you'll tell him what he wants to know so that he can rest easy.'

'Now just you shut your mouth,' snapped his father, 'I've had about enough of this,' and with that he punched the boy, sending him sprawling to the ground.

The messenger saw his chance. Using the distraction, he took a step, bent, scooped up my knife and came at the bully, the blade swinging upwards.

He met his target and Tuta's father screamed in pain as my knife tasted blood in the hands of another.

But the messenger's blow was harried and wild, a first strike aimed at gaining the advantage and sadly failing, while making it impossible for me to help him in the bargain. He had opened a cut in the robber's thigh, the tunic gaping, blood already gushing down his leg, but Tuta's father, injured and drunk though he surely was, was still the more experienced fighter and a better knifeman, and he bit down on the pain and rounded on the messenger, his own blade flashing as he charged forward.

The messenger had no chance of a second attack. In the blink of an eye the short sword was in his stomach, Tuta's father grunting with the effort as he punched the blade in with a thump like the washerwomen on the

Nile beating their sheets, and then another, and then, when the messenger was bent over clutching at his torso, coughing and spasming with the pain, a dead man for sure, again – just out of spite.

Now Tuta's father swung towards me. His leg was awash with his own blood, his blade dark with that of the messenger.

'You stupid little bastard,' he screeched, and I wasn't sure whether he was talking to me or Tuta or maybe both. All I knew was that I was stumbling back, my heels knocking against where Tuta lay sprawled so that I too was dumped to the stone.

My eyes were on the short sword as Tuta's father lumbered forward, dragging his bad leg behind him.

This is it. This is what the moment before death feels like. My thoughts went to Aya, to my mother, and to a Siwa I would never see again.

'No, Father, please,' shrieked Tuta, and threw himself in front of me, just as the blade came arcing down.

Thank the gods – his father pulled back in time, letting out a curse that promised worse punishment later and reaching to haul Tuta off, depositing him once more to the ground and then coming forward again, intent on delivering the deathblow. Tuta had brought me precious time, though, and I had managed to get back to my feet, and was thinking my way towards defending myself.

'Hey, what's going on in here?' came a shout from the tunnel, and while Tuta's father whipped around to locate the speaker, I lunged for my knife. It was one of the theatre workers, alerted by the commotion. With a shout of frustration, Tuta's father abandoned murderous thoughts and turned instead to the stricken messenger, rifling him for his purse. Taking the money, he reached, grabbed Tuta and yanked the poor injured boy to his feet, dragging him towards the exit just as the theatre worker appeared.

The worker began to protest: 'What . . .' before his face fell at the sight of the blade and he was flattening himself to the wall of the seating area, letting robber and his small accomplice barrel past.

Out in front of the stage, I scrambled to the messenger. There I knelt by his side and put one hand to his temple, my eyes going to his tunic, all red and torn and wadded up. Three stab wounds. *Punch, punch, punch.*

All my fault. I'd been such a fool.

He coughed blood, eyes already glazing. When I put my hand to his heart it was beating, but only just. Fluttering like a wounded bird.

He was going to die here – he was going to die here, and it was all my fault, but even so I had to know, and although I hated myself for doing it, for putting my own needs above his last moments, I bent to him, saying, 'Please, tell me, what did the message say?'

He passed out, but before he went, he whispered to me what the message said.

And it meant nothing to me.

14

I sat back on my heels, feeling a potent brew of anger and frustration and hatred. From across the way the theatre worker shouted, 'Now you just stay there while I fetch the soldiers,' but I was doing no such thing. I pulled myself to my feet and, ignoring the worker's shouts, ran into the seating area and dashed up the stairs until I reached the rafters.

I came to an overhang. Jumping, I grabbed it, swung myself up on to the roof of the theatre and crouched there, scanning the Zawty streets from my new perch with a bird's eye view.

The streets were less crowded now that large sections of the city were shrouded in darkness, torchlighters only just beginning their night's business. Even so, I thought I saw my quarry two streets away: an older man and the younger boy hurrying along, the man limping.

I stood, gauging the distance between the theatre's overhang and the flat roof of what was either a shop or house next door. It was a long way down, with no awnings and nothing soft to break my fall if I missed or came up short.

Taking deep breaths, I squatted, feeling my leg muscles bunch – and then took the jump.

I made it, feet finding purchase, forward motion taking me on as I traversed first one roof and then – *jump* – another. On the roofs was bedding, but thankfully nobody settling down for the night. I raced on, keeping Tuta and his father in my sights, leaping from one rooftop to the next.

My heart hammered. What I planned to do when I caught them, I had no idea. What drove me was a sense of injustice, a feeling that I'd messed up, a need to put things right.

On I went. We were coming out of the city now, where there was more housing. Finally, I reached a gap between the roofs which was too wide for me to jump, and that was my cue to let myself down to the street below, keeping out of sight behind a cart as I took stock.

I cursed. There was no sign of them, but . . .

Stepping out from hiding I scanned the ground and, yes, there it was, a blood trail. For the length of a street I followed it and there it ended.

Here was where they had gone to ground.

And now I was standing in front of a house, much like any other on what was a quiet lane. The bloodstains led directly to its door. Coming as close to the house as I dared, I strained to hear through the window.

From inside came the sound of harsh discussion: Tuta's father was cursing. There was the noise of a slap and Tuta crying out in pain that made me clench my jaw with anger.

What to do now? Surely Tuta's father would need to take to his bed and heal. After all, apart from his injury the robbery was a success. As far as he knew there was nobody in pursuit and they had their money.

If I could just get that money back.

I crept to the darkened rear of the house, thankful there were no neighbours to sound the alarm. Sure enough, from one of the back rooms I heard what sounded like Tuta easing his father into bed, the older man complaining, demanding beer for the pain and honey for his wound.

Good. Drink — drink yourself into slumber.

I moved to the darkest part of the rear courtyard, navigated my way through some scattered clay bricks and took a seat on a step, deciding to wait until I thought it was safe.

How long was I there? I did not try to read the stars in order to know, as I'd once been taught. But everything inside the house was still when I slipped around to the front. There I took my knife from my belt, finding scant comfort in a weapon I had never used in anger before but knowing it was better than nothing. With hands that shook, I moved the screen aside and stepped inside.

15

The front room of the house was almost bare. There were none of the stools, cushions or rugs I was used to seeing in the homes of Siwa. None of the home comforts you'd expect. On the one and only table in the room was a clay flask lying on its side, the rusty short sword, a single candle flickering – and the two money purses.

Also in the room was Tuta. He had been sitting against the far wall in the dark, but at my entrance he dragged himself to his feet and let out one short yelp of surprise, 'Hey!' before recognizing me.

I winced at the sound. For a second I thought he might shout again, raise the alarm and bring his father running. After all, I had no real way of knowing exactly where his loyalties lay. But he did no such thing. And instead we stood stock still, our eyes locked as we listened and waited to learn whether Tuta's strangulated shout had roused his father. Tuta's face was badly bruised and he had been crying. The cocky lad I'd met that afternoon was absent now. In his place this frightened, beaten little boy.

No sound came from the back room. I stepped to the table, scooped up the two purses and dropped them into my pouch. Perhaps I could find out if the messenger had family and deliver them the money. I thought I could make my way back to the street where I'd first seen him, perhaps ask some of his friends there.

First, though, I had to get out of this house.

Tuta had been watching me, making not a murmur as I retrieved the money. His face was open, bottom lip trembling, and I knew what he was thinking. He was wondering how his father would react when he woke up. He was wondering how bad the beating would be.

'Come on,' I whispered, 'you're coming with me.'

He shook his head, stepping back to the safety of the wall.

'You want to stay here and be thrashed?' I hissed. 'He'll most likely kill you when he finds out I've been in and taken the money.'

'Then don't take it, sir,' pleaded Tuta.

I shook my head. 'I'm sorry, Tuta, whether you come with me or not, half that money belongs to me, the other half to the messenger – his family at least. Come with me. Earlier you told me you lived on the streets. Any life is better than life with him.'

'He'll find me.'

'Then leave the city with me.'

To go where, I wasn't sure, but what else could I do?

There was silence. Tuta seemed to consider. 'How can I be sure this isn't a trap, sir?' he said, looking at me sideways. 'To pay me back for what I did to you?'

'You saved my life back there. That's what I want to repay *you* for.'

76

At last he seemed to reconsider, nodding and moving across the room towards me.

Just then, his father appeared.

His hair was wild, his leg crusty with dried blood. He roared with frustration, pitching himself forward on his good leg as he went for Tuta, seemingly heedless of the knife I held.

'You trying to take my money, boy!' he yelled, snatching up Tuta by the scruff of his neck like a naughty dog and yanking him backwards. 'You dare! You dare!'

'No, Father, no, Father,' pleaded Tuta, but his father was laying about him with his good foot. In the next instant he stopped, almost as though he had remembered my presence and more importantly the money, and his eyes went to the table, saw the purses missing and then flashed at me. Before I could react he was launching himself across the room at me.

My attempts to fend him off with the knife were useless, and he far outweighed me. He barrelled into me, taking the wind out of me and knocking me down so that I fell hard to the flagstones, a piercing ringing in my head as it made hard contact with the stone. Made strong by anger, he held me down, fingers of one hand closing around my neck, pinning me with his legs. Spittle landed on my face and I felt blood seep through my tunic and realized it was his, and in some far-off part of my brain I wondered if he might simply bleed out and collapse before he was able to finish the job.

His hand squeezed. I tried to drag breath into my

lungs and couldn't. Twisting my head, I saw Tuta lying motionless, his eyes closed, dazed or out cold. My own hands went to grab at the huge, calloused hand at my neck, trying to prise his fingers free. He was reaching behind himself with his other hand now, fingers pawing at the table, going for his short sword.

And then, in a movement of shadow I saw a figure behind him. Not Tuta. Someone new. A hand swept away the knife which clattered to the floor. Next I saw a clay brick rise and fall, splintering over Tuta's father's head a second after he realized his weapon had been taken away. His eyes rolled up, his grip relaxed and he sank to one side.

And in the dim light of the candle that still burned, I saw my rescuer for the first time.

It was Aya.

16

'Gods!' Aya knelt, taking my face in her hands. We looked at each other and I saw that she, too, bore the signs of her long journey across the desert from Siwa to Zawty. Her braided hair was matted and dirty, face grubby.

We kissed, but there was no time for reunions and none for explanations. On the floor, Tuta's father groaned, attempting to pull himself to his hands and knees. Aya pulled me to my feet, dragging me to the door, but I stopped her.

'Tuta,' I called to him, 'come now, it's your last chance.'

And this time he needed no further encouragement, joining us as we raced out of the front door and along the street, feet echoing on the stone as we made our escape.

'How did you get here?' I asked her as we ran.

'Same way you did. By horse. Matter of fact, our horses are currently in the same stables being looked after by a young man who remembered you and knows him,' she indicated Tuta. 'And with a little greasing of his palm he told me where I could find him.'

'Bastard!' exclaimed Tuta then pulled an apologetic face when Aya and I both shot him furious looks.

'Can't say I expected to find you at the same time,' she said to me. 'But who's complaining?'

'Not me,' said Tuta, 'but we're going to have to get back to the stables and find your mounts, get out of here tonight. Father knows you're stabled there, sir. He'll get you for sure if you stay.'

As we collected our horses, the stable boy and Tuta regarded each other warily, Tuta clearly wanting to give stable hand a piece of his mind but deciding against.

Either way, we didn't hang around. We took our horses and a short while later, with no sign of Tuta's father in pursuit, we were riding out of the city, putting Zawty at our backs at last.

For perhaps two hours we travelled, Tuta sharing Aya's mount and clinging on to her for dear life, and it was almost dawn when at last we stopped to build a fire and cook fish that Aya had bought or sweet-talked from a fisherman on the banks of the Nile.

As Tuta built the fire, Aya and I moved a short distance away to talk. We walked like soldiers returning exhausted from battle, supporting one another, and then plopped gratefully down to the sand to sit. Her head found its regular spot, and there we rested, with the sun rising at our backs, watching Tuta busy himself arranging brush into kindling. For some moments the only sound was the scratching of his flint. Otherwise the desert felt uncommonly still, as though we were the only three people in the world.

'Why did you leave?' she said.

'I need to find my father. I need to show him that . . .'

'No, I mean like that. The way you did.'

I paused, all that guilt I felt rising to the surface. 'I wasn't sure I could leave you any other way,' I told her at last. 'I wasn't sure I could leave you at all.'

'Well, don't do it again. Ever. Creeping off without saying goodbye.'

'I'm sorry,' I said.

'Tell me, then,' she said. 'Tell me everything that's happened.'

So I did. I told Aya the full story, beginning with my visit to Rabiah's house and ending where she came in. Everything. I didn't miss out a thing.

'And that was the message, was it?' She said when I had finished. '"Come at once to Location Mother. We fear The Order gathers."'

'That was it.'

'Location Mother,' she said. 'A secret meeting place. Does it mean anything to you?'

'No.'

'And "The Order"?'

I shook my head.

'You never overheard anything while you were growing up?'

'No.' And for a moment, I was speechless. I knew full well how little I had to show for so much effort, nearly dying twice, and the messenger – a blameless, innocent man – dead because of my clumsiness and inexperience.

'And now I just don't know what to do,' I said. 'I don't know where to start, where to go.'

Reassuring arms encircled me. 'Well you *would* know,' said Aya, 'if you'd stuck around to hear what Rabiah had to say. She told you about Khensa, but did she also tell you what happened after Menna's attack on the temple?'

'Go on.'

'There was a priest who died in the attack, yes? You remember that?'

'Yes. Vaguely.'

'Well, he didn't die in the attack.' She stopped herself. 'What I mean to say is, he died, but not in the attack. The Nubians killed him the following day. Your father had asked them to do it because it was this priest who had been working with Menna, passing him information.'

I thought about visiting the Nubians' camp – or should I say the site where the Nubians had been camped – and finding it deserted. 'I never saw Khensa again. Is that why she left Siwa?'

'The Nubians were dispatched on a mission – again, by your father. They were assigned the task of tracking down Menna and his men and stopping them once and for all. According to Rabiah, Khensa has grown to become the leader of this mission, and though she has wreaked havoc on his gang her task remains uncompleted. Menna and some of his lieutenants remain at large.'

'And this is what Rabiah thinks the message was about?' I asked.

I couldn't see her, but I felt Aya pull a face. 'Well, that's what she said, yes.'

'You're not so sure?'

'No, not really. Maybe Rabiah has us just where she wants us.'

'She wants us to pick up a stray and sit in the desert without a clue what to do?'

'That's not strictly true, though, is it? We *do* know what to do, because that's another piece of information you missed out on by doing your moonlight flit. Rabiah suggests we go to Thebes, find Khensa and enlist her help.'

'You'll excuse me if I don't find the prospect of doing Rabiah's bidding too enticing. It hasn't really worked out for me so far.'

'Do you really think that?' she said.

I considered for a moment. 'No,' I admitted, 'maybe not. I guess it was her idea for you to follow me, after all.'

'Then we eat, we sleep, and tomorrow we set off for Thebes,' she said.

'It is at least a plan of action,' I said, 'but our problem is that we know nothing about Thebes. Look what happened when I went into Zawty with that particular philosophy.'

'That's where I can help you, sir,' said Tuta. We had not heard him approach but now he stood before us. Behind him the fire blazed, dancing orange flames mirroring the coppery rising sun.

'You know Thebes?' said Aya. I could tell she was reassessing him in light of everything I'd told her.

'It's where my mother and sister live,' he said, and had the decency to throw me a sheepish look at the same time.

'So there really is a mother and sister, is there?' I asked.

'What I told you was partly true,' said Tuta. 'We did live in Thebes. It's where I spent the first ten summers of my life and I loved it there, but my father made some powerful enemies and we had to leave for Zawty. He used to beat my mother just as regularly and painfully as he beat my sister and me. I bet you can imagine, too, can't you, sir, that he drank a lot too.'

'Can't say I'm surprised about that,' I told him.

'Our house did indeed burn down, sir. Father knocked over a lantern while drunk, and it was the last straw for my mother, who took my sister with her back to Thebes.'

'And you?'

Tuta's reply was a rueful smile. 'Loyalty, I suppose, sir,' he said.

'You can come with us to Thebes, Tuta,' said Aya. 'We'll be glad to have you as a travelling companion. You can prove your worth when we get there.'

'I will, my lady.'

We cooked the fish and then slept, Aya and I curled up together on the sand, Tuta not far away, until the heat of the sun woke us and, tired as we still were, we set off for Thebes. On my mind were the messenger's last words.

What had he meant? What was The Order?

17

'The Order is supposed to think us outdated and redundant, of no threat,' raged Sabu. 'What has happened, Hemon?'

The old man pursed his lips, furious. There was a time he would have shouted right back at Sabu, but though Hemon was still imposing, muscle had become sinew, age had dulled him, and shouting matches no longer held much appeal for him. 'Possibly this is what we need to find out,' said the old man instead.

'Our master thanks you for the efforts you have made on our behalf,' said Sabestet, placing a cupful of hot carob in front of Sabu, who had to fight hard to contain a wave of irritation.

He had done as he had been asked by Hemon and Sabestet, undertaking the journey to Hebenou, where he had found Emsaf's farm under new ownership. The current occupants had been wary of him with good reason: not only was he filthy from the trail, wild-eyed and exhausted, but also he had just learned that Emsaf's farm became vacant when his wife and son were discovered slaughtered.

Sabu hadn't known Emsaf well, but Emsaf was one of his kind, and though they had no contact during the present, their pasts were linked, their futures inextricably entwined. Sabu had always believed that one day they would fight side by side in order to restore Egypt to its old ways, its right ways.

Funny, how an ironclad certainty could be so easily obliterated.

'How were they killed?' he had asked.

'Stabbed, so they say.' Not that the new owners had seen the bodies, of course. 'We had nothing to do with their deaths, you understand.'

'I understand.' The man and his wife were clearly nervous. Sabu had spent his life in Siwa protecting people like this, and he despised being the cause of their trepidation. He hated himself for being its envoy. But his smiles did little to put them at their ease. His only option was to learn what he needed to learn then leave them in peace as quickly as possible.

'There was no body of a man found?' he asked, thinking of Emsaf.

There was not, he was assured.

'And what of the family's belongings?'

Most had been buried with them, as was tradition. They had set aside the rest, they said, nothing of much use but still. Just in case a friend or relative should come, and they were happy to give him the pack with the possessions, for him to look through.

He did.

There was no medallion. Creative questioning also

confirmed that none had been buried with mother and child.

And so he had left, taking the route back to Hemon's home at Djerty, barely stopping until he saw the town appear in the distance. Rising from its centre was the granite pillar of the Pharaoh Userkaf. Not far away was a temple to the falcon god Monthu, the war-god who, when enraged, appeared as a white bull with a black face.

Very fitting.

There, he had found Hemon.

'And you think they're hunting us?' he said now.

The Elder nodded. 'It is the only explanation.'

'Then we fight.'

'We fight . . . ?' said Hemon turning his gaze to Sabestet.

In turn, Sabestet fixed a milky, unseeing gaze on Sabu. 'Our master has questions. He wishes to know the names of the warriors who make up our army for this particular fight.'

Sabu rolled his eyes. He'd known this was coming. 'I have begun to train Bayek, but he isn't ready.'

'It is your duty to make him ready,' said Hemon.

'It'll happen. But don't forget that Emsaf was training his boy also, and it did them no good. Our stock has become depleted. This makes us vulnerable.'

'Quite so,' scoffed Hemon, 'which is precisely why we need to increase our numbers, and one way to increase our numbers is to . . .'

'Yes, yes, I know. Bayek's training will be completed.'

'When?'

'When I say.'

'Too late, perhaps?' said Hemon. 'By the time you decide he is ready The Order will have annihilated us.'

'Leave Bayek to me. Our most pressing matter now is to find whoever it is that would have us all dead and kill them before they finish the job. We strike at them before they can finish what they've started, wouldn't you agree?'

Hemon nodded. 'And how do you propose to do that?'

'I have some thoughts about that. In the meantime – why now? Why is The Order suddenly taking such an interest in our activities that it wants us eradicated?'

Hemon nodded. 'A good question. It appears there have been developments in Alexandria.'

PART II

18

Several Months Earlier

One early morning, an ex-soldier by the name of Raia arrived at the Library of Alexandria. It was so early, in fact, that one of the custodians was still fast asleep, slumped against the stone of the entranceway, head lolling on his chest and a thin silvery line of dribble glittering slightly in the growing light. Raia only just resisted the urge to kick him awake as he passed, unseen and unchallenged, into the great entrance hall of the library.

Inside was a different story. Nobody snoozing in here. Another man might have felt dwarfed by the tall, sculpted columns that stretched away from him, disappearing into foamy morning light to where teachers wandered with their pupils in the garden, and students lined the stone benches of the amphitheatres in order to hang on the sage words of mathematicians and astronomers.

Another man might have whistled in awe at the thousands upon thousands of scrolls racked in hundreds upon hundreds of shelves, left and right and straight ahead like a vast honeycomb of parchment; the sculpture and bas relief, the sense of industry that permeated the building, musty and damp but learned and wise; the awareness that here, within arm's reach, close to where he stood, was the repository for all human knowledge, past, present and probably future.

Another man, perhaps.

Raia stood to get his bearings, watching as young scholars, male and female, moved hither and thither, sandals rasping on the stone. Not that it was lost on him. Not that it didn't impress him. Just that he had once been a soldier, a warrior famed for his steely nerves, iron will and fortitude in the face of the massed ranks of the enemy. To him the library was little more than an affectation.

Talking of which . . .

He had been meaning to ask directions from one of the older workers who made their way among the shelves laden with scrolls — but as it was he had no need. The sound of Theotimos's hacking cough, a noise that never failed to set his nerves on edge the way others felt about the sound of grinding teeth or cracking bones, seemed to float through the library and find him.

He changed direction and made his way towards the sound, glancing to his left and seeing eyes that watched him through the tubular scrolls. A spy? A curious scholar? Coming around the end of the shelving, he satisfied himself it was the latter and fixed the young man with a craggy warning glare anyway. The boy's shoulders hunched, his chin dropped and he turned away.

That cough again. Raia moved towards it, eventually finding Theotimos in a corner of the library where he had seemingly set up camp at a table. Already spread out were several documents, and he was returning to his seat with more.

They were only scrolls, but it was as though Theotimos was bent double under their weight. His progress was slow, one foot seemed to drag slightly on the stone. When he looked up to see Raia his eyes clouded, first with fear and surprise, as though caught in the act of some criminal endeavour, and then with confusion, as he evidently took a moment or so to recognize Raia.

Standing there and looking down on this diminished man who was, at least nominally, his superior, Raia cursed his luck at being chosen for the job of understudy. He'd had his doubts from the very beginning: Theotimos was obviously infirm, more in need of a carer than an attendant. Having worked with him for over a year now, Raia was even more convinced that Theotimos's standing in The Order of Ancients was the result of little more than misguided sentiment and misplaced loyalty.

Centuries old, The Order had been formed to help Egypt adapt to new forms of governance instigated by Alexander at Memphis. Each successive generation of Order leaders had adopted and in some cases adapted the principal ideology of The Order, which was, in a word, enlightenment: a move away from the control-by-fear once exerted by gods, priest and pharaohs, and towards modern modes of self-rule. A new Order to replace the old order.

Once upon a time, Theotimos had been instrumental to its workings, and was among those who had worked hardest to maintain the organization's purpose. Then, of course, he'd been a firebrand. There were, in this very library, transcripts of great oratories given by Theotimos – legendary debates in which he had participated. He'd been a truly great man. A terror to his enemies.

Raia wished he could have known Theotimos back then, when he took his seat among The Order's most eminent thinkers and policy-makers. He didn't like the way he felt about Theotimos as he now was; it reminded him too much of what lay ahead of him, should he live long enough. Neither did he enjoy the surge of contempt he felt every time he laid eyes on the man, a sense of rising scorn whenever Theotimos gave his customary salute, as he did now, rheumy eyes finally resolving into recognition as he resumed his seat at the table.

'Hello, my friend.'

His grey hair was long, his scraggly beard careworn and unkempt. He revealed crooked and broken teeth when he smiled, hopeful as always that the warmth of his greeting might be returned.

It wasn't. Raia managed to conceal a sneer at the scholar's deplorable lack of care for himself, filing it away as yet another justification of his disdain.

'Theotimos,' said Raia, 'what brings me to the library at such an ungodly hour?'

'I've been given a job to do.' Theotimos's eyes had returned to the scrolls before him. His fingers danced over the parchment. It came as no surprise to Raia that he had been 'given a job'. A member of The Order who outranked them both was in the habit of giving Theotimos somewhat tiresome and inconsequential tasks. These jobs were designed to utilize Theotimos's scholarly prowess while Raia's own skills as a tactician grew dusty with neglect.

'What job is that, Theotimos?' asked Raia, inwardly sighing.

'An assessment of sorts, I suppose you could say,' replied Theotimos. He leaned closer, squinting at the scroll he read, using his hand as a rule. 'Aha!' he exclaimed.

'What is it?'

Theotimos beckoned him over. 'You see this?'

Raia ambled across. Some of the parchments were in Greek, a script he knew, and they spoke mainly of Thebes as far as he could see. Others were written in a script he didn't recognize.

He said as much and Theotimos made what was intended to be a jocular tutting sound. 'This is *sekh shat*,' he said, pointing at the scroll, 'an old demotic script, not that I'd expect a pup like you to know.'

'Is there a point you intend to make? Would it be too much to ask that you made it?'

Theotimos chuckled.

At least I'm a source of amusement in your final years, thought Raia. *About all I'm useful for.*

'This word here,' said Theotimos. 'You know what it says?'

'I'm afraid not. Perhaps you might consider telling me before I lose the will to live.'

Theotimos looked up, eyes narrowed and glittering with old secrets and a sudden, disturbing lucidity. He smiled slowly, and Raia kept himself from taking a step back.

'It says Medjay.'

19

Some weeks after Theotimos's revelation, Raia awoke in an Alexandrian brothel, ideas fermenting in a fuzzy head. He paid his dues, took his leave and returned home to make plans – plans that were intricate and involved and, most importantly, would ensure his ascension through the ranks of The Order as smoothly and as efficiently as possible.

His first job was to find a translator.

No, not his first job. There was something else to do beforehand, an act that would give him a great deal of satisfaction.

And then, when the foundations of his scheme had been laid, he packed, said goodbye to his wife and two daughters and left Alexandria, commissioning a boat along the rippling azure river in the direction of Faiyum.

When he was close to his destination he disembarked, bought a horse and made his way to the home of the one they called Bion, killer of men.

He wondered if his old comrade still wore the kohl around his eyes.

And if those eyes were still as dead as they once had been.

*

Bion's house on the outskirts of the Black Desert, close to Faiyum, was one of a few scattered buildings that made up a tiny settlement. The slight dip in which they stood gave the homes the impression of sinking slowly into the ground, and the wind had a habit of picking up great scoops of sand and flinging them at the walls. It was a hostile environment, and the shepherds who made it their home had the good sense to spend most of their time away, which was just how he liked it.

It was, therefore, something of a surprise to return from a trip to collect water, and see a horse tethered outside his house. Draped over the hindquarters of the animal was the standard of the Royal Guard, the Machairophoroi.

Bion stopped.

So, he thought. *He is here. Raia has come to collect.* No one else would even know to come and find him here.

He drew his knife, just in case, looping the leather thong around his wrist, and stepped inside.

Raia had been waiting. When the killer pushed open his woven wicket door, ducked his head and stepped inside, the older man stood, and for several moments they regarded one another in silence: Raia with his arms folded, smiling, the killer with his knife in his hand.

It was the visitor who broke the silence. 'Hello, Bion, my old friend.'

'Commander,' replied Bion, unsmiling in return. He did not need to attempt social niceties with Raia. In fact, he preferred not to. Keeping Raia off balance was always preferable. He stepped out of the doorway, into the shadows. He hid a smile at the way Raia shifted his weight, as though preparing for an attack but not wanting to offend. 'What do you want?'

Raia smiled, practised and polished, indicating Bion's knife, another relic of the old days. 'Can I assume you no longer feel in need of protection? And if so, then perhaps you'd consider slipping it back into your belt? I'm only human, you know, and the sight of a sharp blade in the hand of the great Bion, killer of men, is likely to inspire fear in even the bravest among us.'

'You flatter me, Commander,' said Bion, more from habit than respect, and did as Raia asked.

'You still wear the kohl, I see.'

'To ward off the sun's glare.' He felt Raia's eyes on his scars. He did not move, knowing the shadows only made the marks stand out even more.

'What happened there?' asked his former commander.

'A disagreement,' said Bion, his tone inviting no further questions.

'A funny sort of disagreement . . .' Raia made a crisscross motion with his finger at his cheek, as though to picture the kind of swordplay that might inflict such a wound.

Bion shrugged again, wanting to leave it there. He'd miscalculated on a job. He'd escaped, then finished his work. He would not make similar mistakes again.

'I see.' Raia took a deep breath, closing the subject. 'What else has been keeping you busy in the years since we were last acquainted? It must be ten summers or so now . . .'

Bion indicated his home. Low ceiling. Walls that seemed to close in on them. Bare essentials telling a story of solitude and subsistence. 'And you?' he asked in return.

In response, Raia seemed to glow, as though he'd been looking forward to the question. As well he might. Bion could see his tunic was of the best linen; his belt worn but fashioned from expensive leather. Everything about him apart from the knife at his belt spoke of a life lived in comfort. And that knife, like the one Bion used, was a souvenir of days in the Royal Guard, in itself conferring status upon him.

'Life in Alexandria has been good to me,' confirmed Raia. 'So good in fact that I find myself at the vanguard of creating a *new* Egypt. Do you know The Order? Has word of our work reached you?' Bion shook his head as Raia continued. 'We are a society growing in strength and stature. Our aim is to usher in a new, more modern society. One that moves away from the old established ways.'

Bion waited for him to go on. He did not bother hiding his boredom. Even as one who had once moved in the same circles – in fact, *especially* since he had knowledge of that world – he did his utmost to avoid any talk of political affairs and ideology. He'd known his job was not to sit with those who decided policy, but to protect them and kill for them if needed, and for those tasks – especially the latter – he had been very well suited; he had taken pride in his work. It was the one thing he surpassed all others in. No doubt this was why Raia had travelled so far to see him now. It was certainly not to . . . *talk* to him.

'The Order is very powerful in Alexandria, Bion, and will only become more so. While you have been making home here, I've been busy myself working with them. Not because I am ambitious, you understand . . .'

Bion made sure his face remained impassive. Raia had been playing politics for too long. He'd forgotten who and what Bion was.

'. . . But because I want to work for a better Egypt. A more prosperous, self-governing Egypt. And I'm pleased to say that the elders at The Order have recognized my dedication and integrity. I don't think it's too arrogant or big-headed of me to say that I'm being talked of in certain circles, perhaps even suggested as someone who might one day take high office within The Order.'

Raia smoothed down his tunic, clearly pleased with himself. He obviously expected a response from the man in whose home he stood, and waited for it with smug confidence.

Bion resisted the urge to take out his knife and sharpen it – juvenile, not worth the reaction. He shifted his weight, eyes fixed on the other man, breathing steadily. Idly, he wondered when Raia had become such a talker – he'd been a man of action, once.

When Bion said nothing, Raia stammered, then recovered, continuing smoothly.

'Now, of course, that is not for me to decide, I understand that. And something so far out of my hands is hardly worth my thinking about. My immediate concerns are advancing our aims and improving our good works. I'm painfully aware that with the eyes of Rome upon Egypt, The Order needs to be clever if we want to survive and stay in power – we need to take action. Maybe even what you might call pre-emptive action. Do you understand so far, Bion? Am I making myself clear?'

Bion nodded. He did indeed understand. He understood that Raia was just the same as he always had been: a man who despite his many good qualities was oblivious to his own shortcomings. A man who had grown complacent, and over-confident in his machinations.

'Good, good,' said Raia, 'I knew you would. And it's important you do, because, as I'm sure you realized from the moment you saw my standard, I'm not here merely to catch up on an old comrade. I have a request to make of you.'

A request, thought Bion. That was one way of putting it.

Raia went on. 'In Alexandria I have been appointed assistant to an elder of The Order, a scholar named Theotimos. Not long ago Theotimos discovered scrolls relating to the Medjay. Scrolls that he says point towards a Medjay resurgence.' He paused. 'The Medjay. You know of them, don't you, Bion?'

Bion nodded. He did indeed know of the Medjay, having once researched them out of curiosity, wondering how to belong. And he thought about them now. They were protectors of the old kingdom, guardians of all that was ancient, the men who once upon a time had stood sentry at tombs and temples and carried out duties as bodyguards and peacekeepers. In ancient times the Medjay had been feared warriors, considered as wise as they were skilled in the ways of combat. But that was hundreds of summers before, when times were different, and so were the preoccupations of Egyptians who lived in those times. With a new era came new guardians and protectors, and such is the way of things that neither the representatives of the modern world nor their enforcers were prepared to tolerate those who represented the old one, and in that regard the Medjay were one of the most visible examples of a way of life that was increasingly regarded variously with contempt or outright hatred. Over time that status of the Medjay had changed. They'd moved from being protectors to almost apocryphal entities. Mostly rumours now. In some parts of the country they were considered quaint but irrelevant, while in other areas of Egypt, where they'd been outright persecuted, they were firmly considered extinct.

Perhaps they would have simply remained an old, out-of-date force, gradually to be forgotten, were it not for the fact that, as the Medjay's numbers and their visible presence had dwindled, their reputation and influence had somehow increased in scholarly circles. Though they no longer physically protected anything, their name had come to represent a form of preservation, a noble ideal. A safeguarding of the 'old' way, which was, by implication, a better, less corrupt and simpler way of living.

As Machairophoroi, he and Raia had supposedly been among those moving away from the ancient pharaonic rule – and thus the ways of the Medjay. He'd never met one, but what he'd heard about them had intrigued him, at the time. Thinking about it now, it made perfect sense to Bion that Raia would join The Order. He was always eager to embrace modernity and was unsparing in his criticism of 'the old'. It was inevitable that he would consider the Medjay his natural enemy.

As for Bion, he had no thoughts on the matter, other than mild curiosity. He had been paid to guard, and sometimes to kill. Not to think.

'A Medjay resurgence?' he said now, still wondering how it involved him. 'That's what your boss Theotimos thinks, is it?'

'He's not quite my boss,' bridled Raia, 'but yes, in a word that is precisely what he believes.'

'And what do you think?'

Hopefully this time Raia would be to the point.

'I can't read scrolls written in fancy ancient

languages,' said Raia with pride, 'I'm a soldier, not a scholar. This is why we have historians like Theotimos, so that they can tell us what the scrolls say.'

'And what does Theotimos say the scrolls tell him?'

Bion was patient in many situations. Now, he found, was not one of those times.

Raia pulled a pained face and shifted weight. He'd noticed Bion's irritation. 'I'm afraid that Theotimos did not get very far with his translations of the scrolls before illness indisposed him.'

'I see.'

Bion made no comment regarding soldiers and poisons. After all, he did not know for certain, and Raia would not tell him anyway.

'I hope he will recover soon, and can resume his studies.' He went on hurriedly, sparing Bion the trouble of prodding him onward. 'However, what he's been able to tell me from his sick bed is that the Medjay are not defeated. Perhaps I should say: they refuse to admit defeat and plan to manoeuvre themselves into a position where they will once more be vying for power in Egypt, which, as you might imagine, will bring them into direct conflict with The Order.' He paused. 'And as you might also imagine, Bion, we want to prevent that occurrence.' He held up a hand as though Bion had been about to interrupt him, although Bion was about to do nothing of the sort, 'You might ask when the Medjay plan to make their move. We do not know. Only that it is a long-term plan, something involving future generations of Medjay warriors. As I say, we would like to strangle such notions at birth.'

'We?'

'The Order.'

'Yourself and Theotimos?'

A small flicker of irritation on Raia's face was dismissed as quickly as it appeared. 'Does it matter? Either way it's to the benefit of The Order that the Medjay are stopped before any such plan can gather momentum. I would very much like to see to that.'

In order to increase your own standing, thought Bion, saying instead, 'So there is nobody else in your organization who knows?'

'This is a strategic point, soldier. The fewer people who know what we intend, the less likely it is that the Medjay can take action against us. We need to hit them quickly and hard. Our actions must be covert.'

'And that's the only reason?'

Raia's eyebrows knitted together. 'What other the reason might there be? These people are dangerous. We need to give them the respect they deserve.'

Which is why you're here.

'Which is why I'm here. Did I come to the right place?'

'You need me to kill Medjay for you.'

Raia chuckled. 'Bluntly put, but yes, that's *exactly* what I need you to do, Bion. Any surviving Medjay, you put them to the blade. Not just them, but their bloodline: man, woman or child . . .'

And here he paused, as though waiting to see if Bion would flinch, which he did not, because he had killed man, woman and yes even child just the same, making no distinction for age or gender.

Bion had no care for such details. Killing was killing.

'I want them dead, Bion, and I want you to collect the Medjay medallion to prove it, bring it to me in Alexandria so that I may have proof of the job done.'

'And in return?'

Raia preened. 'As I say, I think I am being primed for a leadership role in The Order. Of course, I would be extraordinarily grateful to anybody who had helped me and my ascent, and I might confer upon them greater status within The Order itself.'

'You mean me, do you, Commander?'

His visitor rolled his eyes. 'I mean anyone who helped me, Bion, just as I say.'

'What if I have no wish to return to the city or its ways, or revisit my old life?'

Raia folded his arms, looking at his old comrade carefully. It was clear he did not believe Bion wanted to stay there at all. 'Is that really your wish?' he said knowingly, and then, when Bion failed to reply, added, 'Do I need to remind you . . .'

20

They had been in Naukratis. Bion remembered it well. Like Alexandria, Naukratis was one of the modern cities, the Greek-built ones. Nevertheless, it still had some of the old problems, one of them being – as Raia and Bion were to find out that day – the constant conflict between landowners and the peasants, the *sekhety*, who worked their fields.

Bion and Raia had been in charge of guarding the child of a lower-ranking civil official within the pharaonic government, a little princeling by the name of Qenna.

They were there as a gift to the mother, a sop to convention, the child considered low risk. However, both were professionals and they didn't intend to let their guard down.

That day they had come with the boy into a square surrounded by cracked stone columns on all sides. Being from Alexandria, neither Raia nor Bion realized it was at least twice as busy as usual, and that the atmosphere was more fervent. What they saw was a bustling square, with a raised stone platform at its centre, and steps on which men stood delivering impassioned speeches to a lively crowd.

One orator in particular seemed to have gained a large audience. 'Why should we put up with this?' he was shouting, bent forward, one hand held out as though begging for the crowd's attention. His dirty robes seemed only to emphasize the significance of his message. 'Why must we stand by and allow ourselves to be treated this way!'

They had watched as the orator continued to speak against what he called the godless methods of a land-owner named Wakare. It wasn't until a little later that Bion conducted his own investigations into Wakare's working practices and found that they were indeed unethical and exploitative, and that the anger and hatred he had experienced that day in the square was entirely justified.

But for now . . .

'We must rise up,' bellowed the speaker. Bion saw the boy look startled, taken aback by the strength and passion of the man's message. Maybe they should leave, he thought. After all, the crowd seemed lively, these situations had a habit of spiralling quickly out of control.

On the other hand, maybe it would do the boy some good, he thought. Let him see life as it is truly lived.

'We must take back the land that we farm, on which we break our backs. Why should our hard work line the purses of those who have done nothing to deserve it? How is our work rewarded?'

The speaker reached into his tunic and he must have had a small sack hanging at his side because he brought out a handful of soil that he let crumble between his fingers, the crowd roaring its approval in response.

And then it happened.

Perhaps Wakare had only just been made aware of the orator's rabble-rousing; more likely, he'd been told in advance and had enough time to raise a mob of his own. Either way, as the speaker brought the crowd to fever pitch, their excitement threatening to boil over, three men appeared from the left-hand side of the square and made their way towards him, shouldering their way through the crowd.

Reaching him, one of the men drew a sword and waved it to ward off the crowd as his two companions set about the speaker, a blur of flailing fists as they pummelled him to the ground. The crowd reacted with cries of outrage, surging forward but deterred by the waving swords as the men delivered a pitiless beating, silencing the speech with the orator's blood.

Bion's first thought was his only thought: *The mission*, and then *Protect the boy*. Raia the same.

'Stay with us,' said Raia, his voice more commanding and harsh than Qenna was accustomed to hearing from a man who was his social inferior, his employee. But the child, imperious as he was, was no fool; moreover, he'd been schooled by his father, who had always instilled in him the necessity of obeying the commands of his bodyguard at all times, so this is what he did, scooting behind Bion and waiting there as his protectors gauged the situation.

And then came a renewed shout from the crowd and a ripple of fearful expectation, as a second group of men appeared from the opposite side of the square, seven or eight of them armed with long blades, swords and pitchforks – all manner of weaponry. They seemed to bristle with it, a skyline of dark, pointed, death-dealing instruments brandished overhead as they closed in.

Raia had swept back his robe to reach for the sword that hung at his belt. Bion, thinking ahead and seeing how the situation might be inflamed, reached to stop him, but it was too late; the new arrivals were wide-eyed and angry, drunk on beer or bloodlust or simply seething with injustice, and they saw the Royal Guardsmen and began rushing towards them. Either they didn't know the two men were protectors, expert swordsmen, ruthless and precise in combat and, more pertinently, prepared to lay down their lives as necessary for members of the royal family. Or, perhaps they simply didn't care. What they saw was three members of the elite – people who were, in some small way, architects of their pain. And even though Bion and Raia wore no uniform, just clothes befitting their royal appointment, that was enough to mark them out as rich and well-to-do. It announced them as belonging to the wrong side. Bion drew his sword. He knew what was coming.

'Royal Guards!' Bion shouted. 'We are Royal Guards!' They were foolish, these people, he thought idly. Did they not realize how easily they could be killed?

'We have no wish to fight you,' called Raia. Bion stood steady, hoping this would be over soon, though in truth other than the danger to the mission, he did not care whether any single person in that ragtag bunch lived or died. So when the first of the mob reached him he simply ran through the protester, who dropped with blood saturating his tunic, dead before he hit the flagstones. The sight of it enraged the group further, and as bystanders scattered, the battle intensified, the two guardsmen fighting with their backs to the platform, shielding the boy.

With his free hand Raia signalled to Bion, trying to execute a retreating manoeuvre. Those bystanders sufficiently curious not to have fled formed a circle in order to watch the fight and it was into their ranks that Raia was hoping to escape. Now, seeing an opening, Raia whirled a finger and pointed. Bion grabbed the boy and they pushed their way into the crowd, using their hilts to bludgeon a path between onlookers.

Now Raia was through, surging past the protest's fringes, beckoning for Bion and the boy to follow. But the crowd they hoped to leave behind was vengeful and hostile and legs snaked out, tripping them up.

Bion crashed to the ground, covering the boy, and then with a lurching shock he realized that the unthinkable had happened: his sword – as much a part of his arm as his own hand – had slipped from his fingers. He was unarmed.

He scrambled to protect the boy, using his body as a

shield as the first of the land workers burst through the crowd, a scythe held two-handed above his head. Bion saw rotten teeth and straining sinews in the man's neck. He saw hatred and the need to kill, and he threw up a useless arm in defence as the implement sliced the air towards him.

It never met its target. Raia had stopped, turned back and used his sword as a spear, and the attacker fell with the blade embedded in his chest. Plunging back towards them, Raia stooped, snatched up Bion's sword and felled a second man, wrenching his own sword free, tossing Bion's blade back to him as his comrade scrambled to his feet, dragging the boy with him, the three of them continuing their escape to safety. And at last they ran from the square, losing the last few pursuers in the streets of Naukratis.

Bion remembered the grateful eyes of the boy when at last they reached the Royal Court. He himself had thanked Raia for saving their lives, but had done so with annoyance. Why? Because he knew Raia well: a good soldier, perhaps, but lazy too. Too ambitious. Always scheming. Eager for more, for things beyond his station. And Bion knew that one day he would be reminded of the fact that Raia had saved his life, and be honour-bound to repay that debt.

When Raia had left to begin his return journey, Bion's feelings were like a blanket in need of unravelling. He knew Raia hadn't told him the full truth. He knew he now had a job to do, and though he had no wish to be bound to the man in such a manner, Bion was not a man to leave any obligation unfulfilled. It was irksome. His life, though frugal, was pleasing to him; he had no desire to leave his small home for what would be months, maybe even years on end. He had no desire to kill again.

And yet . . .

Why was it, he wondered, that he felt a tingle of anticipation? That he remembered the smell of blood so easily, how flesh parted before a sharp blade so readily?

And as he'd made the preparations that were to take him away, first to Hebenou, and then on the trail of Emsaf, he had wondered, *Do I miss the killing?*

21

Aya was taking long, frustrated strides back and forth in front of the rock that we'd called home for the past two days.

'I can't believe we let him fool us,' she was saying. 'A little street rat, letting him get the better of us like that. He saw you coming in Zawty, he saw you for the inexperienced mark you were then, and he hasn't stopped since, I'm telling you . . .'

'You don't understand,' I told her, squinting up at her from where I sat cross-legged. 'Tuta and I have been through a lot together.'

'Brothers in arms, is it?' she said, not unkindly. She sat down next to me, leaning against my shoulder. 'You think there's honour among thieves?'

Was I worried?

I wasn't sure.

Our journey had not been an easy one. We'd crossed rocky terrain, our horses' hooves slipping on shale beneath our feet, making camp and hunting for food. Those survival skills that had been taught to me by my father and Khensa, and in turn passed to Aya during our expeditions in Siwa, we now handed on to Tuta. In doing so, we amazed ourselves. We took pride in our subsistence. This was unforgiving land that gave up its fruit begrudgingly. Survival was not easy and ensuring Tuta's well-being as well as our own was an added challenge. We felt ourselves harden beneath the unforgiving sun. The fear that we felt being so far from home, cast adrift of those things that usually provided so much security, became resolve.

I had lain awake at night wondering whether this course of action – to find Khensa – was the right one, but pleased we were taking action. And even if one day I was forced to return to Siwa with my mission a failure, then I would at least return as one more suited to the role of protector.

I would know I had tried. That I had not turned from the task merely because it seemed insurmountable. That I had become the better for it.

Then, on the horizon, we saw columns like broken teeth and knew them for what they were: the Theban pillars – the Great Hypostyle Hall – and we saw the shape of a temple that seemed to form itself from the desert before our eyes, gaining mass the closer we came. The river span curled in the distance, a bright blue thread through sandstone buildings, while beyond it lay the Thebes Necropolis, stretching from the banks almost as far as the eye could see.

We'd been exhausted, hunched over on our horses, but the sight of the city in the distance straightened our backs. This was Thebes. To me in Siwa it had been as remote and legendary as Alexandria, and yet the two cities could not have been more different: Thebes, the once-proud Egyptian capital, had suffered during a series of revolts from which it had never quite recovered. Spread out like a tattered patchwork blanket to the left of the temple, the city's ramshackle collection of houses and buildings looked as though they'd been tossed like dice to the desert floor and left to rest, or maybe rot, gradually becoming at one with their surrounds.

It was only up close that we began to see flashes of colour from the awnings and lines of washing, but from afar it had simply looked like a huge grey structure at once crumbling and foreboding. The great pillars seemed to brush the clouds above and yet looked exhausted, as though in danger of simply collapsing to the sand below: awe-inspiring yet damaged and ageing. A symbol of strength succumbing to age and neglect – much like the city itself.

On the fringes of the city we found the shade of a tree and a rock that would serve as a windshield, and decided to make camp. 'You wait here,' Tuta told us both. He wanted to venture into his old home city alone, in order to find his mother and his sister, Kiya, and he took the horses, the idea being to barter them for food. Aya was suspicious but Tuta and I prevailed, and off he went.

The first day out there in the shadow of Thebes Aya and I talked of home, as we often had on our journey, recounting our camping expeditions, reliving them;

the second day, the conversation had turned to the whereabouts of Tuta, Aya growing more suspicious. What did we know of him? On the one hand, he had not only once lived in Thebes but also was used to living by his wits on the streets. Who better to find his own family, and then Khensa?

They were the positives.

On the other hand, Tuta had been young in Thebes. Very young. In all likelihood his family would have moved, left the city, maybe even died.

Khensa? She could be anywhere. I wasn't even convinced of the wisdom of looking for Khensa in the first place.

But more than all that, Tuta had our horses. And he was a thief.

True, I'd saved his life and he'd saved mine. But he was still a thief.

The third day – well, the third day I sat watching Aya worry, part of me thinking she had no grounds for concern, part of me sharing it. Then, on the fourth day, Tuta returned.

22

Much time had passed since Bion's blade had tasted blood. He had travelled along the river to Alexandria, needing to speak to his employer but wishing it were not so, thinking that he'd rather be anywhere than back in the nest of snakes that was Alexandria. He hated politics.

There was, however, one thing to be said for returning to Alexandria, and that was the look of discomfort on the face of his old commander, who had expressly told him to contact him by messenger, and not to visit him at home.

'What are you doing here?' Raia had snapped.

Bion looked over his shoulder. He saw a large room, ivy along a far wall, a table set with food and fire in braziers. A woman, Raia's wife perhaps, stood with a silver tray of bread and fruit, two little girls on chairs sat with their legs swinging, all looking his way. He thought how disquieting he must appear to them – the scars, the kohl-smeared eyes, the dirt from the trail – and was not surprised when they made themselves scarce with barely any prompting from Raia. Or perhaps he had just stared too long.

Recovering his composure, Raia invited Bion inside,

ushering him to a place at the table, offering him bread. In return, Bion offered something to Raia. He took out the medallion he had taken from Emsaf and let it fall to the tabletop. Raia's eyes gleamed as he pounced, picking up the metal, turning it over in his hand, inspecting it as though hoping to see bloodstains. A second later his brow clouded. 'Just one?' he said, and let the medallion drop, a glare at Bion indicating that he didn't consider one trophy worth the break in protocol.

'So far.'

'And yet you're here?' said Raia. 'Wasn't the plan that you were to use Emsaf's family in order to get the information we needed? This is why I sent you, Bion. This is easy work for you. Or should be.'

'He had been warned of my coming.'

'Perhaps you are out of practice.'

Bion looked at Raia patiently. 'These men are dangerous. They're different from men we've fought in the past, Commander. They're not indentured servants who want a better deal, workers campaigning for a better treatment from their landowners.' Though to some it might look as though the kill had been easy, Bion had had to work to track down Emsaf. Use trickery to get close enough for the kill. It had gone well because Bion was very good at what he did. Not because the quarry was incompetent – far from it.

Raia shrugged. 'They're men of conviction, nothing you haven't faced before.'

'They are men of conviction who are also highly

trained, highly skilled. They have everything we have up here,' Bion tapped his temple, 'and probably more of what we have here,' he tapped at his chest.

Raia chuckled. 'You do yourself a disservice, my friend,' he said, reaching forward to give Bion a friendly punch to the shoulder, failing to notice Bion tense in response. 'If anybody can do it, you can.'

'Would it not be more prudent to make this a two-man mission? Three, even?'

Raia shook his head definitively, the smile slipping from his face. 'Absolutely not.'

Of course not. Raia knew Bion would not talk. He had no such certainty about anyone else. Bion tucked the information away. It could be useful some day.

'But if these men are as dangerous to The Order as you fear . . .'

He pressed, curious above all to see Raia's reaction.

'Dangerous to The Order they may be,' replied Raia, 'but to men like you and I,' he waved his hands, bringing them both into his theoretical world, 'they merely represent the old ways given human form. You're quite right, old friend, we must not make the mistake of underestimating our foe, but neither should we fall into the trap of giving them too much respect. This is a job we can handle, you and I, I have no doubt about that. Either way, I haven't forgotten that your natural preference is to work alone, even if you have. Now, come on, how can we root out the last of these vermin?'

Bion looked at him. Wasn't it obvious? 'You have

a leak. Find the leak, you can find the last of the Medjay.'

'Are you sure we have a leak?' asked Raia. His eyes hardened, both of them knowing full well that it was Raia who had impressed on Bion the need for secrecy. And yet, if there was a leak then ultimately it was his responsibility. Bion would not talk. They both knew that.

'You said Theotimos was unable to continue his translation. Who was to do it instead?'

'A translator. I used a student from the library.'

Fool. Bion rested his hand at his side, fingers lingering on the pommel of his knife.

'Then I think I had better speak to this translator.'

23

Bion had let himself into the home, made his way up to the roof and found the historian Rashidi and his wife asleep on rush mattresses beneath the stars.

Bion watched them for a moment, considering his options. The usual would do well enough here. They were mere civilians, scared into his bidding easily enough. He flicked the shawl he wore back over one shoulder and drew a dagger that he placed to Rashidi's throat, put his other hand over his mouth and shook him awake.

Moments later they were back inside, where Bion bid Rashidi take a seat on a pile of cushions and then sat down himself. The uneven lighting in the room served only to make him look more sinister, his shadowed features doing the work of a thousand threats.

Rashidi was rigid with terror, his mind empty of all reason, his mouth dry. All he could focus on was the knife in Bion's hand. At last he found his tongue, 'What do you want?'

'I want to know about the Medjay.'

'Well, there is no such thing as the Medjay,' blurted Rashidi. 'Not any more. They don't exist, and haven't existed for hundreds of years. The Phylakes now stand where the Medjay once did.'

'But you do know of the Medjay?' asked Bion evenly. 'Your specialist subject is the Medjay, these . . .' Bion shrugged, 'protectors, scouts, soldiers of the Old Kingdom. Yes or no?'

'Yes.'

'Have you seen documents recently?'

Rashidi's eyes flickered. He swallowed. There was a pause in the room, a silence broken only by the sound of a candle guttering.

'I see documents all of the time in my line of work.'

Bion leaned forward. 'I think you know what I'm talking about. Have you seen documents *recently*? Something new? Something interesting, perhaps? You see, I spoke to a translator last night. He told me that he was having difficulty with some work and sought your advice. Is that right?'

'No,' said Rashidi.

It was a lie, of course. The translator had been very clear as to what had transpired. Still, he took another angle, for the moment. 'The Medjay are supposed to have died out, centuries ago,' he said. 'But they haven't, have they?'

'There are those who still proclaim a loyalty to the Medjay.'

Bion held up a hand to stop him. 'I'm not talking about them, I'm talking about the real ones. I'm talking about the ones to whom you sent a message not long ago.'

Rashidi shrunk back, as though he could disappear

to a safer place, a small keen of terror and knowing his only answer.

When Rashidi had given Bion the information he needed, Bion held him against the wall, flipped his dagger into an overhand grip, rammed it through his left eye into the brain and let the body slide to the floor before wiping the blade clean on Rashidi's hair.

He checked the cesspit, thinking he might use it to dispose of the bodies, but it was too small for his needs. At the rear of the house he found a walled courtyard area used for cooking, as well as olive oil stored in tall vases, and decided that would do instead.

Next he took the steps up to where Rashidi's wife slept on the roof beneath the stars. His promise to Rashidi had been empty, of course, but the relief the man had found in thinking his wife safe had granted information he'd otherwise perhaps have withheld. People trusted stupidly, Bion knew, when they thought loved ones might be saved.

He bent to her and she awoke instantly, alerted by the feel of his hand over her mouth, and her eyes widened as his dagger blade plunged deep, her good eye fluttering as she died.

Bion pulled her body to the side of the roof, heaved it over the side and down to the courtyard, and then descended the steps. He then dragged her corpse and that of Rashidi outside to the cooking area, doused their bodies in olive oil, set fire to them and everything around them. He waited a moment, to make sure everything was burning nicely, then slipped away into the shadows, returning to his own lodgings.

Back in his room, he took stock. He packed his things neatly, readying himself to leave at first light the next day.

When he went up to his roof and looked across the city, he saw the smoke in the distance. Across the rooftops came the sound of commotion as the fire alarm was raised. He settled down to a restful sleep. He knew where to go next.

24

Looking back, and I feel guilty admitting this, but when Tuta had returned and said 'I've found her', my first thought was that he'd found Khensa.

He hadn't. But he had found us somewhere to stay and that somewhere was with his mother and his sister. The family had been reunited.

As we headed into town and through the markets, I found myself assaulted once more by the sights and sounds of the city. The sun above our heads shone just as brightly, uncaring of the difference between prosperous Zawty and a Thebes that felt as if it would forever bear the scars of war, but was it my imagination or were the people somehow grubbier and less cheerful than they'd been in Zawty? One thing was for sure, we stood out less, the three of us, ragged and dirty from travelling.

Into the slums we went, where houses butted up against each other and there was a permanent stench, perhaps from the river but just as likely a result of sewage that ran in the streets.

'These are the people I told you about, *mouty*,' said Tuta to his mother when we arrived at his home. From the outside it had looked just like any other house in the slums, but inside it was pristine and filled with a love that was so tangible it hit you the second you walked through the door, as though the sun were shining inside the house.

Tuta's mother was a large, redoubtable woman with an open smile, eyes alive with the same mischievous light I saw in Tuta. She stood with a little girl whom I guessed to be about five summers old – too old to be seeking refuge in her mother's skirts, unless one knew what she must have seen when her father was still there. She regarded us with wary curiosity, but without fear. Tuta had gone to stand beside them. Looking at them together, it was difficult to believe they'd ever had anything to do with that drunken brute back in Zawty; they looked like a normal enough family, though after a moment of careful watching I could see the signs that they were people who had left a darkness behind, exchanging their ill fortunes for better ones.

'I am Bayek, son of Sabu of Siwa,' I told them, reacting to Tuta's silent prompting.

'And I am Aya, of Alexandria and Siwa.'

Tuta's mother acknowledged us gravely, and introduced herself as Imi, and the girl as her daughter, Kiya. 'I have you to thank for my son's life. You saved him from that horrible man,' she said.

I smiled at Aya, and quickly clarified that I had not done all the saving single-handed. When it came to the story of how Aya had rendered Tuta's father – his name was Paneb, we discovered – unconscious, Tuta's mother's eyes went to Aya, appraising her carefully in a way I couldn't quite decipher.

The moment passed, and I said, 'Wepwawet, the protector god of Zawty, brought us together, and now I hope that the gods of Thebes will be just as kind and aid us in our mission.'

'You're looking for an old friend from Siwa, I hear. A tribeswoman who lives here in the city with members of her people, is that right?'

'It is,' we said in unison, and she nodded decisively.

'Then you shall be our guests here until such time as you may find them. And if anybody can find them, Tuta can. No doubt his skill in making contacts among the city's undesirables will be most useful.'

She threw a playfully admonishing look at Tuta, who pulled a face that was somewhere between a blush and a smile.

'However,' continued Imi, 'you might also consider making your way to the Temple of Karnak. There you will find the priestess. I have every faith that she will be able to help you. Whether you'll be able to even speak to her is another matter.'

I raised my eyebrows and Imi took a deep breath, expression serious and a touch concerned. 'As you might have noticed from the look of our city, Thebes is in a somewhat depressed state. The Greeks have been harsh towards us – they continue to be so – and there is much resentment and jealousy among the local people. Bear this in mind as you travel through the city.'

The next day Tuta bade us farewell, evidently looking forward to acquainting himself with the underbelly of Thebes, pointing us in the direction of the temple before he went. 'The priestess is as intelligent as she is mystical, so I've heard it said. I'm sure that if anyone can convince her to help, then you can.' With that he flashed us a grin and was off, leaving us to explore Thebes together.

We set off, in no hurry, wanting to get a feel for this strange, dilapidated city and the people who lived in it. Just as we had been on the approach, we were struck by its washed-out appearance. It was clear that Thebes had once boasted vibrant colours. We saw vestiges of it on painted columns and pillars and walls. Now, though, time, sun and general neglect had taken their toll. The fading and peeling paint adorning the carved figures and the bases of the columns was a sad reminder of another, more prosperous time.

Only nature was undaunted. In Thebes, colour was provided only by foliage and the occasional glimpse of the glittering water. Its denizens, meanwhile, appeared as worn down as its buildings.

'Do you notice anything?' said Aya, as we trod its streets.

'Like what?'

'Imi is right.' She lowered her voice. 'There is a certain tension about the place.'

'You mean the state of it?' I indicated some daubings in Latin and Greek that we passed. Crude statements of discontent that served only to underline the shabby look of the place.

'Not just the look of it, but . . .' she rubbed her fingers together as though testing the quality of herbs, '. . . a certain feel. As though the whole city is on edge.'

Sure enough, we passed Greeks with indentured Egyptian servants trailing in their wake, and then a high-born Greek with a coterie of Egyptian body-guards, either oblivious to the townsfolk who watched him with such dislike, or uncaring of it.

We finally reached the Alley of Sphinxes, baked by the sun as we walked between the huge black cats that lined the way to the Temple of Karnak. Before we neared the sprawling, vast temple complex, we stood for a moment, entranced by it. Like everywhere else this expanse of buildings, precincts and quadrangles had seen better days, but even so, it was a feast for the eyes. The columns were twice as tall as anything we'd seen in Thebes so far and three times as wide, the carvings even more intricate and ornate.

We climbed steps and made our way inside, asking after the whereabouts of the priestess from temple workers who looked at us with mild curiosity and then waved us on, further into the complex, into the inner sanctum.

Passing among the tall pillars and the washed-out marble we came to a worker dressed more finely than others.

'We'd like to see the priestess, if we may,' asked Aya

sweetly. I stood by her side, not needing to adopt a look of godly devotion. The temple had that effect on me anyway.

The man eyed us up and down, his head arriving at a position in which it was perfectly inclined to look down his nose at us. We'd cleaned ourselves up since our travels, but even so he judged us inappropriate to see the priestess and was shaking his head, about to tell us no, when there came another voice. 'Wait,' it said, and we looked up to see its owner materialize from the shadows at the far end of the auditorium.

25

At first I saw the silk and gold and beauty and was rendered almost speechless by it, thinking that she was truly resplendent, sumptuous with riches and colour. But then she came closer and I saw that her linen was frayed and the gold leaf on her staff and the tall headpiece she wore was flaking. As she approached I realized that she was in many ways the embodiment of the decaying temple and thus of Thebes itself. I found myself wondering what effect she had on the city. For even though her clothes were down-at-heel there was a presence about her. There was nothing at all stricken about the way she carried herself, nor was there any hint of defeat in the slow, measured manner in which she turned her gaze on us. Her command to wait had been clearly intended not just for us, but for her servant as well.

'I am Nitokris, God's Wife of Amun, High Priestess of Thebes and guardian of the Temple of Karnak. Tell me, what brings you here?' she asked.

I bowed my head in return. 'I am Bayek of Siwa,' I said, 'and this is my companion, Aya of Alexandria.'

Aya and I looked at one another. Aya nodded, even as I shifted slightly, deferring in this conversation to her. Considering she'd been at the temples in Alexandria,

Aya was obviously best placed to reply. 'We come to Thebes from Siwa,' she said, and then stopped at the knowledgeable way the priestess nodded, as if already in possession of that information.

'We come in search of Siwa's protector, a man named Sabu.' Aya indicated me. 'This is Bayek, son of Sabu. I am Aya. Sabu may not be in Thebes, but we hope to find a Nubian named Khensa who may be here with her tribe. She might know where he is.'

'Indeed,' said Nitokris. She led us to a bench along one wall, dismissing her underling first.

'So, you are the protector's son,' she murmured – a statement, not a question.

I nodded in confirmation anyway.

'And do you hope to be protector yourself one day?'

Her lips quirked even before I answered, from the look on my face alone I would guess.

'Yes,' I said. 'My father is training me to take up the role.'

'Is that all he has told you? That you will one day be Siwa's protector.'

The question was neutral, without judgement or insinuation. I couldn't help but instantly wonder.

'Is there anything else to know?'

Her smile returned, though her gaze was still serious. Intent. 'Yes,' she said, 'there is much to know.' Though this could have been anyone's reply, about life and anything else, I knew she was being specific. There were no airs about her, no self-aggrandizing mysticism.

'Your friend Khensa. Perhaps she will give you answers that you seek. If she does, return to me, for I should like to talk more.'

Was that the end of our audience? I found myself eager to spend more time in her company, wondering at the wisdom a woman with such presence might have to share. And then, as though she sensed that need in me, she turned her gaze towards me. 'I am the God's Wife of Amun,' she said, answering a question I hadn't asked with a touch of amusement which quickly faded to gravity, 'and one day I hope to see Thebes rise again, and once more be the force it was.'

'You cleave to the old ways – to the ways of the Pharaohs?' asked Aya. She was clearly intrigued, ever wanting to know more about everything.

'To the ways of the gods and the good of the people,' Nitokris answered, simply. 'To Amun, who rules by listening to the poor, not by using them. Amun, who is of service to the people, rather than insisting on being served by them.'

'But there are new ways now,' said Aya. I could tell that she was interested by the priestess, despite being one to favour the logic of philosophers over clerical politicking. 'The word coming from Alexandria is that Ptolemy Auletes is selling Egypt to the Romans to stay in power.'

Nitokris laughed, low and confident. 'Ah, but hasn't Egypt been invaded before? The Persians, the Nubians, the Greeks. And yet, it is our country that changes people. Our people endure. We will change the Romans just as we changed Alexander. It is up to us to see that Egypt always retains that power.'

'Us?' I asked.

'Oh yes, protector's son.' She sobered once more, one hand lightly coming to rest on my shoulder for the briefest moment. 'You may one day find yourself with more than just Siwa's temples to protect.'

She rose from the bench and with that, the meeting was over. As we left, I found myself looking forward to the time when we might return – and she could give me answers to questions not yet formed. Beside me Aya was thoughtful too, both of us lost in our own worlds.

Tuta, meanwhile, continued looking for Khensa. Weeks passed, during which time Aya and I became further acquainted with Thebes, spending our days joining Tuta to forge contacts and ask questions, or going to the out-skirts of the city with wooden practice swords that we'd whittled in order to work on our swordsmanship.

At nights we would all convene at Tuta's house and sit around a fire, or perhaps outside if the night was warm, drinking milk, beer or wine. Tuta's little sister, Kiya, had developed an affection for Aya. Her mother didn't mind, being more than happy to let the girl sit with their visitor, her legs drawn up, head resting on Aya's tunic.

Tuta, Kiya and Imi were a family again, but although Aya and I were outsiders we were greeted and treated like royalty, and I know that Aya loved it there just as much as I did.

I was happy. I wanted to find Khensa and my father, and learn what else the priestess had to say. Even so, I liked the simplicity and the day-to-day joyfulness of this new life I now led. Each day, Tuta would return from his investigations, telling us that he hadn't found Khensa, 'Oh but, sir, I will, don't you worry about that, I will. If she's in Thebes, or if she's ever been in Thebes, then I'll find her.'

I'd often wondered how much Tuta had told his mother and Kiya about the circumstances in which we'd met, until one night, when we sat in the yard with jars of wine, the sounds of the slum in the air around us, talking and drinking, and the conversation had died, and we realized that Tuta's mother was looking at Aya in a strange fashion – a look I recognized from the day we had arrived.

Kiya had been sitting with Aya in her usual pose, resting her head, thumb in her mouth. But as she became aware of the awkward silence she sat upright, wondering what was wrong.

And then Tuta's mother came out with it, addressing Aya. 'So you gave my husband a good hit on the head, did you?'

Aya shifted uncomfortably beneath the intensity of her gaze. 'I did. It was . . . I mean, there was a fight . . .'

'It's like I said to you, Mama,' said Tuta, and then tailed off as she held a finger to her lips.

'I know, I know you did, little Tuta, I just wanted to hear it in Aya's own words, that's all. I just wanted to hear her say it.'

Aya wasn't sure how to react, throwing me an awkward glance.

'You might have killed him,' continued Tuta's mother.

And now Aya swallowed, not sure what to say in reply. I could tell she had no regrets, but neither did she want to cause grief. 'I was just trying to save Bayek,' she explained, 'and Bayek was just trying to save Tuta.'

Tuta's mother laughed, loud and clear, hands to her knees while she rocked back and forth. 'No. I mean you *should* have killed him.'

'He would have had a very sore head the next morning,' grinned Aya, relieved and a touch proud as well.

'Is that right? Well, he's no stranger to that. Perhaps it'll be such a sore head that it will make him mend his ways, though I doubt it.'

Tuta shook his head sadly. 'He won't mend his ways, Mama.'

'No, I don't suppose he will. Bullies like him never do.'

'He's not *just* a bully, Mama,' insisted Tuta. 'He's worse than that now.'

Tuta's mother shot him an indulgent look. 'Well, he's not here, is he? Nothing he can do to us now.'

We continued our training, until one day Tuta came to us, and this time when he said, 'I've found her,' he meant Khensa.

26

Khensa was found, and suddenly I was forced to confront the fact that I was about to see my childhood friend again. I had to ask myself, how did I feel about that?

I wasn't sure. The last time I'd seen her she was ensconced with her people in tents constructed from carved wooden supports and garish canopies. Theirs was an arrangement that was at once both permanent and transient, befitting their nomadic status in the region. When one day I arrived at the camp only to discover that they'd packed up and left I was upset to lose my friend, but it came as no great surprise. They were a wandering people, untethered by locality.

I'd missed her, of course. From Khensa I'd learned virtually all I knew about survival. Our relationship was ... well, I wouldn't have said it was odd, but it wasn't particularly normal either. A nomad training a small-town boy in survival skills? While we become friends, no less? Thinking about it now, though, I had to admit that Khensa had moulded me in many ways, long before my father finally decided to train me himself.

'Like I said to you before, I was beginning to think

they were a rumour,' said Tuta as he led us outside Thebes, heading towards the river. 'Seems like a lot of people had heard gossip of this group of Nubians in Thebes, but not many would admit to having seen them. I was pretty sure they'd lived here at one time or another. Of that I was almost certain. But did they *still* live here? Nobody knew. Which is all a long way round of making my excuses for why it's taken me so long.'

'You've done well, Tuta,' said Aya fondly.

'Well, that's praise indeed, that is,' beamed Tuta, knowing Aya never praised without merit. He was rewarded with a smile from Aya.

As we travelled, Aya and I kept expecting to come upon the Nubians' lodgings. Yet Tuta led us past the boundaries of Thebes and through the bulrushes to the very edge of the river, to the landing of a ferryman. The man was well known to Tuta, judging by the way they greeted one another.

Next thing we knew, the boatman was pushing us across with a pole, and on landing we crossed into the necropolis, from which the souls of the dead travelled onward to the *Duat*.

Tuta pulled a face. This was new territory for him too. We made our way through the necropolis until we came to a tomb driven into the ground.

This was the place, indicated Tuta, chewing his bottom lip and standing aside as though he expected Aya and me to jump down and go bounding inside.

We looked at him in disbelief. 'In there?' I said.

He nodded.

'But it's . . . they can't be.'

'They are,' insisted Tuta.

'How do you know?' asked Aya.

I looked around. After all, this particular tomb looked like any other tomb in the necropolis, as though it had been hewn into the very landscape itself, the squared-off entrance the only real indication of human activity.

No – in fact there was something else – something Tuta drew to our attention. Further back along the ground there was some kind of vent that, when he pulled us over to it, we saw was emitting smoke.

'I've listened at it,' whispered Tuta. 'They're definitely in there. More than one of them.'

I was still reeling. 'How could they?' I blurted. 'How could they make this their home? It's . . . It's not right.'

'It's a terrible thing, is what it is,' agreed Tuta sadly.

'Oh, don't be ridiculous,' said Aya. 'Tuta, whose tomb is this?'

'I'm afraid I've no idea,' said Tuta. Aya had asked, though, and he gamely tried to answer anyway. 'It could be that it's . . .'

'Nobody's tomb, isn't that right? They wouldn't set up camp in somebody's tomb, now, would they?'

I stared around, frantically trying to divine whether there were markings on the walls surrounding us, so far making nothing out at all. It did not make me feel better.

'Even so,' I spluttered, 'to make their home here is . . .'

Aya cut me off, smiling slightly as she surveyed our surroundings. She was taking all of this with far more equanimity than I was. Of course.

'What? Sacrilegious? No, if you ask me it makes perfect sense. This, after all, is the one place *nobody* would come looking for you. Nobody but Tuta, it seems.'

Aya had the last word on the subject. Whatever my feelings on the matter I'd need to make sense of them alone.

Tuta, meanwhile, was happy with any outcome that involved praise from Aya, still grinning and blushing as we returned to the entrance.

'What do we do now?' I asked. Could they be in there? Was there even a possibility that my father was inside?

'I don't know,' admitted Tuta.

'They might not let us in,' I said.

'Even if they do, how do you know they're not going to cut us down the minute we step inside?' said Aya.

Tuta looked worried. This he had clearly not expected. 'Wait a minute. Wasn't I told that the Nubians and Bayek were great friends, from not so long ago?'

We pointed out that 'not long ago' was ten summers and that people change, factors which made turning up unannounced and letting ourselves into their underground hideout – evidently a place they wanted to remain undiscovered – a very bad idea.

On the other hand, as Tuta was all too ready to point out, what else did we expect? What other choice did we have?

And then, as we stood close to the entrance trying to decide what to do, the decision was made for us, because a figure appeared at the threshold: a woman who carried a spear and squinted up at us from the hollow of the dark interior.

'Hello, Bayek,' she said. I recognized the mischievous gleam in her eyes only too well.

I blushed, slowly raising my hand in a sheepish greeting. How many times had Khensa told me about whispers, and how sound carried in walled-up places?

27

She clambered up to greet us, and at first I thought she was just the way I remembered her: the coloured braids in her hair, feathers, the tribal scars. She had the same bearing, the same dark and smoky eyes, a gaze that would brook no argument.

But she was older. Not just in years but in other ways as well. When I knew her as a young girl she had worn a necklace decorated with bones, and other trophies were woven into her hair, but now?

'Hello, Khensa,' I said, indicating her necklace of lion's teeth, as well as what must have been a hippo tusk woven into her braids. 'You've grown in stature and prowess.'

She acknowledged the statement with a nod, and it was then that I sensed something different about her, a distant, preoccupied air that I didn't remember from years ago in Siwa, as though she had the cares of the world on her shoulders.

Nevertheless, and although the smile never quite reached her eyes, she greeted me effusively, exclaiming, 'My friend, my brother,' and giving me compliments of her own. I had grown, she said. I had developed muscles, and she prodded them, doing the same to my belts, pulling an impressed face. When she last saw me I was a boy. Now I was grown. A warrior.

I introduced Tuta and Aya. She and Khensa eyed each other. Their characters were not opposed – in so many ways they were much the same – but their outlook could not have been more different.

'Have you heard from him?' I asked once the introductions had been made, eager to know.

She looked at me. 'From . . . ?'

'From my father.'

At this, she looked surprised. 'No. Why would I . . . ? Wait, is that why you're here?'

I tried to control a wave of disappointment. 'Are you sure?' I said to Khensa, as stupid as I sounded. 'You haven't heard from him? He's not here?'

Khensa shook her head, confused. 'I would know, Bayek, if he was here. I'd remember something like that. He would only have come here if I'd asked him, and I haven't. Nor have I approved any message sent. Perhaps you'd better tell me what's going on.' She stood to one side indicating the opening that led into the tomb, 'Come in,' she said. 'Let's drink.'

'You really do live in there?' I asked.

She nodded. The corner of her lip curled, but I couldn't help but press on, even though I knew she was already amused at my reaction.

'But it's a tomb. It's sacred.'

She shook her head and started to walk, one hand trailing along the wall.

'A looted tomb,' explained Khensa, 'no longer sacred. Nobody respects the tombs any more. Come on.'

I'm not sure what I expected as we put the sun to our backs and trod down into the tomb below. Something dark and dank and cramped, I supposed, but nothing could have been further from the truth. The ceiling was low, but not so low you were forced to stoop, and it was draped with awnings that took me back to Siwa with a rush of recognition and a sudden yearning for home. It was warm without being unpleasant. A fire at the far end gave it a – and it seems strange to even think the word – 'homely' feel, and was far from the only source of light in the room, as there were lanterns hanging from the walls on either side. How easy it was to forget that we were in a tomb.

I could see at once that the Nubians' numbers were much reduced. An older man covered in a shawl, weathered face heavily scarred, sat coughing, raising his head to look at us without much interest. A younger man, slightly older than Khensa, sat next to a woman his own age, who was pregnant. There was also an older woman busying herself at the other end of the cavern.

Other than that?

'This is it,' said Khensa, seeing my face fall. The man coughing, she explained, was her grandfather, the tribal elder. The other woman was her mother. The young man was Seti, a warrior, the pregnant woman his wife. There was a scout, too – Neka his name – but other than that this was the remains of her tribe.

I was trying and probably failing to keep my shock to myself. I had never known any of the tribe in the old days. When going to see Khensa, my usual method had been to hang around on the boundaries of the camp waiting for her to appear. Even so, I could tell that there had been up to a dozen of them back then; the encampment had been a place of light and life and colour. Some of that still remained – the canopies overhead – but a strange sense of diminishment seemed to have settled over those assembled here.

'Where is everybody?' I asked, looking around, unable to keep the dismay out of my voice.

'Dead or gone,' explained Khensa, matter-of-factly.

'How?'

A weary look came across her. 'The simple answer is a war – one that shows no sign of ending. Let us sit, drink, catch up first. I want to know what you're doing here – and why you're asking after Sabu.'

Beer and a place around the fire was the accompaniment to our storytelling session. I went first, a tale that began by assuring Khensa that little had changed since she and her tribe left Siwa.

'Had your father begun your training?' asked Khensa.

'He had,' I told her, adding, 'but it progressed slowly. He never seemed to want it to happen. He'd always say I wasn't ready. According to Rabiah he had doubts about training me, since the night of the Menna attack. He worried about leading me down the same path he followed.'

I went on to tell Khensa about my father's departure, and how it had left the town in disarray. Rabiah mystified as to his reasons for going, my decision to leave in pursuit, my desire to keep pursuing a path toward protectorship of Siwa.

'You still want one day to become protector of Siwa?' asked Khensa bluntly.

'Yes,' I said, and my voice shook with conviction. It was the truth I could finally own, without any doubt hampering my certainty. 'I think that I've changed. Maybe I just played at it before, but now I know. I want to be the protector of Siwa, to follow in my father's footsteps.'

'So you think you know your destiny?' asked Khensa. I wasn't sure if it was a statement or a question, only that I felt under scrutiny. But my certainty didn't fade.

'I know my path,' I told Khensa, meeting the directness of her gaze with one of my own. 'It is to train as my father's apprentice and serve as Siwa's protector. That's all I want.'

That, I thought, *and Aya*.

'What do you know of the Medjay?' said Khensa.

Her question came out of the blue, and I stared in puzzlement. Aya answered for me, and I was thankful, though also a bit surprised. 'Why?'

Khensa nodded slowly, acknowledging Aya and her timely intervention, while still focusing on me. 'The fact is, Bayek, that if you know nothing of the Medjay then you know nothing of your path. Everything you believe – well, I wouldn't go so far as to say it's been a lie, but it certainly hasn't been the whole truth.'

I fought irritation, close to becoming anger. 'Then why don't you tell me?'

So she did.

And then I understood.

28

'Your father is a Medjay.'

I swallowed. I didn't even know what a Medjay was, but even so I heard myself say, 'He can't be,' confusion evident to my own ears.

'Nonetheless, Bayek, he is,' said Khensa.

'But they no longer exist,' said Aya quickly. 'The Medjay died out years ago.'

At least Aya knew something. It was reassuring, somehow. A truth I could use to calm myself. While I recentred myself, Khensa spoke.

'They didn't, not fully.'

'Wait,' I said. I needed to know, before the conversation swept past me. '*What* exactly is a Medjay? A soldier of some kind? A protector?'

Khensa nodded. 'A protector, indeed. They are – or were – the reason that people respected the tombs, for one. They were the protectors of such things. And as a protector your father was sworn to guard the temples at Siwa, thus the whole village, from any forces willing to act against it or against the aims of Medjay.

'But what you must understand is that his role as Medjay went much further than that. It made him a *guardian*, not just a guard. It made him a protector not only of Siwa but also of an entire way of life. A protector of Egypt.'

Aya looked doubtful. 'What way of life?'

'The way our enemies like to think of as "the old way", as though that's a bad thing, as though its being old makes it somehow out of date.'

The shadows of the flames flickered against the wall, as though pantomiming a story I could not fathom. I glanced at Aya and kept quiet, letting her ask her own questions. She was as much part of this as I was.

'Well, then, maybe they're right, maybe it does,' responded Aya, drawing herself up. It wasn't quite a challenge, but it certainly was blunt.

Khensa shook her head, serene. 'No system, new or old, is without its flaws,' she said. Of all the things Khensa excelled at, knowing and understanding people was one of them. Confidence clearly shone through as she went on. 'No doubt the old ways were in need of modernization; clearly some thinking needed reappraisal but . . .' And here she held up a finger, 'but they existed for thousands of years and they existed in a belief that we are on this earth to work together in our worship of the gods rather than simply to increase our own wealth and prestige. I know what you're thinking,' and here she turned her attention to Aya. 'You're thinking of yourself as an enlightened one. Perhaps you have given up on the gods.'

'I haven't given up on the gods,' replied Aya instantly, though we both knew it wasn't strictly speaking true and her words rang hollow. Even Tuta gave her a surprised sideways glance.

But Khensa smiled. 'It is good, to be full of questions. I know that you see it as a sign of your intelligence and enlightenment that you question, and that's something I can fully understand.'

As I raised both eyebrows at her, remembering being scolded far too often about all my pesky questions during survival training, Khensa rolled her eyes at me and deftly nudged a rock, causing it to bounce off my foot and ricochet into the fire.

'Hush, you.' I had heard those fond words many times from her, and I grinned, unrepentant, and feeling on familiar territory once again.

'My people question things, too. Everyone does. Change is growth. It's the only way to survive. But it doesn't mean we have to cast everything aside.' She looked into the fire, eyes distant. 'There is grace to be found in ritual, and in tradition. It has kept my people alive. We rely on it. What we cannot afford, however, is to let tradition become a yoke that slows us down, drags us under.' She hooked her fingers, miming a driver pulling back a team of oxen. 'Being in the city, never moving – in a way, that's one form of stagnation already. It makes certain things even easier: selfishness, venality, corruption. Cities are beautiful.' She offered Aya a crooked grin, an honest gleam of admiration in her eyes. 'But they also make it easier for bad things to fester. They can quickly become a world in which the wealthy and powerful fashion artefacts, and whole cities in some cases, in praise of themselves, monuments to their own vanity.'

'It's not the gods who have failed us.' Aya's voice was subdued, and she sighed – though she'd never shared this thought with me, it did not seem a new one to her. 'It's people.'

Khensa gave her a sympathetic look and turned her attention to me. 'Bayek, that is what your father as a Medjay believes, and that is what we in our tribe also believe. There are still many who believe in the ways of the Medjay. Our scout, Neka, tells me of a man claiming an allegiance to the Medjay imprisoned in Elephantine. There are pockets of us, Bayek, pockets of resistance. But all of those who feel drawn towards the ways of the Medjay are in need of guidance, and whether they know it or not they need guidance from the bloodline, the true Medjay. They need guidance, Bayek. That could be you, someday.'

I thought of what the priestess had said: *You may soon find yourself with more than just Siwa's temples to protect*, and I felt infused with a sudden sense of purpose.

'But I'm not ready.'

'The best leaders are never ready.' She tilted her head, inspecting me. 'And I concede, you do have much to learn yet, before you can properly lead.'

Khensa sat back. The firelight danced, and what I saw was a look on her face that convinced me I was doing the right thing by naming my path and following it. It was an expression that spoke of something deeper than emotions we wrestle with every day, our usual aches and pains and gripes as human beings; it spoke of something deeper, something more ancient. What I saw in her face was knowledge. I felt it myself, even though just a little bit. Though uncertainty still nagged at my heels, I wanted this. I wanted to know more about the Medjay. I wanted to help people – all the people of Egypt. It felt good. A fervour and resolve. The overwhelming conviction that I had found my path. I just needed to keep learning. To become more.

'Are you Medjay, too?' I asked her.

She shook her head, snorting in amusement. 'Of course not. My clan and I, we are our own people. But many ages ago we discovered that our principles were aligned well enough with those of the Medjay, our ideology the same.'

'My father?'

'An ally, yes.'

'I think now I understand what I was up against,' said Aya suddenly. 'This is it, isn't it? To Sabu I represented the new ways. The ways that destroyed the Medjay. Is that why he didn't complete Bayek's training . . .'

'No,' Khensa interrupted, 'though it took me a long time to understand why.' She flicked her gaze towards me, inscrutable for a moment, then shrugged. 'Being Medjay, it is about something more than you or I. It's about the greater good, about looking beyond today, tomorrow, next week even next month and asking what happens in ten years' time, fifty years' time. The Medjay is a way of life. It's a way of being, a way of saying that I reject values forced upon me by a society I no longer support. It's a better way of being at one with the world and with the people in it. It is about giving everything, sacrificing everything if needed.' She paused and shrugged. 'I think that's why Sabu held back on the training.'

Aya listened intently and I caught a look of dawning understanding in her eyes. Though Khensa had always been skilful at hunting, and I lucky to have her to teach me, her skill at reading people is what had always awed me. But I didn't understand what Khensa was trying to tell me. I did not ask her to elucidate further – she'd just be annoyed at my thick-headedness.

'So why did he leave?' I heard myself say. 'Why did my father leave Siwa?'

'I don't have the answer to that. I can see why Rabiah sent you to me, but as for why your father has left Siwa unprotected, I don't know. Find him and you'll find out. And also, when you find him, then perhaps your induction can continue.'

'Do you think I am to become a Medjay?' I was perhaps a bit breathless as I asked, but I valued her opinion. And she was a mentor of mine as well, after all. My first dedicated teacher.

She laughed, and I had to admit I'd likely earned that. 'I know that your father was training you in the ways of the Medjay, even as he worried. But, you see, it's not just a matter of learning combat, or subterfuge and surveillance. It isn't just a series of skills such as those I once taught you in Siwa. Becoming a Medjay is about adopting a new way of life. It's about changing your way of thinking. Medjay isn't something you choose, like whether to eat bread or fish. Medjay is something you are.' She thumped her own chest, the sound like the beating of a drum in the cave. 'It's something only you can define. Whether you like it or not, Bayek, you are the son of Sabu. In that you have no choice, along with everything it brings. But being Medjay? Well, regardless of what Sabu believes, that's entirely up to you now, isn't it?'

29

How did I feel about setting out on a path that would make me a Medjay?

To be honest, it seemed just a step further than being a protector of Siwa. Ironically, that was exactly why my induction had not been completed. My father's doubts and worries had likely been exactly along the lines: even if he taught me how to protect Siwa, how much more would it take for me to learn, and protect if necessary, the Medjay ethos?

On the other hand if I were to reject Medjay ways, just as Egypt herself had done, what would it mean? For all Khensa's talk about the Medjay being in my blood, it wasn't as though I could somehow magically embody their ideals overnight.

Belief wasn't something you carried in your blood.

Conviction was part of one's spirit and ideology. That much I knew with certainty. I was confident Aya would agree with me on this – she was the one who had exposed me to modern philosophers and poets, after all. In the meantime, there was still much to learn.

'What will you do now?' asked Khensa.

I shrugged. 'Do what I've been doing. Continue to

teach myself what I can as I search for my father. Keep learning.'

I could practically feel Aya's approving smile – a quick glance in her direction confirmed I was right.

'This Medjay in Elephantine,' Aya said. 'Could he help us?'

Khensa looked doubtful. 'It's unlikely the man they have in prison is a legitimate Medjay. No doubt he's a pretender, someone adopting the mantle and claiming adherence to its ways without true understanding of the history. There are plenty of those about. Besides, how would you reach him?'

'With your help.'

She was nodding, thinking. Unsurprised by my presumption.

'We thought Sabu leaving might have something to do with you being here,' prompted Aya.

'I'm sorry to disappoint you.'

'But you are here because of my father, aren't you?' I probed. 'It's true that your people decided to go after Menna?'

Khensa nodded.

'Then where is Menna? Dead? Close by? Where?'

'He is near,' agreed Khensa. 'Menna has been at his current location for almost six years but we believe he may now be on the move. My scout, Neka, is looking into it now.'

'You can't lose him,' I said quickly, perhaps a little

too sharply, wincing immediately afterwards. I had no right to order Khensa in such a high-handed way.

She pulled a face, clearly agreeing with my regret. 'I ought to slap you just for suggesting such a thing. While you've been in the sun wondering why your father hasn't been teaching you to play swords, I've been out here watching my family die at the hands of Menna's men. Ours has been a long war of attrition, Bayek. I have no intention of letting him go, and if you think you're going to arrive here and start telling me my business . . .'

'I'm sorry,' I said. I was sincere. For all that had cast a long shadow over my life, as well as the man with the crooked eye who had crept through my window the night of the attack . . . the consequences were a bit more immediate for Khensa.

'He exists, then?' I said at last.

'Menna?'

'I mean, he's not an idea or a group of people. Some means of scaring children to go to sleep at night?'

'Oh no, he's none of those things, said Khensa. There as a long pause as she seemed to think, poking at the fire with a stick and blinking slightly as the flames leapt in response. 'You found your way here,' she said at last, directing her words at Tuta, 'do you think you can find a horse and cart?'

Tuta nodded enthusiastically.

Two days later, we had a horse and cart.

30

Before we left, Aya and I went to see Nitokris once more. We made the journey to the Temple of Karnak, navigating the guards and temple workers to her inner sanctum, where she greeted us as though she had known we would appear, leading us to the same spot to sit.

'So,' she said, turning a serene smile on us, looking from me to Aya and back again, 'you return.'

'When you said there was much more to things . . .' I trailed off under her knowing gaze, then smiled somewhat ruefully. 'I understand now. We know of the Medjay, and that my path involves being much more than just Siwa's protector,' I told her.

'And you embrace that path, do you?' asked the priestess.

'I wish I had known earlier,' I said. The shade of the temple was soothing, wind blowing gently through the hallways, cooling our skin. For all my resentment at having had this hidden from me, this place calmed me down, moment by moment. I needed the focus.

'It is no small responsibility, embarking on the path of a Medjay,' she said. 'The Medjay is no mere guard or protector. You will have been told that the Medjay uphold an ancient ideology, I'm sure, but your duties go beyond even that. Your task as a Medjay is not merely to protect old things, but to provide balance, justice and equilibrium. As a Medjay you will revere Amun. You will be the living embodiment of Ma'at, the ancient beliefs in truth and harmony.'

I was holding my breath, I realized, and forced myself to exhale, then breathe slowly and regularly. Finally. Simple, straightforward information. Something I could rely on.

'Once upon a time, every Egyptian would apply the principles of Ma'at to their own lives and follow them, but these things along with so much more has been lost in the rush to modernity. These things are what make us good, Bayek, son of Sabu, and as a Medjay you are not just charged with preserving and promoting those principles, you *are* those principles. Do you understand?'

I nodded. This I could cleave to. Information I could absorb and draw conclusions from. This was something to aspire to, to craft an entire life from. Be good. Protect the innocent. Take down the corrupt. Focus on the day to day, but also look to the future.

'I know you do,' said Nitokris. She spoke with utter certainty and, in that instant, reminded me of Khensa, and her uncanny ability always to know what truly drove someone. She angled her head slightly, then stood, the meeting at an end. 'Do you know the symbol of Ma'at?' she asked me.

I shook my head.

'It is the ostrich plume.'

As she left I reached into my pouch and pulled out the items I had been gathering on my travels.

In my hand were feathers. White feathers.

Khensa led us on a journey of many days. With us was Seti, the scout Neka having yet to return. The five of us must have made a strange sight, wedged in between supplies on the cart as we trundled over land to the west, away from Thebes.

We described a circuitous route. An approach from the west was too dangerous according to Khensa and Seti, so when we reached the low, shallow mountain that was apparently our destination, we kept our distance and took a long route around the base of it, coming at it from the east.

We left the cart in the foothills and made the ascent on foot until we reached a vantage point – a plateau offering a view of the glittering sea over to the east as well as what looked like the beginnings of a large hollow through the centre of the mount below.

There we gathered, crouched, in a circle, looking to our guide for advice. Khensa had warned us of the need for quiet when we reached the top, and when we arrived she pressed a finger to her lips and fixed us with one of those fearsome, tight-lipped stares she was so good at, reserving special intensity for Tuta, who had proved to be a bit too excitable for her liking during the journey.

She commanded us to go on our bellies and we edged to the lip of the plateau, looking down into what was part-hollow, part-valley – an almost circular gash in the mountain falling to a basin below. There on the valley floor, hidden by mountain walls on all sides and accessed by a single road leading in from the east, was a collection of buildings. The buildings were badly constructed, but they were buildings. They spoke of permanence.

Lying there, Khensa turned her head to me. I lay between her and Aya. 'And that,' she said, in a low voice, avoiding a whisper that could carry in the distance and betray us, 'is where Menna has been hiding for . . .' She thought. 'Five summers now. A long time, but he hasn't got careless. Yet. Look . . .'

Pointing, she directed our attention to a ledge directly below us, where a sentry with a bow slung across his back kept guard, pacing back and forth along the outcrop. As we watched, he stopped, turned to face over the settlement below and then cupped his hands to his mouth and let out a bellow, a strange sound like the call of a hawk, but also unmistakably human.

In return came an answering bellow, another hawk sound in reply.

'From the sentry at the other side of the mount,' explained Khensa. 'They do it at night to keep each other awake, and by day just to check in.' She pointed at the buildings. 'The smaller one is a storeroom of some kind,' she explained, her voice still low. Aya and Tuta strained to hear. Seti was elsewhere, looking for other routes. 'Next to it, the larger building, is where Menna's men are billeted, six of them, including two sentries, one out east, the other just below us. The third building, that's Menna's personal quarters. He shares it with his lieutenant, a man we believe is called Maxta. Most of them I don't recognize but Maxta was there that night. You probably would have seen him. He has a crooked eye.'

It was as though a giant hand gripped me, and for a moment I couldn't move, held hostage by a powerful and overriding memory. The same man who had crept into my room the night of the attack? It had to be.

Khensa ushered us away from the edge, and we formed a circle, doing all our talking in low voices. 'And what of Menna?' I asked. 'Is he the horror of rumour? Have you seen him up close?'

Squatting there in the shingle on the mountainside, Khensa chuckled drily. 'Don't tell me you ever believed all that stuff about sharpened human teeth?'

I shook my head, but my burning cheeks betrayed the lie. I didn't need to look to know that Aya's face had broken into a broad grin. Next thing I knew, I felt her taunting finger poking into me. I shot her a look and she smiled back, the moment sending a warmth through me.

'No, I'm sorry,' continued Khensa, 'much as it pains me to destroy any childhood myths, but Menna has normal teeth. He is still powerful, though, but his influence has receded. Ten summers ago he had three times as many men at his disposal, not to mention adherents all over the country. This summer? We kill him. Soon.'

She held her breath for a moment, and finally let the

air out, slow and measured. The strain of her self-imposed mission clearly had taken a toll on her, but she still carried on. Resolute. Unyielding.

'Menna may have lived on in the memories of those in Siwa, but out here, out in the real world, he is a spent force, and the reason for that is my people. All this has been achieved at such great cost. And Menna lives because, although we are both reduced in strength, he is less reduced than we are. It's as simple as that. We've been watching him, waiting for the right moment to strike, and one of the things that Neka has told us is that Menna and his people may be about to leave . . .'

Khensa tensed, listening. From below came the noise of a chariot arriving. It was followed by the sounds of a struggle, and a cry that seemed to flutter up towards us, as though seeking our ears. In the next instant, Khensa had scrambled to the edge in order to look out over the encampment, with the rest of us not far behind.

Looking down, we saw two men dragging another, a Nubian, from the chariot to the smaller of the three buildings. His head hung between his shoulder blades. Even from this far up we could see he was in a bad way.

'Neka,' hissed Khensa. 'Gods, they have Neka.' Her hand curled into a fist against her thigh, and in the second or so before she composed herself, I saw that it shook with rage and frustration. 'They tortured him,' she said, and I heard the anger in her voice, underlined with frustration and impotence.

Just then Seti returned. He'd taken a different route at the mountain to check for Menna's sentries. Khensa scooted over to him. He saw straight away there was something wrong, angling his head slightly to look at her with a guarded expression. 'What is it, Khensa? What is wrong?'

She didn't waste words. Didn't bother trying to honey-coat the news. 'They have Neka in one of the buildings. He's already been tortured. They will likely torture him more.'

The effect on Seti was profound: agitated one second, looking as though he was about to throw himself over, the next moment about to scramble down the mountainside.

'We go,' he was saying. 'We go to rescue him.'

'Not yet,' said Khensa firmly. She was younger than him – it occurred to me that, of our group, only Tuta was her junior – but her words had authority and they were enough to silence Seti – for the moment at least.

With him quiet, Khensa drew us in. 'Right, we get down off the mountain and then we discuss what we do before we go attracting attention to ourselves. And you,' she indicated Seti, 'don't do anything rash or we all die.'

Reluctantly he agreed. The five of us turned and made our way back down the mountain.

31

At the foot of the mountain, Aya, Tuta and I stood to one side as the two Nubians faced one another, neither in the mood to back down.

'I'm going in there,' roared Seti. It had all been stored up as we descended and now it came pouring out. 'Neka is my brother. He's not just my brother in the tribe, but my brother in blood. Remember your words by the fire? Remember how you talked about the importance of blood and how bonds cannot be denied? Well, don't deny it to me now.'

Khensa put her hands to his arms and they shook with his fury. 'Not without a plan. You'll be cut down. A sentry at the entrance road. One above your head. Not to mention the men billeted in the camp. Oh, you're the best I've seen with a bow, and by the gods you'd take a few of them with you, but you are still just one man. You would die, your child would be fatherless and Neka would die, too, and what would be the point of that? Menna would rise again.'

He pulled free of her. 'Then what do you suggest? Leave Neka there? Or perhaps we should return to Thebes and ask your sick grandfather and my pregnant wife to join us? I'm *not* alone, don't you forget. What about you? What about your friends from Thebes?'

Khensa planted the shaft of her spear in the ground and swung to look at us as though seeing us for the first time, and I opened my mouth to speak, wanting to impress on her that we could be useful to them. But it was Aya who replied, 'We can do it. Let us prove it to you.'

Khensa shook her head, levelling a finger. 'There are so few Medjay left, you think I want to be responsible for killing the one who might be the last? No thank you.'

'You'll be responsible for helping his transformation into one,' insisted Aya. Her words surprised me, yet warmed my heart. I didn't think she'd believe in what the Medjay represented. Perhaps it was that what I wanted was enough for her.

'It's suicide. Of the five of us, only two have . . .'

'What?' probed Aya.

Khensa took a deep breath, fixing her with a steady gaze. 'All right. Have you ever killed anybody? Has he?'

Aya shook her head and took a deep breath. I knew this. I knew she was settling in for an argument that she would not give up.

'Is that what being a Medjay is all about, then? It's all about killing people? That's the qualification you need?'

Her words were pointed, but not angry. An honest, sincere question.

'No,' shot back Khensa, though I could see she was

listening to Aya. 'But when killing is required then Medjay must be able to do so without flinching, without second thoughts, and in the full knowledge that his or her course of action is the only one available to them. Could you do that, Bayek?' She came close and put her hand to my chest. 'Is it in there to do that?'

I thought about the man with the crooked eye – Maxta, I now had a name for him. I thought about Menna, and my father, and being a Medjay. I thought about Tuta's father, and how he'd terrorized his family for so long. A family which, not long ago, I had seen happy and safe.

I straightened, ever so slightly – I knew my answer. And Khensa being Khensa, she saw before I could even speak. She gave me a look, acknowledgement, a touch of relief, and then Seti chimed in before she could speak again, quaking with restrained emotion. 'You know what they'll be doing, don't you, Khensa? You know what they'll be doing to him?'

'Yes,' she said quietly. 'But our brother won't talk. Neka will die before he'll tell them where we're living.'

'*Die?*' blazed Seti. 'I'm not going to let that happen, and nor should you.'

Khensa clasped both hands at the shaft of her spear and rested her forehead against it. Her tribal feathers hung like palm fronds; strips of leather dangling from her wrist bracers danced in the breeze as she thought hard. Then suddenly she roused herself, strode to our cart and, to my surprise, plucked from it my bow. I started to speak, to protest, when she tossed it to Seti. 'Look at it,' she snapped, 'feel the tension.'

I coloured as the Nubian inspected my bow.

'It's not a bad attempt,' said Seti, though you could tell he wasn't impressed. He passed it back. 'The tension needs improving, that's all. My sister, all that matters here . . . Do you trust these people?'

She nodded.

'Then trust them to do this for us.'

Khensa was about to reply when we heard a noise that carried from within the mountain.

Something that silenced us.

Something that ended the argument there and then.

A scream.

32

We waited for night to fall. It was a full moon. Khensa and Seti had disappeared briefly, and when they returned both wore white face chalk. I pulled a quizzical face. 'To honour our gods,' she explained, and then added with a toothy grin, 'and to inspire fear in our enemies.'

Now we split up: Seti working his way upwards, his job to silence the sentry on the ledge; the rest of us were to travel around the base of the mountain to the east and neutralize the sentry there.

After that, it was a case of being quiet and waiting until Menna's men had eaten well and drunk even more fulsomely so that they would be dead to the world when we made our move.

The five of us crept around the mountain until we reached a point where it opened out into the track that led into the encampment. As we came closer to our destination, Khensa moved ahead, indicating single file to ensure we hugged the stone, making ourselves part of the landscape as we beetled slowly and quietly nearer the entrance. She blinked and I could see she was still mentally counting.

Now we were as close as we dared. We were some fifty feet or so away from the sentry who was leaning on an outcrop with a bow across his back, facing away from us. We'd been hearing the hawk call as we approached the entrance but now I wondered if he'd fallen asleep, because it'd been a while since the last one.

But no.

It came. A sound that seemed to fall from the heavens, echoing into the vast blackness of the desert beyond – a sound that was in its own way lonely until the sentry not far from us stood from where he reclined on the outcrop and responded.

I looked at Khensa. Her eyes were half closed in concentration, counting still, but that last alert seemed to have been the one she was waiting for, and I saw her swallow. Ready. She glanced to us, nodded affirmation. Ready. Stay there. Wordless commands.

And then, silently, she hefted her spear and set off at a run, feet padding silently on the hard ground, moving like a ghost through the night, spear hand drawing back ready to let loose on the run.

He can't have heard her. It was inconceivable. Either way, something – perhaps some extra sense – made him stand and turn, and in the light of the moon he saw Khensa approaching and opened his mouth, perhaps to yell a warning to the sentry, perhaps to challenge her. Who knows? Neither course of action would have helped him.

In the next second the only sound in the night was of his gurgling, a death rattle exhaled from around the point of Khensa's spear which was embedded in his neck. He fell, feet scrabbling, just as Khensa reached him and knelt. She obscured our view but I saw a knife and the gurgling stopped.

For a moment or so we all listened, wondering if Seti had done his job and taken care of the first sentry. Each of us dreaded the sound of the hawk call, but it never came. Satisfied, Khensa passed the sentry's bow and arrows to Aya, a look of mutual understanding passing between them.

Now, conscious of a moonlight that threw our shadows along the path, we moved fast but quietly towards the compound. Here the track opened out and the buildings that this afternoon we'd seen from our vantage point above were now close at hand. Inside them the enemy slumbered – hopefully with sufficient soundness that we would not wake them.

Away to our left were stables, chariots, horses. Khensa gave a low whistle, at which Tuta and Aya came together and then, keeping to the wall of the bowl, moved around in the direction of the stables.

Khensa touched my arm. 'It's good to have you here, Bayek,' she whispered.

I was remembering her reservations. 'You really think so?'

'I do.'

We looked up and saw that Seti had taken up position on the ledge opposite. Just seeing him there with his bow in one hand and an arrow in the other gave me fresh confidence. Khensa too, I think, because at that moment she indicated to me and we began to make our way to the cluster of buildings in the middle of the basin.

We were out in the open now, feeling exposed and vulnerable as we crossed to the storehouse, I glanced to my left to see that Tuta and Aya had begun their work, harnessing a horse to one of the chariots. We'd need it: with Neka hurt we would require transport. Besides, the plan was to leave Menna and his men without means of returning to Thebes.

We reached the storehouse and stopped, looking at one another as we steeled ourselves, half expecting a cry to go up. Nothing came as we breathed easy and inspected the storehouse door, which was locked with a wooden spike hammered into a loop in the sturdy wood. Wordlessly we began to loosen it, moving it as gently as we could from side to side, working it loose. Some moments later the spike was free and the door unlocked. It squeaked and we screwed up our faces at the sound, which to us was like a clap of thunder in the camp.

Then the door was open, and for the first time we were glad of the moonlight which flooded inside as we stepped in the door and saw Neka.

He would have looked like his brother Seti had it not been for the eye closed by a huge bulbous bruise and the grazes on his cheeks and forehead. On his chest was a series of knife wounds, as though delivered one agonizing, painstaking cut after another.

And yet, when he saw us, his good eye opened wide and his parched lips drew back in a smile, the sight of it sending a wave of relief over us. Even though his hands and feet were bound he managed to sit up.

'Seti?' he whispered.

'Covering us from the ledge,' replied Khensa, going to her knees, drawing her knife and opening Neka's bonds in one movement.

He massaged his hands, touched his eye and winced.

'How bad is it?' asked Khensa. Hesitant fingers went to the wounds on Neka's chest but he caught her hand and held it there.

'Yes,' he said, his good eye clouding over, 'they hurt me, but they were only just getting started. Tomorrow, they said, that was when the real fun would begin.' He indicated me. 'Who's this?'

'This is Bayek, son of Sabu,' said Khensa quickly, helping him to his feet. 'He and his friends are helping us. Come on, it's time to get you out of here.'

'Oh, I'm leaving all right,' growled Neka, his expression turning dark, 'but I'm leaving with Menna's head on the end of that spear you're carrying.'

Khensa shook her head, fast and determinedly. 'No,' she said firmly. 'We're outnumbered. You're hurt. This mission is to get you out of here safely and that's exactly what I intend to do.'

'What do you think my brother would say?'

Khensa thinned her lips. I think we all knew exactly what his brother would say if he were here now.

'We've been waiting for an opportunity to hit him . . .' pressed Neka.

'We need a better opportunity . . .' She trailed off and I could tell she was starting to think about it. Despite the risk to the few of her people left, she was seriously considering it.

'It's here, Khensa, it's here in the palm of our hands, the chance to take down Menna for good. You brought reinforcements.' He jerked his head at me, sensing he could convince her. 'We're already inside the compound. The sentries are dead, yes?'

'Yes.'

'That leaves seven more men. Five in that building, Menna and his lieutenant in the other one. We've got the area covered from above. We've got warriors here. We've got the element of surprise. Now is the time, Khensa. Let's finish this.'

She raised her chin. Needed no more persuading. 'You want to kill Menna for what he's done to you, do you?' she said, her fingers tracing the wounds on his chest.

He flinched. 'Yes, sister of mine, yes. I do.'

She looked at him for a moment, gaze piercing and steady. And shook her head, ever so minutely.

'This I refuse. The killing of Menna falls to me. Those are my terms. Accept them or not, it's up to you.'

There was the beginnings of a smile. He nodded, weaving back slightly – trusting her judgement. 'You drive a hard bargain. I agree to your terms. Give me your bow and let's go.'

She did as asked, and after Neka took a few gradually steadying steps, we headed out.

33

Easy success was quickly taken from us. It was all for the sake of a man having a piss. Whatever plan formulated by Khensa and Neka might well have worked were it not for that bladder bursting with beer.

We had crept outside of the storehouse, back into the basin, where across the way Tuta and Aya were crouched in the stables.

They were waving at us. It took me a moment or so to see what they were doing, my eyes adjusting to the night, maybe having difficulty believing what I was seeing. But no, they were definitely waving. I squinted, trying to make out why.

Waving and pointing to . . .

My eyes went to the other buildings in the encampment, and there at the larger of the two huts I saw one of Menna's men relieving himself against the side of the wall. On the ledge Seti stood with his bow drawn back and ready to fire, but right now the guy was on the wrong side of the building. His chosen urinal was in one of the few areas Seti couldn't cover, and now, if he looked to his right he'd see Tuta and Aya, but if he looked to his left he'd see me, Khensa and Neka.

Shit!

Khensa began silently and frantically indicating for us to return inside the storehouse. The only sound in the basin was the henchman's stream of piss against the side of his hut.

He'd be in trouble for that, I thought crazily. They probably had rules about going out to the boundary but he was too tired to bother.

Steam rose. He stopped.

And then started again.

And then stopped, let his tunic drop until he stepped backwards, unsteady on his feet, either with drink or sleepiness.

Terrified of a movement that might catch his eye, but just as terrified of staying out in the open, we froze – even Khensa, who gave up on trying to shepherd us back inside, simply crouched, motionless. Likewise. Tuta and Aya had fallen still on the other side of the hollow. I didn't dare turn my head to see Seti.

All of us were petrified of being seen, praying the man would simply stagger back into his quarters.

But he didn't.

He'd stopped, cocked an ear, and then he put his hands to his mouth to make the hawk sound, or at least a drunken approximation of it.

We held our breaths, watching as he once again cocked an ear, listening, waiting for the answering hawk call and seemingly irritated that it didn't come. Next he appeared to take stock, and with his chin raised and his chest puffed out he took a look around himself like a drunken king surveying his realm. His eyes passed the stables and didn't linger there, Tuta and Aya concealed by the shadows. But then his gaze came to where the three of us crouched outside the door of the storehouse and suddenly I felt terribly exposed, thinking, *This is it, Bayek*. The friendly moon shining down on us pointing us out. *There they are.*

Surely we'd been spotted.

Khensa thought so too. She gestured to Seti. Both started to move slowly, weapons at the ready.

But the unthinkable happened. Finally coming to a decision, the man shouted once – beginning to raise the alarm. Khensa faded into the shadows and Seti stood, no longer hidden. The man saw him and launched himself forward, his second shout delivered with more volume and urgency, throwing himself at the door to his lodgings and battering them with both palms.

For him, it was too late. Moving to the door of the billet had brought him into the sightline of Seti, who fired. An arrow pierced the man's cheek, his barrage of blows stopped and his yells were cut off by the shaft in his oesophagus.

But the damage was done, and in a moment the door of the billet was flung open. 'Hey,' came a cry from within, a voice filled with sleep that became a shout of shock when the man inside saw his friend's body sprawled on the ground.

He charged out. Foolhardy. Khensa's spear caught

him as she lunged out of the shadows, the kill neat and quick. My knife in my hand, I kept watch still, alert and attentive. I felt movement at my side, turned to see Aya arrive, Tuta there too, lurking and grinning at me as they settled nearby.

On the other side of the camp, Seti had used the lull in combat to jump down from the ledge. The Nubians, reunited, embraced, but then almost immediately a strange sense of indecision was cast upon them: *What to do now?* We knew there were four or five men still inside the main building. And in the other building . . .

Menna.

It was as though we all woke at the same time. It wasn't over. Khensa was gesticulating for Neka: *Get over there. Cover the door.* Meantime, Aya had notched an arrow in the sentry's bow. 'Seti,' whispered Khensa harshly, 'check the back. Make sure there's no way out of the rear.'

Though the Nubians clearly had known patterns to rely on, the rest of us were at a loss. Already unprepared, we'd been caught off guard by the pissing man; now we were desperately trying to play catch-up with the seasoned hunters.

The first we knew of more trouble was a sound we heard from the stables where Menna and his lieutenant were already clambering into a chariot.

I heard myself shout, *'No!'* even as they pulled out of the stables in a thunder of wheels and hooves, and for the first time I got a good look at Menna's lieutenant.

It was him. It was the man who had come into my bedroom window all those years ago, the man who had rendered me rigid with fear. I saw the crooked eye. I saw the terrible twist of his lips, enjoying himself, even now, when the odds were so horribly stacked against him.

At his side Menna seemed to be nothing by comparison. A small man. Lean and weathered, his skin the colour of the leather belts that crossed his chest.

Neka levelled his bow, checked himself, then darted to gain a better position, loosing on the run. But his bad eye hindered him, and his arrow slapped into the side of the chariot, piercing the basket and lodging there harmlessly as the chariot turned, thundering towards the camp approach road.

I tensed, waiting, hoping, no, *praying* for Seti's own response, when from the other side of the building came a scream of pain that told us he was otherwise engaged. And now it was too late.

Gods! Curses!

Khensa had snatched her bow and quiver from Neka. 'Stay here,' she yelled at Aya, 'contain them.'

At the same time she set off in the direction of the stables. 'Bayek, with me!' she commanded and I didn't need telling twice, staying on her heel as we sprinted to the chariot. When I glanced behind I saw Aya, training her bow on the hut. Seti came racing around the back wall, notching an arrow to take aim at Menna's chariot, already slipping out of sight, and then in the same movement swinging back to cover the rear entrance. They had their hands full but between them they'd be all right: two experienced Nubians; Aya, new to this still but smart and confident; Tuta, who no doubt had a few tricks up his sleeve.

'Can you drive this thing?' yelled Khensa, jumping into the chariot. I grabbed the reins, shook them in response and steered us out of the stables, wheels cutting a groove in the sandy ground as we described an arc around to the entranceway. One of the few things my father had been unstinting about was this, at least. We were behind Menna, it was true. But we had one major advantage.

We had Khensa.

Our horse snorted, mane fluttering. I held on tight, painfully aware that it was a long time since I'd last driven a chariot – back in Siwa, of course, and that seemed like years ago now – as well as the fact that it was so dark.

I could have laughed at how the moon alternated between being our enemy and our ally. Now at least it illuminated Menna and Maxta ahead. Maxta was driving, casting frequent looks over his shoulder as Menna crouched in the basket on the board, arms braced along the sides.

I shook the reins, used the switch. Were we gaining? Out there, right then, it didn't matter. My teeth were bared, numbed by the same wind I felt in my hair. But through me coursed a feeling of utter exhilaration.

And if we weren't gaining just yet, then we would. I knew it in my bones, and anyway . . .

Beside me, Khensa had been crouching like Menna, finding her balance as we thundered along, each dip and rise of the uneven ground threatening to tip us over to one side, buckle the wheel, crack its wooden spokes. These old things were better for sedate trips to the market, maybe even as far as Thebes and back, not for racing over the desert at night.

Ahead of us the whip cracked. I heard Maxta urging on their horse. I did the same. Menna stood up, planting her feet apart, one leg behind mine so that our thighs touched, bracing each other. I saw the muscles in her forearms tense, bow held. In her right hand was an arrow and she notched it, drawing back the bow, riding the board of the chariot, bracing herself against me and on the basket, doing everything she could to keep herself and her aim steady.

But it was not quite enough.

Her first arrow sailed past the escaping pair in front of us. She looked at me, and I back at her, and there was no screaming, no shouting, no cursing, just a silent mutual assurance that, whatever happened, we would get the job done.

'Next one,' she yelled above the drone of the chariot wheels, and notched a second arrow, her muscles tensing as she drew back the string.

She was yelling with the effort, arm trembling with fatigue when she finally loosed her second arrow. This one found its mark, spinning Maxta around in the basket as it sank deep in his left shoulder.

He fell, yanking at the reins, causing the horse to stop and rear. In the same instant the chariot snapped round, wheels spinning in the air as the entire contraption twisted then crashed to the ground, the occupants still inside.

We pulled alongside. Khensa had notched another arrow and I had my dagger in my hand, and we stepped from our basket and went to investigate.

Their chariot was upside down, one wheel smashed, the other spinning lazily to a halt, both men trapped beneath. Trying to get to its feet, their horse was whinnying painfully and as Khensa kept her bow trained on the overturned chariot, I moved towards it, cutting the leather straps that held the animal, setting it free. I then walked to the rear, crouched to see underneath, wincing at the sight that greeted me. There was a lot of blood.

At first I'd thought both men were alive. Their eyes were open, seemingly regarding me dispassionately. My attention was drawn to Menna. There was something odd about the way he simply regarded me. And then I realized he was unblinking and also that his head was at a strange, unnatural angle to the rest of his body, as though stuck to the side of the basket.

At that moment his jaw dropped open and I saw something inside his bloodied mouth and realized that he was in fact pinned – during the crash he had tumbled against the point of Neka's arrow, which was now embedded in his face. Had it killed him? Or was it a broken neck? Either way, he was dead.

As for Maxta, he was still alive. And unlike Menna he was staring at me with eyes that saw.

'Who are you?' he asked, and though his voice dripped with malice it was forced and weak. A line of blood ran from his mouth into his beard.

'It doesn't matter,' I said, still crouching. 'You're beaten at last. And by a Medjay's son.'

His eyes widened in horrified recognition as he coughed his last, a bubble of blood appearing at his lips and then bursting as he died.

34

Bion had met Raia on one final occasion before leaving Alexandria, this time at a location with which Raia was more comfortable: a grove of fig trees deserted but for clouds of insects, drooping foliage and a stone bench on which they sat, able to converse in peace without fear of being overheard. Without Raia worrying about all the things Bion's presence within his life could bring.

Bion had inhaled the sweet scent of figs and watched insects among the trees as he updated Raia on his meeting with the scholar Rashidi, telling him what he'd learned about Hemon and Sabestet, this blind boy and his master living in Djerty.

'An ancient, eh?' Raia snorted with scorn, and Bion was glad they sat side-by-side, sure that his distaste for Raia was written all over his face. It was strange, he thought. The commander he knew from the old days was ambitious and prone to bouts of misplaced self-belief, but not stupid, not one for unthinking, unquestioning acceptance; the man he saw now, especially in his home surrounds of Alexandria, who sat beside him, occasionally closing his eyes and turning his face to the last of the afternoon sun, was a very different beast indeed.

'So you leave for Djerty soon,' Raia said, 'to continue our mission?'

Bion wondered which part of the mission was *our* mission. 'At first light,' he replied, his mind going to a task he planned to undertake beforehand.

'Good, good. I shall look forward to news that the ancient and his blind helper are dead by your hand.'

'Yes,' Bion said simply, thinking, Yes, they would die soon, the fact as inevitable as the rising of the sun. They would die soon and then, he knew, Raia would have another mission for him. Raia would always, he suspected, have another mission for him.

Bion found that the thought did not displease him.

This, his legacy. His gift to the world. Death. There was rebirth after wars, after all. And if he hastened the timing a little, well, so what? Death visited everyone, sooner or later. Peace awaited his victims there. Was it such a terrible fate, to find respite from life, to move on to the next one?

'Something of a coup, don't you think?' Raia was saying, and Bion set aside his wonderings to focus on the man, plotting away before him. 'To find the ringleader this early into our mission? Feels like cutting off the roots before felling the tree?' Raia settled back, raising his face to the sun, pleased with his turn of phrase.

Bion's scars itched. He wished to be elsewhere. 'Yes,' he said, uninterested.

There was a pause, the kind of silence that allowed a

little awkwardness to sidle up beside them and make its presence known.

'I don't detect within you a loss of heart, do I, Bion, killer of men? You know how important this mission is to me. You know how grateful I will be when it is complete.'

'You have one medallion,' Bion said, wondering how Raia could not understand that he cared little for rewards, that the killing itself sufficed. 'Soon you will have several more.'

'Don't let me down, Bion,' said Raia. His eyes had taken on a steely texture. Bion was amused, though his features did not shift.

'I won't, Commander.'

Raia flashed teeth as a smile returned to a face that said *Life is treating me well and I intend for it to stay that way.* 'Good, good.'

For some time they sat side by side, until at last Raia spoke. 'You remember Naukratis, Bion?'

You reminded me about it in Faiyum, thought Bion, but instead of saying so, merely nodded his head.

'The landowner, Wakare, you remember him?'

'I do.'

'He was murdered not long after that. Murdered in his home. Did you know that?'

Bion remained silent. It had no bearing on today.

Raia stood to go, looking down at where Bion remained seated on the stone bench. 'I wonder,' said Raia, 'whether if I were to investigate further, then I'd discover that Wakare was killed by a knife through the eye socket into the brain.'

I wonder, thought Bion, but said nothing, watching Raia leave until he was out of sight, listening until his steps faded away to nothing.

That night, before returning to his lodgings, Bion wandered across the city, marvelling at its newness, its Greekness. Yes, Alexandria reminded him of his time in Naukratis, it had that same haughty air of its own importance, except even more so, if such a thing were possible. Here you had to hunt high and low to see the peasants, the *sekhety*, the poor, the *shouaou*. A dirty face was a rarity in Alexandria; those who made their way along the streets and narrow passageways were well-to-do and assured of their own importance, happy and safe in the security of a consensus. These were the rich, the opposite of the *sekhety*, the people who could count upon fortune's good grace. Once upon a time he had killed for their like. And despite believing that he had left that life behind, he was doing it again.

His walk, purposeful, brought him to the door of a well-appointed home, nestled among those occupied by the very rich he had been watching before. He knocked and the door was answered by a servant. He asked for the master of the house, or perhaps the lady of the house if the master was not available, which he wasn't.

The servant stood nervously to one side as an elderly

but well-dressed woman appeared and eyed him with suspicion. 'Yes?'

'I was wondering if I might speak to your husband, Theotimos,' said Bion.

She was a woman of some bearing, and if she was intimidated by Bion's appearance she gave no sign, regarding him from along the bridge of her nose before replying. 'My husband is dead,' she said simply, with only a faint trace of emotion.

'I see,' said Bion, and then when he realized she was waiting for his condolences added, 'I'm very sorry to hear that.'

He made as if to leave and then stopped, shoulders dropping as he turned to regard the widow in her doorway. 'How did he die?' he asked.

'He was set upon by a gang of thieves,' she said.

'What did they take, the thieves?'

'Nothing.' She shook her head sadly. 'Just some scrolls.'

35

Before he died, the scholar Rashidi had told Bion that Hemon and Sabestet were to be found in Djerty, and so that is where he went.

In Djerty he paid for information, and from what he could gather, Hemon and his ward lived outside the community. He had also discovered that the old man was reputed to be something of a mystic, and also that Hemon had taken in Sabestet at a young age. The blind orphan had been begging, performing a cups trick in the streets for money, when Hemon had passed by, seen him at work and been even more impressed when he realized the boy was blind.

The two had struck up a relationship and Hemon had taken Sabestet off the streets to live with him out east. Sabestet was now in his early twenties, but despite the fact that his blindness seemed barely a handicap to him, he'd never shown any inclination to leave in search of adventure or the big city, the way young men are prone to do.

That was interesting, Bion had thought, *the bond between them*. He did not understand.

And so at market he bought a belt, small cage, a basket and a two-handled copper bowl to which he attached the belt. He baited the cage and caught a rat, which he placed into the basket. When night fell he rode out to the homestead and waited in the dark until he felt confident that the two occupants of the house were asleep, before making his move.

Taking the rat, basket and bowl, he moved to the front door, placed the items on the ground, drew his knife and listened. In the distance was the cry of a scavenger bird but otherwise all was silent. As for any noise from inside the home, there was nothing, not a sound. Silence.

Stealthily, the killer let himself in, sliding into the door like smoke and standing there, listening and letting his eyes adjust to the pitch-blackness as he took stock and gathered himself for his next move.

He felt a blade at his neck.

'I am blind, intruder,' came a young voice from behind. 'My world is as dark as yours, but I have the advantage of this knife at your throat. What's more, I know this house, and you do not.'

The killer went still, sensing that the young man with the blade at his neck would use it if necessary, but knowing also that as soon as he allowed himself to be disarmed he was a dead man, his mission a failure, his legacy of death superseded by one of defeat, and he could not let that happen.

He was, after all, Bion, killer of men. If one listened to Raia, anyway.

He sensed another figure standing before him, the

old man who spoke now, a disembodied voice in the blackness. 'Take his knife, Sabestet.'

Don't try anything, said the prick of pain he felt as the pressure of the knife increased at his neck and a hand snaked across the front of him, reaching for the knife he held.

'I'll take that, please,' Sabestet said close to his ear. Bion's eyes had adjusted now. He could make out Hemon standing beside the table, which had been put there, it seemed, to create a barrier. Clearly the pair of them had known he was coming. Not such outcasts in Djerty as Bion had been led to believe, they had evidently been warned about him. He for his part had been careless. Meanwhile, the old man held something, a lantern, ready to light it when Bion was disarmed.

But that wasn't going to happen.

Bion wasn't going to allow that to happen.

He let the blind boy take his knife, having allowed its leather retaining loop to slip from his own wrist, bringing his arm up slightly as though to cooperate.

And then he made his move.

With a flick of his hand he slipped the leather loop over Sabestet's wrist, turned it fast to make it excruciatingly tight and yanked forward. Sabestet's knife dug into his neck but Bion had pulled back, rendering it useless, and the boy gave a yell as he was dragged sideways and forward.

Hemon cried out. Sabestet swung wildly with his knife hand, his other one out of action, but Bion had control now, and he used the table that had been placed there to help stop him, surging forward with Sabestet, writhing, ahead of him, snatching at the flailing knife hand, running him against the side of the table at the same time.

Again, a howl from Sabestet – a cry of frustration followed instantly by one of pain as his spine slammed into the tabletop. The old man was on the move now, a curved sword gleaming dully. In a second he'd be upon Bion, who shoved Sabestet over the tabletop, ramming the boy's knife hand on to the table, once, twice, hearing the jangle of the blade as it span away and at the same time switching his efforts to the boy's other hand, held fast by the retaining loop of his own blade.

Sabestet was dazed and in pain – too dazed and too pained to stop Bion from twisting his own arm across his chest and jamming the blade through his shoulder into the tabletop, pinning him there.

By now the old man had rounded the table, seen that the momentum of his attack was lost and switched his stance.

His speed impressed Bion, but even so, he was old, and though he was faster than his years, he wasn't as fast as Bion. When he darted forward with an attacking jab, Bion ducked beneath it easily, feeling the sword whistle over his head as he dived, took the old man's legs from beneath him and jerked upwards at the same time, upending The Elder and slamming him upside down to the stone, his head making painful contact with the floor and knocking him out cold.

The skirmish was over. Bion felt for blood at his neck, a small cut there, nothing to worry about. Groaning, the boy lay pinned by the knife to the table, his top half bent over it, his feet scrabbling weakly to the stone for a moment or so before he lost consciousness.

Good.

Bion knelt to the old man, feeling for a pulse. Excellent, he was alive. He needed them both alive for what he planned next. Ensuring the boy was pinned to the table, he left them for a moment or so, fetching the basket with the rat and then returning inside the house, lighting the lantern and closing the door.

Work to do.

36

'Do you know who I am?' said Bion.

Light was provided by lanterns and a fire bimbling in a freestanding brazier not far away. There were only two chairs in the room and the old man was tied to one of them, his arms behind his back and dried blood on his face from his head wound, his white beard caked with it.

'I know *what* you are,' said Hemon groggily. He pulled at the rope that bound him to the chair, and then regarded Bion with a blank stare. 'You are the end of life. You come here to take away all that we are.'

Yes, I am death, thought Bion. It was nice, when his targets understood. But to Hemon he just nodded. 'I am that, yes, and more.'

'He won't tell you anything,' said Hemon, inclining his head towards the table, where Sabestet lay splayed across the top, as though for sacrifice. Bion had unpinned him before tying him to the legs and then cutting open his tunic to expose his stomach and chest. Next he'd placed the rat inside the upturned copper bowl and strapped it to Sabestet's chest.

They could hear the rat moving inside the bowl, scratching, trying to find a way out.

Lifting his head every now and then, Sabestet was trying to be brave, but was unable to stop himself emitting nervous little sounds. He could feel the trapped rat on his bare skin. He probably knew what Bion had in mind.

'I know he won't talk,' said Bion to Hemon. 'It's not him I expect to talk, it's you.'

'I shall not either,' The Elder shook his head.

'I think you will,' said Bion, 'Now tell me, where is the rest of your kind? The last of them.'

Hemon shook his head, bitter. He knew that both he and his ward were as good as dead. 'There is no *rest* of us. You're looking at them. You should congratulate yourself when you leave here that you leave the Medjay extinct.'

'I'm not sure about that,' replied Bion evenly. 'I think there are plenty in Egypt who share your ideals, plenty who call themselves Medjay.' He moved around to the brazier to blow on the hot coals, which glowed in response.

'These people you speak of are not the original Medjay, merely pretenders, idealists, those on the fringes of society who like to see themselves in opposition to the prevailing consensus.' Hemon spat to the side, in disdain. 'I'll grant you that these people do exist, but they are not the authentic followers of our creed.'

'They don't share the bloodline, is what you're saying?' asked Bion.

Hemon nodded. 'And the bloodline has died. The

bloodline ends here. It ended with the death of my wife and my just-born son many years ago. Kill me, extinguish the last weak flames of our order and your job is complete.'

Bion sighed. Inside he was full of admiration for the old man's courage, his ability to stick to the story even when the odds were so severely stacked against him. But he had to be sure, and besides . . .

'You're right, the Medjay is close to its demise,' he said, 'but my employers have found documents in Alexandria that suggest your kind plans to rally, that a new generation of Medjay is being prepared to take over from the old. You claim that you are the last rightful Medjay. I have already recovered one medallion that proves the opposite. Now, please, before I am forced to take this further, tell me where I can find the last of you.'

Hemon shook his head and Bion knew his plans would not go to waste.

'Well, then, I think we both know what happens next,' said Bion. 'I place hot coals on the copper bowl. The bowl heats up and the rat inside tries to escape, which it begins to do by trying to gnaw at the bowl before giving up and tunnelling out another way. How do you think the rat escapes, Hemon?'

Sabestet groaned. Hemon shook his head at the savagery of it.

'It is painful, Hemon,' continued Bion serenely. 'A terrible pain that, depending on which route the rat chooses to take, can be extraordinarily lengthy. I have seen it before. I have administered it before. It is a death I would not wish upon anyone.'

He paused, thinking that he in fact did not really care, but he'd learned over the years – over the kills – that pretending sympathy unnerved his prey even more, for some reason.

'Now, tell me,' he said, wondering at what Hemon's deepest, most private thoughts were at this very moment, 'where is the last of your kind?'

The old man shook his head. A little more unsettled now. 'You have no need to do such a barbaric thing. There is no *last* of our kind. I've already told you. You're looking at him.'

Bion used tongs to place a hot coal on top of the copper bowl. The rat inside responded straight away and the scuttling, snuffling sound seemed to increase in urgency. Sabestet whimpered. Bion added another coal, and then another. 'Unfortunately for you', he said evenly, 'I believe you are lying.'

The scuffling sound from inside the bowl became more and more frantic. The copper began to glow, Sabestet moaning as the copper heated, but while that would be painful enough, it was nothing compared to what was coming. Bion had seen rats gnaw their way to freedom. He had heard the screams of the tortured. He had seen a burrowing rat nose its way from between a man's ribs.

Sweat had broken out on the old man's forehead. 'It's me you want,' he tried weakly, but Bion just shook his head, leaning over the bowl and blowing on the coals which flared red in the flickering light of the room.

The rat was squealing in pain now. Soon it would begin to worry at the skin. It would start to chew the flesh. Sabestet was steeling himself, as bravely as he could. Bion would have been impressed, if he'd cared about such things.

Tell me, thought Bion. *They always do. You will as well. Why fight?*

'You haven't got long,' he warned the old man. 'Soon it will begin and there will be little I can do to stop it.'

'All right then, all right,' gabbled the old man, 'I'll tell you. Please, just remove the coal, I'll tell you.'

Bion looked into his eyes and he believed him. Reaching for the tongs, he removed two of the hot coals. One remained.

'Please . . .' prompted Hemon.

'We're close,' said Bion. 'Just tell me, let me decide if you're telling the truth and then we'll see about the last one.'

'There is one other Medjay,' swallowed the old man. 'One other true Medjay. One who is, as you say, at the vanguard of a resurgence.'

Bion shook his head. 'Try again,' he said.

Inside the bowl the rat was still trying to escape.

'What do you mean?' stammered Hemon. The sweat shone on his forehead now. Still they could hear the rat.

'There is a bloodline . . . ' pressed Bion.

'There are two,' agreed Hemon, nodding his head vigorously. 'A father and son.'

Bion looked into his eyes, saw the man was telling the truth. 'Good, good,' he said, 'and what else?'

He dropped the second coal back into the brazier and then removed the last one, but held it there poised above the bowl. The boy had been holding his breath, his back arched awaiting the moment that the rat began burrowing, every sinew in his body anticipating the agony to come, but now he relaxed a little. The bowl itself, which had been glowing, seemed to calm. 'Names?' said Bion.

'Their names are Sabu, and his son Bayek.'

The old man bowed in defeat. Bion suspected it was shame he was seeing in those old eyes. Shame in himself, for failing his calling, for the sake of his ward, whom he knew would die anyway once he had disclosed the last Medjay's whereabouts.

37

It had been several weeks since the battle at Menna's hideout, and I'm not sure any of us had fully recovered. Cuts and bruises had healed – or almost so in the case of Neka, who had suffered the most – but as for what went on in our heads? Aya, Tuta and I had returned to Tuta's mother's house in Thebes after the battle. As we walked in, she'd rushed over from the kitchen area to take him in her arms.

'Gods! Tuta, my son, where have you been all this time? I've been so worried. Feverish with worry I've been.' She'd enfolded him so tightly in her arms that all I could see of him was a squished face, his eyes gleaming with newfound light and life.

Seeing him there in his mother's arms, the edge of a smile that he was directing at me, brought to mind a conversation we'd had on the journey back from Menna's settlement, when he'd taken me to one side: 'What we did back there at the tomb-robber's place was just about the most exciting thing ever in my life, sir,' he'd said, and then tailed off, shaking his head in disbelief.

The thing was, he didn't need to say anything else because I'd felt it myself, racing along the plain in the chariot, something that had been building within me these past months, maybe even since I'd left Siwa.

Yes, I knew the feeling. I knew exactly what it was.

It was a feeling of purpose.

And Tuta was right, it felt good. It felt good to have it in our lives.

We'd left the bodies of Menna and Maxta on the desert, food for the scavengers; the remainder of Menna's men we'd barred into the storehouse before scattering their horses and then leaving. The storehouse wouldn't hold them for long but it gave us enough time to make headway. In any event, with no paymaster to offer a bounty, a pursuit was unlikely.

Ever since the battle I had watched as a strange kind of lassitude seemed to descend over Khensa and Seti. The emotions of peace and triumph I had expected to see now that their years-old struggle with Menna was finally over were curiously absent. I wondered if, in killing Menna and fulfilling the pledge they'd made to my father and to the Medjay, the Nubians were now at a loss. Without purpose.

On the way back Khensa had been quiet, deep within herself. She'd promised that when Neka was recovered he would find out more about the Medjay imprisoned in Elephantine – this man, after all, was the only lead we currently had – but other than that? What could they do? What *would* they do? Resume their nomadic ways, once Neka was fully healed and had investigated the Medjay rumours in Elephantine?

Likely. I had a feeling I would soon be bidding a fond farewell to Khensa.

In the meantime, things had, for the time being at least, gone back to how they were before. Neka pronounced himself fit for duty and departed south. Time stood still as we awaited news.

And now he had returned, and Khensa had come to Tuta's door, seeking us out and summoning us into the street, where I couldn't help but notice a difference in her. The listlessness and melancholy that had descended over her after our battle at Menna's hideout seemed to have diminished. In her eyes was a new vitality, a rekindled spirit.

Khensa fixed me with a look – a look I knew well. An important look.

'Neka brings news of the Medjay imprisoned on the island of Elephantine,' she began. She took a deep breath before continuing. 'It seems that I was wrong,' she said. 'The Medjay imprisoned in Elephantine might not be an impostor. Neka has unearthed information that indicates he is the scion of a genuine Medjay bloodline. This man is currently imprisoned in a pit in the gatehouse of the Temple of Khnum on the southern side of the island.'

I sensed something important was afoot. I hardly dared allow myself to believe as her eyes and their newfound fire found mine, wanting to gauge my reaction when she delivered her news.

'Bayek, if Neka is right . . . the prisoner is your father.'

38

Tuta had no idea he had been followed. Not until he was halfway along the narrow passageway, heading towards the slums, and a figure stepped out in front of him.

Before that, he'd been excited. Why? Because he was due to join Aya, Bayek and the Nubians on another adventure – this time on an expedition to rescue Bayek's father from a pit in Elephantine.

Why was Bayek's papa in the pit? Tuta didn't know and, truth be told, he didn't really care. Oh, he had heard all about the Medjay, and it all sounded pretty important and very exciting to him, not that he pretended to understand any of it. The thing was that it was important and exciting to Bayek and Aya, which made it that way for him too. These days he felt as though he were a part of something, as though he had a contribution to make. As though he mattered.

But that feeling was nothing compared with the thrill of the battle itself. Was 'thrilled' the right word, when people had lost their lives? Who cared? The *right people* had lost their lives. That was all that mattered to Tuta, because while he was doing good, being a part of something, mattering, he was also doing important stuff. That boy who had spent his time in Zawty trying to part strangers from their money and goods, scraping around for food and the odd bronze coin? He was gone. New Tuta was here, and he was about to embark on a fresh adventure.

And then the figure stepped out in front of him and Tuta knew at once that things had gone from being mended to broken again.

His father's eyes, rheumy with drink and bitterness and loathing for himself and for Tuta, bore into him like twin augurs. It was a look that promised nothing but more pain and despair.

'So I found you then?' Paneb leered, and Tuta's mind raced, trying to think how on earth his father could have found him in all of Thebes. Trying to calculate how he was expected to behave.

So he did what he always did. He broke out into a grin. 'I'm glad you're here, I've missed you, Papa, I really have.'

Paneb scoffed, burping. 'Missed me, have you? That's a good one. That why you left me behind in Zawty?'

'Oh come on, Papa, admit it, you would have killed me that day. I wouldn't be here now if I'd stayed behind. It was self-preservation that took me to my toes. Surely you of all people can understand that? Besides, you knew I was going to come here, to Thebes. Where else would I go, after all? All I know is Zawty and Thebes, and Zawty was out of the question. I knew you'd come and find me here when you'd calmed down.'

His father leaned in. 'And I suppose since you've arrived here you've been up your old tricks, eh?'

Tuta nodded, quickly forcing a grin on to his face as though he and his old dad were pals together.

But Paneb wasn't falling for it, and he lunged forward, grabbing Tuta's upper arm, fingers squeezing the flesh in an iron grip that Tuta had forgotten in his new-found happiness but now remembered afresh, and slammed him to the wall of the passageway.

'Where is she, that bitch?' came the rasp at his ear. A familiar smell.

Thank the gods for presence of mind. 'That's what I'd like to know,' said Tuta. 'I've been told my mother and the little brat left some months ago. No one knows where they were bound.'

'You'd better not be lying to me, boy. What have you've been doing with yourself, then? Where are your friends? I want to have a word with those two.'

'You're hurting me . . .'

The grip relaxed. 'Come on, talk.'

'The two from Zawty, I don't know what happened to them. They aren't my friends and, as for what I've been doing, I've been surviving on the streets, just as I always have, just as I did in Zawty, what do you think?'

'What do I think? What I think is that you look fairly well nourished and clean for someone who's been living on their wits in a slum like this, that's what I think.'

'I have lodgings, of a sort,' tried Tuta, who'd just had an idea.

'Oh really? Where would that be, then?'

'Over the river, in the necropolis. An old tomb there.'

The slap came after a disgusted pause, but it was hard and sharp and as familiar to Tuta as the grip and the beer breath. 'It's nobody's tomb,' Tuta yelled in pain, 'looted or never been used, no desecration, no sacrilege, I promise. It's dry and it's warm at night when the cold bites and what more could you want? Papa, I'm telling you, it's a good place to live. Why don't you let me take you there? We could be together again.'

At last the grip was released. But if Tuta had any thoughts about making a run for it then he was denied, his father blocking his way with his body.

'Well, that's very nice of you to say, son,' he said, his head lolling slightly, drunkenly, giving Tuta hope that he might simply pass out and allow him to slip away, 'but yer old papa has somewhere to live right now, and either way, I don't intend spending much time in this cesspool.'

Tuta looked at him and forced a grimace as though he was disappointed about that, his father pulling a disbelieving face in return. 'Don't bother,' he spat. 'If you had any affection for me you wouldn't have left me for dead back in Zawty, would you?'

'No one was left for dead, Papa; you were yelling all kinds of murder. If I'd stayed I would have been the one dead, you know that, the mood you were in.'

His father nodded. 'Either way,' he said, 'I need you

208

to do something for me,' and he'd given Tuta the address of his lodgings, a time he wanted him there, and details of some theft he planned to carry out 'where we need a little scrap like you to get in somewhere for us', and a dire warning, 'Don't be late.'

Then he'd left in search of more beer and wine, and behind him Tuta had screwed up his eyes, and stood for a second, trying to not to cry there and then, in the middle of the city.

39

The next night came shouting, and Tuta gasped with frustration. He was on the outskirts of the slum, about to make his way home, when he'd heard it, and his heart broke, because he recognized the voice immediately. It was his father.

Oh, and not just the voice. Oh no. Tuta recognized the tone too. He knew what that tone meant. It meant Papa was drunk and he was angry, and it meant that Tuta himself had miscalculated.

'I know you're here, you lying little shit,' he heard bellowed from somewhere among the houses. Residents were poking their heads out of windows, wondering what was going on, and Tuta heard somebody telling his father to pipe down – for all the good it would do. He experienced a strange moment of guilt, as though it were his fault that the peace (Ha! Peace!) of the slum had been destroyed. As if those who peered out of their windows would see him and know that he, Tuta, was responsible for all the commotion.

Just as quickly, his main concern was for his mother and for Kiya. Last night he'd hurried home from his encounter in the alley and the first thing he had said to his mother was, 'He's here.'

'What do you mean, little one? Who's here?' she'd asked him without concern. Not even when he told her, because she remembered the man she had last seen, and even though he was drunk and ill-tempered and prone to resort to the fist in order to settle his arguments, he'd never been as bad as he was now. No matter what Tuta had tried to tell her since his return to Thebes, she hadn't quite grasped that fact.

'Mama, he's dangerous.'

'Oh, you don't need to tell *me* that.'

'No, Mama, he's badder than that, he's more than a mere rat, he's changed for the worse. He's evil. And even if he isn't evil then he's downright dangerous. I don't think I should go. I should stay here, make sure nothing bad becomes of you.'

She had shaken her head vigorously, telling him that she'd had years of having to handle the terrible Paneb, and if he came round again, well, then she'd just have to handle him again.

And even though Tuta wasn't sure she could do that, he so powerfully wanted to go to Elephantine that he let himself do something he was at this very moment beginning to regret. He let himself believe it would be OK. And the price of his delusion was this: Paneb in the slums, drunk and raging, incensed that he had failed to turn up to the agreed meeting place. No way was he going to let that pass.

Right, Tuta, he thought to himself. *Get a grip. Think*

this through. The only way you can sort this situation out is to meet it head-on. And at the same time, whatever you do, keep him away from the house.

But Aya and Bayek were there. Together they could handle him, surely?

Mind still racing, trying to explore all the angles. No. If he led Paneb home then he'd know where Mama and Kiya lived. They would have to leave the house that they had made their own.

So Tuta took a course of action that scared him but was the only one he could think of. Instead of taking off in the opposite direction to all that shouting he could hear, he went towards it.

Some moments later, there he was, his father, hammering his fist against the house while he shouted for his son. What Tuta would have done for an incensed homeowner to appear. No, an incensed and very tough homeowner. An incensed and very tough home homeowner in an especially bad mood.

Unfortunately for Tuta, no such saviour appeared. There was just his father, his drunken father, leaning on the house, then squaring his shoulders to resume his cries for Tuta when he caught sight of his son standing watching him.

Tuta swallowed but stitched a smile on to his face, greeting his father, trying to stay jovial. 'Why are you making so much noise, Papa?' To which his father had thrown back his shoulders and turned to look exaggeratedly around the area, at the crumbling walls, peeling paint and the tattered awnings, as though he were accustomed to great luxury, this man of taste. Tuta felt bile rise just looking at him.

But keep smiling, he thought. *Keep smiling*. This slum was home to his *mouty* and Kiya and what happened next would be vital when it came to keeping it that way.

'Where were you, boy?' growled Paneb.

Tuta, still grinning, trying to bluff it out, said, 'I came to your lodging, ready for the job and keen to earn coin, just as you said, but you weren't there. Thank the gods you're here now. Is it too late?'

His father wasn't having it. 'What are they like, my lodgings?'

Still trying to bluff. 'Better than you deserve, old man. Come on, let's get out of here and go to some more salubrious part of the city. You look like you need a drink.'

But now his father fixed him with a beady-eyed stare, his beard glistening, his mouth wet as he spoke. 'They're here, aren't they? Your liar of a mother. My little Kiya. They are, aren't they? I'm going to find them. They're mine. They had no right to leave.'

Tuta felt his heart skip a beat. This was bad. This was the worst. Fear inched up his spine and, as he spoke, he smiled still, brightly. Coaxing.

'No, Papa, just as I told you, they're long gone, and so should we be. Come on. Something tells me you've got some stories to share.'

A look crossed Paneb's face, something unreadable.

In the next instant he stepped forward and punched Tuta in the stomach.

Tuta shouted, groaned, his hands going to his belly as he staggered back, and then, looking down, he saw blood – blood on his hands, on his tunic. He saw the knife in his father's grasp dripping with it, and realized it was his own blood. His father was shaking a befuddled head, as though unable to choose between anger and fear and regret and then taking flight instead, running off down the street, even as somebody from a window overhead was shouting for the soldiers.

Tuta went to his knees. His mouth dropped open. His head emptied of all thoughts apart from, *I've got to get to them. I've got to warn them before I die.*

40

'Where is he?' Aya was saying, fond and amused. 'Where is that little scamp?'

'I don't know,' I said. Tuta made his own rules, that's what we all liked about him. He wouldn't have been Tuta otherwise. 'Tell you what, I'll go and have a look for him,' I said, and bent for a kiss from her before she went to return to the backyard, where Kiya and her mother were enjoying the last of the evening sun.

I stepped out, looked left and right along the street. One end of it opened out on to a square with an old disused and overgrown fountain at its centre, the other took you deeper into the slum.

I couldn't see all the way down the street, a large cart was in the way, as well as a stack of boxes. But from that direction came the sound of a commotion, and somebody shouting over and over, 'He's dying.'

I started off down the road, boots slapping a rhythm on the wet and dirty stone as I picked up speed.

'He's dying, he's dying!'

And now, rounding the cart, I saw a crowd of people, one woman who stood there with her hands held in front of her, hands that were covered in blood, another man who looked my way as though I might know what to do.

And I knew, even before I arrived and shouldered my way through the crowd to see who they were talking about, that the blood belonged to Tuta.

I knew instinctively that it was he who lay dying on the street.

I fell to my knees by his side. His eyes had been flickering but they opened now and focused on me. I could see him trying to smile, his lips parting to reveal teeth stained with blood, and my guts turned to liquid. Emotions I couldn't name thrust their way towards my fingertips so that for a mad moment it felt as though I could simply touch Tuta and with all of the love I felt for him heal him.

But my hands went to his face, his cheeks burning hot beneath my palms, and no healing came, just a dying – a dying that originated from his stomach. His hands were at the wound and the front of his shirt was saturated with blood. Wringing wet with it. A trail of it leading away in the streets. Far too much blood, his face paling as the life-force seemed to drain away from him before my very eyes.

I'd saved him once but I couldn't save him again.

Oh, please, no.

'Gods, Tuta, please, stay with me.'

His eyelids were still flickering but I put my thumbs to them, roughly enough to elicit gasps from those standing around us, but I didn't care, because all I knew was that I had to keep him awake; I had to prevent him from sleeping because sleep was the brother of death, and if he closed his eyes he might never wake up, and at that very moment there was nothing – *nothing* – in the world that was more important to me than making sure Tuta lived.

'Tuta, who did this?' I asked him, as much to get him to focus as anything else. I wasn't thinking then of revenge, just of preserving his life.

'Papa,' he managed, the word a whisper that hit me like a slap.

'Gods, no,' I spat.

He took his hands from his stomach and with what felt like an unfeasible surge of strength reached to grab me, bringing me closer, clutching at my belts and dragging me to him, 'Don't let him find Mama and Kiya,' he begged. 'Please, Bayek. Do what you have to do to keep them safe.' He gave me a location, each word forced from between his dying lips.

'Tuta, stay,' I said, and I don't think I've ever meant anything so deeply and fervently as I meant those words, but that passion wasn't enough, and I saw the light ebb from his eyes, and all of that emotion, all that love I felt for him, I wanted him to take with him on his journey to be with the gods. I wanted him to be safe now – safe from what had killed him.

His hands slipped from my face. His eyelids fluttered and then closed. His head lolled to one side.

From my pouch I took a white feather. Tuta had

loved them; he'd always been fascinated by them. I wasn't thinking now. One had appeared in my hand and I pressed it to his blood-soaked shirt, whispering my pledge as I did so, telling Tuta's departing spirit that his blood would soon be mingling with that of his father.

'Hey!' cried one of the bystanders as I pulled myself to my feet and set off at a run. I'd briefly considered returning home to break the news, and perhaps I should have put the feelings of his immediate family before my oath, but may the gods forgive me, I didn't. Instead I took off running in the direction of Paneb's lodgings, Tuta's blood a heart-wrenching trail which confirmed my destination.

As I dashed through the streets, I thanked the gods for Thebes's down-at-heel appearance. I attracted a few glances as I flew along the streets: people recoiled from my bloody face, one or two even called out after me. But nothing too intrusive, nothing that stopped me.

And then, suddenly, he was there. He hadn't made it home yet, was just dragging himself along the street. Was he armed still? There was no sign of a knife. From behind he just looked like any other shabby old drunk. I could see darker, fresher stains on his hip. Where he'd wiped away Tuta's blood perhaps.

The mark of a murderer.

I pulled up and stopped, staying behind him. Now I had him in my sights I began wondering, could I do it? My knife hung heavy at my belt. To pluck it out and use it would be an action altogether different from the battle at Menna's settlement. I hadn't killed Maxta. I had no idea whether I would have done it. The decision had been taken out of my hands.

But here I was creeping up on a man – a drunken man at that – about to be an assassin.

No, not just a drunken man, I told myself, trying to steel myself. *Much more than that, much worse than that. A murderer.*

And I had promised revenge. Was this the Medjay way? I didn't know. I had a debt to pay. A brother's family to protect. It was all that mattered.

I drew myself up. Paneb had stopped on a corner, hand going to the distressed sandstone for support, moving around the corner into a side street, shuffling, his feet knocking vases that toppled and fell with a loud clatter. I turned the corner behind him, to where he stooped, trying to set the vases back up straight. It was only us, the air quiet and still.

'Turn to face your killer,' I said, and my voice fell like a stone.

He froze momentarily, and then continued with what he'd been doing, one hand swinging by his knees as he reached for a jar.

I heard something else as well. Snuffling. The sound of crying.

I took a step closer. 'I come to avenge your son.'

'Come on, then,' he said through a wet mouth. 'Come and finish it. Do it.'

'Turn to face me.' My hand gripped the knife and I took another step closer, wanting to end this but even so knowing that despite the depths of my hatred I couldn't stab him in the back, not like that. I thought of what Khensa and the priestess had told me. I wondered if stabbing a man in the back was true to the Medjay way. I wondered if it mattered.

I wanted Paneb to know. To see. To understand what was happening to him, and who was responsible for it.

'You can't do it, can you?' he said, his sobs ebbing. 'You can't take a life without looking into my eyes. I can I understand that, boy, I can respect that.'

'Turn to face me,' I said through gritted teeth, the knife like a red-hot poker in my hand, gripped so tight I could feel the bones of my fingers. A man who would kill a child understood nothing at all, I thought.

'All right, all right,' he said. 'I'll turn.'

Slowly he began to rotate and face me. I saw hooded eyes, his straggly beard, a face that reminded me of Tuta even though looking at him only increased my loathing.

And then, like a snake, he struck.

I almost didn't see it. His arm angling, a vase in his fist and a grunt as he hefted it from the ground and swung it towards my head.

I reacted in time to ward it off and the jar shattered on my forearm, pain numbing my arm, making me cry out. At the same time a knife had appeared in his other hand and he came towards me.

Those hours spent with Aya practising our sword-play, our wooden swords clacking, rehearsing the same moves over and over again. We'd laughed and kissed and played, just as we always did in Siwa, but we never stopped training, never stopped working.

And the strange thing was that we'd talked about Tuta's father all the time. The invisible unseen opponent we trained to fight, the man we had in mind when we practised our steps and rehearsed our moves was him. All that time – since I'd first encountered him in Zawty – he'd haunted my thoughts.

And now here he was, leaping at me, not with a wooden sword but a real knife, and instead of the fear I'd felt in Zawty when I battled for my life, I fought with the knowledge that I was capable of beating him, and the fear I felt wasn't a desire to take flight so much as it was awareness of possible consequences. I had trained. I was ready. It was a rudimentary, self-taught training, but all the same it worked, and it made parrying his attack second nature, my knife hand slamming down on his wrist so hard that his own blade span away with a clink to the stone.

It was all the advantage I needed. I stepped towards him and thrust home, surging forward and at the same time wrenching the knife from just below his rib cage up into his heart, cutting off his one cry of pain.

His mouth formed a circle. His eyes went wide and fixed on mine, fingers rising to try and claw at my face, the dying man's final act before the gods claimed him.

And as the feeling in his body flooded away and his feet slipped from beneath him, he fell backwards, pulling me with him to the ground.

I leaned over him, still holding the knife that remained embedded in his chest.

'This is for Tuta,' I hissed, and I twisted it once. His body jerked and he gave a final grunt and that was it. I had killed him.

Later I would think long and hard about that, how I'd killed a man. I'd think about how I watched the light of life die in Paneb's eyes, and how I took the feather that was already dark with Tuta's blood and dipped it in the blood of his father, whispering that the oath had been served.

Many nights I would be wrenched from sleep, and once I even awoke holding my hands in front of me as though they could never be responsible for something so ghastly.

Aya would help me, of course. We talked it through. I knew I had kept a promise. I knew I had protected a family. She supported me, and when one night I woke up with images of light fading in a dying man's eyes, she asked me, 'Was it him? Were you thinking of Paneb?'

'No,' I told her. 'It was Tuta. I was thinking of my friend and brother, Tuta.'

41

We delayed our trip, it seemed only right to stay with Tuta's mother and Kiya and help them deal with his death. But there was nothing we could do apart from mourn, and I think his mother knew that.

In the end, she came to Aya. 'You and Bayek should leave, you've got work to do, it's what Tuta would have wanted, you know that.'

And, of course, she was right, and so we did as she said, travelling across the river to the necropolis where we joined Khensa and Neka, bidding goodbye to Seti who was to stay with his pregnant wife. Once they were done, we began what we expected to be five- or six-day journey to Aswan and then the island of Elephantine.

I didn't forget Tuta. I never would. At nights by the fire, I took a feather from my pack in order to remember him. Even so, and though he always stayed with me and always would, the more we put Thebes at our backs the more focused on the oncoming mission I became.

What had Neka been able to tell us about the Medjay prisoner in Elephantine? Nothing much. The island's government was invoking ancient laws that had once been used to persecute the Medjay in that region, when they were deemed by their corrupt administration to pose a real, tangible threat to society.

They probably thought my father was a pretender just like the rest of the false Medjay that had sprung up of late, a man to be punished even for invoking the name of Medjay and possibly encouraging others to follow its doctrine.

I wondered, how would they have felt to know that they had in their clutches one of the last remaining true protectors of Egypt?

We travelled downriver to the village of Aswan. There we moved past the canopies and washing lines, and across the square in the centre of the village to the docks, from where we could see Elephantine. We took a boat across the river to the island and then, in order not to draw too much attention to ourselves, made a fireless camp in a well hidden hollow not far inland.

The Temple of Khnum was on the southern shore, and it was there Neka had said my father was kept, in a makeshift pit in the gatehouse.

On the first day, Neka left to explore our surroundings. He returned that afternoon and we sat in a small circle to make plans. As feluccas passed by, their sails fluttering in the breeze, boatmen calling to one another, he used a stick to draw in the dirt, sketching out a picture of the great Temple of Khnum that dominated the southern area of the island.

'Here,' he said, pointing to where he'd sketched out

the gatehouse. 'In there is the pit in which they keep the prisoners. Your father is the only one in there.'

'Is he suffering?' I asked.

'He won't have been treated well, no,' said Neka, shrugging. 'But he's a Medjay. He'll manage.'

I felt a hand on my arm. 'But how?' said Aya. 'How was he captured?'

Of us both, Aya knew most about the Medjay. She'd shared what she knew during our travels, and she was aware that they were likely to face various forms of persecution up and down the country. She had never been close to my father, but I sensed her opinion of him had shifted since the discovery that he was a Medjay. While I wouldn't say she'd taken to liking him, now at least she respected him.

What she couldn't understand now, though, was why my father had allowed himself to be captured.

'Medjay are the great warriors of Egypt,' she argued, 'protectors of the people, highly skilled fighters, the elite. I can't see him being captured by officials more used to dealing with the self-proclaimed Medjay, who are little more than glorified protesters who don't even understand the implications of the title they claim. Even if they had managed to get the better of him, how did they discover his secret? Bayek, you lived with him for fifteen years and you didn't know. Now, we're supposed to accept that he accidentally gave himself away while travelling in hostile territory? It just doesn't make sense. Isn't the purpose of the rightful Medjay that they remain hidden and out of sight, influencing from the shadows?'

Khensa shrugged. 'Perhaps he was careless or . . .'

'Do the Medjay get careless?' said Aya doubtfully.

'. . . Or unlucky. Even a Medjay can be unlucky.'

'But what does this have to do with him leaving Siwa?' asked Aya.

'Maybe nothing,' I said. But even I knew that was unlikely.

She shook her head and returned to studying Neka's drawing in the sand.

As it turned out, I should have listened to her. We all should.

42

That same night the dream came to me again. It wasn't one where I watched myself plunge a blade into Tuta's killer, only to realize at the last moment that it was Tuta himself I was killing. No. Another, much older one. The one with the rats in the cave, scrabbling to get me.

We were in our shelters: I was with Aya in one, Khensa and Neka in the other. By silent agreement Khensa and Neka had built both shelters while Aya and I made a fire, then caught a hare to cook on it. Funny, I thought, as we watched them labour. I learned shelter-building from Khensa, and I in turn had passed that knowledge on to Aya. But watching the two Nubians at work we were both made aware that, like stone overgrown by ivy, our skills had become obscured so that while they retained their shape and form they were not quite as vivid as they had once been. Watching how they fashioned tent poles from branches they found, cutting and whittling them quickly and precisely, fitting them together, was like being given the lesson again.

They had worked quickly, muttering about oncoming weather and how they wanted to ensure our shelter was as sturdy as possible. Every now and then they'd stop and bicker before continuing to build, sometimes doing it Khensa's way, other times Neka's, and in a short time the shelters were built, and we ate hare and agreed that we needed another day in which to gather information. We then settled down for the night, with the moon throwing silver on to the river at one side of us, the island's foliage spreading out on the other, the air crackling with the threat of a storm to come.

And, yes, I dreamt. The dream of rats. Only this time I found myself turning in order to run in the opposite direction, desperate to escape the cave full of writhing vermin and thumping over uneven ground slowly – so very, painfully slowly – until I realized that what I thought was an earthquake was in fact Aya shaking me, kneeling over me, whispering, 'Bayek, Bayek, wake up.'

I sat up suddenly, jerking awake with a force that sent Aya rocking back on her heels. At the same time I heard it, the storm outside, and saw the frame buffeted by a fierce wind, sand scraping on the shelter like the claws of some monster trying to gain entry.

'What's wrong?' she said, looking at me strangely.

I pushed a hand through my hair, registering that it was long and felt dirty beneath my fingers, scratching at my chest, trying to bring myself into the present. 'Oh, nothing. Dream.'

'About Tuta's father?'

'No. The rats. Look, why are you waking me up?'

'Because there's a storm,' she said simply.

I looked at her, mouth trying to find words that

wouldn't come, and then gave up. 'It'll pass,' I groaned, dropping back to my sleeping mat and pulling the cover to my chin. 'Don't worry about it. Go back to sleep.'

She huffed in quiet laughter, eyes bright in the gloom. 'I had an idea.'

I woke up at her words, alertness seeping through clear to my bones.

'Tell me.'

'It's the direction of the wind . . .'

A moment or so later we were shaking the Nubians awake and I saw them do the same groggy, trying-to-make-sense-of-things that I had just done.

'There's a sandstorm,' said Aya.

Khensa focused and smiled slowly. 'You have an idea. Tell us,' she said.

As Aya began to speak, Khensa's smile widened.

43

Bion had stood in the empty house with the bodies of Hemon and Sabestet lying by the front door.

He'd found The Elder's Medjay medallion concealed beneath a leather band on his upper arm. Then he'd strangled the rat before carrying the basket, the rat trap, the belt and the bowl to where his horse stood waiting for him.

There he'd made a fire, cooked the rat and eaten it. On the fire he'd burned the cage. He'd buried the copper bowl and the belt.

From the home of Hemon and Sabestet he had taken two jars of wine and a bowl from which to drink. As he had sat drinking the pale wine, he had replayed the old man's confession in his mind.

He had names. The mission could continue.

The Elder had told Bion that Sabu and his son were in Elephantine, and so that is where he set his course.

Coming into this part of the country he had noted that he was in an area famed for its hatred and persecution of the Medjay. History was not on the side of the old protectorship in this part of the world. That in itself made it an unusual choice of hiding place.

Accordingly, after a day in the village of Aswan, Bion learned that a Medjay by the name of Sabu was imprisoned at the Temple of Khnum, across the water on the island of Elephantine. Of Bayek there was no word. It occurred to him how peculiar it was that people knew of a Medjay imprisoned in the temple but looked blankly at him when he asked after the son. That was interesting.

'So, old man,' he said to himself, 'what was your game?'

44

'What are we doing?' said Neka. All four of us were crouched in an abandoned and otherwise empty outhouse set some distance from the main entrance of the grand Temple of Khnum and separated from it by a stretch of barren ground. In any normal circumstances we would have been able to throw a stone and hit the temple frontage, but these were not normal circumstances: we couldn't even see the temple, and if we had thrown a stone, well, then it would have been taken by the shrieking wind.

Sure enough, we had been lacerated by sand as we made the trip from our camp to the temple. A trip that no sane person would attempt, alternately scoured and blasted every step of the way. We had swaddled ourselves from foot to head against the onslaught, using thickly covered hands to shield our eyes and keeping our backs to the maelstrom, until at last we reached the shelter that Neka had revealed was waiting for us.

The severity of the storm had prevented any chatter on our journey, which meant that Neka hadn't been able to voice his reservations. Of those he had plenty, and he was making them known now.

Khensa grinned at me. 'Don't worry about him, he's a scout, he's cautious. It's in their blood.'

'This is madness,' he railed. 'Madness to be out in such conditions, attempting something like this.'

Khensa's eyes shone through the slit of the blue scarf she had wrapped around her head. I thought back to the Khensa of a few weeks ago, laid low after the battle at Menna's base, and although she'd never have admitted it, she'd been reinvigorated since embarking on the journey to Elephantine. She'd embraced Aya's idea with enthusiasm: let's use the storm as cover and go in now, while chaos reigned. The direction of the wind was right. The gods were smiling upon us. She'd snatched up her spear while Neka was still rubbing sleep from his eyes. Moments later, as though to truly symbolize her rebirth, she was wearing her white face chalk.

And as if to mark his own resistance to the plan, Neka had not applied his own.

'Every guard in the place will be awake,' he argued now, trying to shake sand out of his clothes.

Khensa screwed up her nose. 'Will they? We weren't – not until these two woke us. And besides, everybody in there will be far too busy with the storm. Look, let me tell you something, Neka. Back at Menna's base when we saw you'd been taken captive, it was I who wanted to wait and Seti who persuaded me otherwise. And if we had waited – what then? Can you imagine the tortures you would have had to endure? You have a lot to be thankful for when it comes to making impetuous decisions. Make your choice, Neka. Accompany us on our mad mission and share in the glory, or go home alone and watch from afar. What's it to be?'

He rolled his eyes. 'You forgot the third option.'

'Which is?' Khensa's voice was wry, but she was smiling, as though she knew exactly what he'd say.

'To die here with you,' he grumbled, determined to stay in a bad mood.

'Don't you want to do that?' She grinned. For a moment he resisted and then on his face appeared the beginnings of a smile, and seeing him begin to relent, she took white chalk from her own face and applied it to his.

'There's nothing I'd like more,' he sighed, a touch over-dramatically, reaching for his bow.

We did not know much. Nothing, in fact, other than that my father was being kept in a pit in the gatehouse, and even that, as Neka was quick to remind us, was old information, just the sort of thing we should have checked on the day we made our move.

The plan, then, was simply to storm the gatehouse as two Nubians, two Siwan and a sandstorm.

What could possibly go wrong?

We left the outhouse. There was at least no need to creep. Stepping out into the storm, we were hailed by sheets of sand that swept across our vision. Any lookouts at the temple would have seen nothing. Even if they had been able to make out shapes coming towards them it would have been impossible to say whether they were human or animal. As Aya had pointed out, our true advantage was the element of surprise. After all, who would be stupid enough to venture out in weather like this?

Sure enough, the wind howled. Sand seemed to pelt us in relentless, merciless waves.

As we approached the temple we were acutely aware of a guard on the gatehouse ramparts. A bowman was posted there day and night, according to Neka. With gusts of wind throwing sand at the temple frontage, any sentry with a sense of self-preservation would be taking cover behind the ramparts, and if he did pluck up the courage and risk a look he'd see nothing.

But what if the wind dropped? What if it stopped for long enough that the sand settled and the vision cleared and the lookout remembered to do his job and do some looking out?

That thought was uppermost in our minds as we made our way to the temple, feeling exposed and vulnerable, cursing the wind that whipped at us but needing it to hide us. And when at last we came to the foot of the gatehouse we took a moment to savour the relief.

We looked at one another. Our faces stung beneath the cloth that we wore, battered by the storm. Neka was focused, all reservations aside; Khensa radiated intensity and focus; Aya had never looked more resolute.

We edged our way to the gatehouse entrance. A huge wooden affair with double doors that would open to admit carts and chariots, it was inset with a smaller wicket door. The noise of the storm was different here, the sand rattling off the wood. Khensa looked at us, gauging our readiness. We were nothing but four sets of eyes, but those eyes said yes; those eyes gave her permission to do what she did next.

Which was to see whether anyone was home.

Khensa raised her fist, knocked. We waited. Would they even hear the summons above the storm's din?

But hear it they did, and from inside came an answer. 'Identify yourselves.'

The voice was muffled, indistinct.

'For pity's sake, open up, or have the blood of a mere child on your hands,' replied Khensa pitifully.

'In this storm. Are you mad?' came the indignant reply.

Khensa rolled her eyes, but kept up the act. 'That's why I need shelter, sir. Please will you accommodate me? I can slip inside this door, sir, before you feel the brunt of the storm, you'll see.'

As though to emphasize the severity of the situation the wind picked up. A huge gust of it thumped at the wooden door, shaking it on its hinges.

'All right, all right,' came the voice from the other side, grudgingly, as though Khensa were controlling the storm's ferocity.

I heard a bolt thrown. I caught Aya's eye. I wondered if she knew what I was thinking and supposed that she did, because, of course, I was thinking that I was mere moments away from seeing my father. And not just seeing him, but *rescuing* him no less.

Maybe she was thinking none of that. Perhaps her mind was going back to the reasons why Sabu had allowed himself to be captured, and imprisoned, by the clod-hopping oafs of Elephantine. Perhaps she was still puzzling on what she was certain was wrong.

And then the door opened.

45

We rushed in: the four of us and the storm. Khensa led, shoving the door into the face of the man on the other side, and he stumbled back, arms pinwheeling, no weapon drawn, his face falling in shock at the sight of us as the wind slammed the wicket door back on its hinges.

Just behind Khensa, Neka was already turning, snatching an arrow from his quiver, bowstring drawn back, bow angled – all in one dizzyingly fast and fluid movement as he targeted a sentry overhead. In the next moment the lookout came tumbling from above to land with a messy, bloody squelch on the stone in front of us.

The storm rushed into the square in which we now found ourselves, as much a benefit as ten extra warriors in our favour. Aya and I heaved open the double gates to allow the wind greater entry, its presence more effective than we could have imagined. As though in reply, there came a shout and another guard rushed out of the haze, this one with his weapon drawn.

Khensa stood, having dealt with the guard at the door, felling the new arrival with a swift-thrown spear before he could reach us. Neka waved to usher us forward, shouting for caution, knowing the edge of the pit could be anywhere, and we felt our way carefully forward even as an arrow came whistling from within the swirling, eddying sand. Loosed more in hope than with any considered aim, it went wide and we edged further forward on our bellies, finding a pocket of calm beneath the storm as we searched for the pit's opening.

We could hear shouting. I imagined the gatehouse guards reassembling as they tried to work out what was happening. Another arrow came slicing out of the mist. They were getting themselves together. Assembling. At the same time we were making noise, the four of us pretending to be dozens, letting the storm work for us.

We finally reached the pit, where I pulled myself to the edge, dragging myself by my fingertips in order to peer down into what seemed like an abyss.

'Father,' I called, and I was sure that I was rewarded with a movement in the darkness below. I saw eyes shining in the blackness. Down there it was safe from the storm that we had allowed into the gatehouse and which now raged around us.

Neka came scrambling around the lip of the pit cradling a length of rope.

'Nice of them to leave this lying around for us,' he said with a grin.

Close by, a stake driven into the ground was grooved in a way that left us in no doubt as to its purpose. Seconds later the rope was wound around the stake and tossed into the pit.

'I'll cover you,' said Neka and pulled away.

'Grab it, Father,' I yelled into the black hole as around me came the shouts and screams of further battle.

There wasn't much time. Neka was fitting arrows into his bow and letting them off. I heard the twang of the bowstring and through the maelstrom I saw his face twisted with determination and effort as each arrow in turn left his bow. Again, he did the work of an army as Khensa, Aya and I, with all our might, dug our heels into the ground, rope burning our palms as we pulled backwards, one step at a time, heaving, yelling, adding to the noise, a mix of triumph and effort, knowing that the end of our mission was within our grasp and hardly able to believe that the four of us had been able to pull off such a daring rescue. Victory so close at hand.

Later, when it was all over, Aya told me that she had glanced into the hole and seen the prisoner helping himself out of his jail, climbing up the wall rope with his feet on the sides of the pit.

I didn't see him. I didn't realize.

But Aya did.

Even before the prisoner reached the top of the pit she knew.

It was not my father.

46

The storm seemed to die in response. As though it too were sharing a dumbfounded air that descended upon us as we looked at one another and then back at the prisoner. Temporarily silent, we forgot to ask his name, what he was doing in the pit or whether he really was Medjay. Just knowing that it was not Sabu of Siwa, not my father, I felt numb, my stomach lurching.

Neka came skidding back towards us, aware that the lull in the storm would inspire the gatehouse guards to greater bravery. 'Come on, let's go, let's get out of here,' he urged before throwing a look at the rescued prisoner. 'Hello, Sabu,' he introduced himself.

'It's not Sabu,' said Khensa, finding her voice. 'It's a decoy.' She reached to the man, grabbed a bunch of his dirty tunic in her fist. 'I ought to throw you back in there face first. Who are you?'

Terrified, the man was shaking his head, mouth working uselessly. He was old, greying, his lips were wet and his eyes rolled crazily.

'*What?*' Neka was saying, diverted from battle by the sudden turn of events. 'What? I was told it was Sabu. A Medjay from Siwa called Sabu.'

I pulled Aya to one side. 'You knew,' I said, piercing her with my gaze. 'You knew, didn't you?'

She shook her arm free. 'Of course I didn't *know*. I suspected.'

'Well, you should have . . .'

'*I tried*,' she insisted. She had. I took a deep breath, and let go of my burgeoning resentment. It wasn't her fault.

'Who's this, then?'

She shrugged. 'I don't know,' she said, and then turned her eyes on the terrified prisoner, still held in Khensa's grasp. 'What's your name?'

'Sabu, Sabu,' he jabbered. His jaw was slack, lips moist, eyes wide with fear and confusion. 'Medjay, Medjay.'

We both sighed. Asking this madman anything would get us nowhere, that much was obvious.

'We've got to make tracks,' Neka was warning from feet away. The storm no longer provided as much cover, and soon it would provide none at all. He let two arrows off into the area across the pit and was rewarded with a scream of either surprise or pain; enough, hopefully, to keep them at bay for some moments more. 'We've got to get out of here, do you hear me? We can have this conversation later.'

And he was right.

An arrow came whistling out of the darkness and embedded itself into the ground beside him. It was followed by another and then another. In the next instant we were pulling ourselves to our feet. The tempest had subsided, visibility was clearing, and we heard the unmistakable sounds of the gatehouse guards regrouping. 'Who goes there?' came the cry, a little cautious at first and then repeated with more authority. But we were in no mood to reply, a ragtag squad, disappointed and battleworn, we retreated out of the gate and ran headlong into the storm, which was less fierce but still lashed at us, as though admonishing us, punishing us for our stupidity.

I threw a look at Aya and saw nothing in her eyes but the great pain of wishing she had been wrong. Outside the gate the wasteland stretched before us, sand whirling in our vision, but I hardly registered the tumult. There were warlike cries and a group of guards came rushing from around the side of the gatehouse with their swords drawn, others taking up position with bows.

'Halt,' they demanded in unison, and if the idea was to stop us in our tracks then it failed, because our blood was up, our survival instinct keen and sharp, and though we checked ourselves at the sight of them, we pushed on.

Neka snatched an arrow from his quiver, twisted his torso and loosed it, all in one movement. His shot found its mark, dropping one of the bowmen. At the same time a swordsman, running, tried to block Khensa's path, but she swung with the spear, bringing the shaft of it up and under, impaling him.

From the corner of my eye I saw a second bowman take aim at Aya. My warning shout was snatched away in the swirling storm and I changed course, trying to reach her, thinking, *No!* and shouting at the same time. 'Aya! Dive!'

And then the bowman was dropping his weapon, clutching at his neck, from which protruded an arrow. Where had it come from? Not from Neka or Khensa. I had no idea. I just kept on running, screaming at the others to speed up as, thankfully, we left the last of the guards behind.

I ran to Aya. 'Someone's out there – and whoever it is just saved your life.' She looked at me and I wondered if she was thinking the same thing I was, and then we kept on running, peering into the murky, swirling darkness as we plunged onwards, with still no sign of our mystery bowman.

Ahead of us were Khensa, Neka and the prisoner; behind us the temple, the shouts of the guards becoming more distant now. With the moon lighting our way, we kept running, joining up, keeping pace, until at last Khensa gestured and we headed off the wasteland and into trees at the perimeter of the island, crashing through dry undergrowth until the going became wet beneath our feet and we found ourselves at the waterside.

There, Khensa stopped us with a raised fist, crouched and indicated for us to gather around. Her chest heaved, her breath was ragged and she surveyed her crew with eyes that shone with danger and excitement.

'We're being followed,' she said, and then gave a start as a voice came from the darkness, weapon instantly at the ready.

'Not difficult, the noise you were making,' it said, and a figure stepped forward, making us scramble to our feet, the others reaching for their weapons.

Not me, though. It was a voice I recognized, and a familiar figure who strode into the clearing, angrily brushing undergrowth aside and looking around at us, an exasperated look on his face. 'You're dead, all of you,' said my father.

47

When he strode into the clearing, he looked almost the same as when I'd last seen him, maybe slightly less tidy without my mother's guiding hand. His long hair was gathered back, his beard a little straggly, his face just a touch more weathered and craggy than it was before.

And unhappy. Father was not quick to temper; he tended to smoulder. Mother always said he kept it hidden, that he was like the slow-moving water, calm on the surface but with dangerous, fast-moving undercurrents. Oh, but now the surface calm was broken and the colour was in his cheeks, his eyes afire as they swept across us accusingly.

'Sabu,' Khensa said a touch wryly, dipping her head in a greeting that was also a tacit acknowledgement that he and I had things to discuss – matters that did not involve her. Neka, too, seemed to withdraw, stepping away from a reunion that was between my father and me.

My angry father.

Gods! I thought, as he turned to me, pinning me with a stare. How different this was compared to the scene I'd pictured. The dreams of a small boy, buried deep inside me. I'd been naïve. There was no embrace. No greeting. No gratitude. Just . . .

'What the hell are you doing here?' he snapped.

'We came to rescue you . . .' I said uselessly.

He threw up his arms, bow in one hand. 'Do I look like I need rescuing?'

'You don't,' said Aya flatly, and then indicated the poor creature who crouched at our feet and stared up at us, cloaked in fear and confusion, as though cowering in the face of an oncoming rockslide. 'But *he* did.'

Father knelt to address the erstwhile prisoner, his voice softening along with his manner. 'You performed your duty well, Bes, and I'm sorry if you've been caused any distress. My thanks go to you and to your family, and I hope you can all enjoy your reward.'

'Thank you, Sabu, thank you,' managed Bes, nodding furiously. His wide eyes skittered and, if he wasn't exactly calm, at least he seemed to have collected himself.

'Why?' I asked. 'Why did you need him?'

Father sighed, straightening with a resigned air. 'The short answer is that I needed to set a trap, and I needed bait for that trap.'

'A trap for what?' said Aya.

'For a killer – a killer hunting Medjay.' He stopped himself. 'You know of the Medjay, I take it, if you've got this far?' I nodded and a look passed between us.

'And that's why you left Siwa?' pressed Aya. 'Nothing to do with Menna?'

'Menna . . .' Father seemed to remember and threw a look to Khensa, who nodded confirmation from where she still stood a distance away.

'Menna is dead, Sabu.'

'Thank you, Khensa, thank you. That means a great deal.' He turned to Aya. 'No, the reason I left Siwa had nothing to do with Menna and everything to do with a message saying the Medjay are under threat.'

'The killer?' I said.

Father nodded. 'A man who knows his trade, Bayek. He got the better of Emsaf, an expert and talented Medjay, a great fighter, scout and tracker. This killer is methodical and he is ruthless. That's why I hoped to draw him out.'

'I'm sorry, Father,' I said. My face fell and my head dropped, but he put his hands to my arms.

'There'll be plenty of time for reprimands later – and there *will* be reprimands.' He paused. 'But for now, I'm pleased to see you – all of you – and I'm gratified that your skills have improved since I left Siwa. A few bad habits that we need to look at, mind you, but we'll make a –'

'Wait,' whispered Khensa, holding up a hand for silence.

'What?' said my father.

'Somebody close,' replied Khensa. 'Your trap may yet work. Someone's coming.' She narrowed her eyes, nodding slowly. 'And they're good.'

'It must be him. We finish it, here and now,' said my father, hoisting his bow, grim-faced and steadfast with the rising sun at his back. He indicated for Khensa and Neka to take the flanks while he took the middle, in order to come at whoever was stalking us from three directions. Aya and I stood, ready to take our places. He nodded. 'Join up, form a party just behind. Keep watch in case he tries to work his way in from the rear.'

'He won't be able to do that . . .' started Neka.

'He's got this far,' snapped my father. 'Emsaf underestimated him. I won't make the same mistake.'

We fanned out and began to move away from the waterline, leaving Bes behind. Looking to my left, I saw Aya tense, skirts clinging to her legs with the damp. Ahead of me a cluster of flies danced in the early morning cool.

No noise now. The Nubians and my father were out of sight. The temple guards had clearly decided to give up their chase. If this Medjay hunter was as good as my father feared then would he be so easily snared? I was doubtful.

We moved further forward, painfully aware of even the quietest squelch and crackle as we trod through the undergrowth. Within me was the same excitement I'd felt at Menna's base, a knowledge that I was part of something – something worthwhile. I wished I could somehow communicate that to my father, to prove to him that I had grown, that I was making my own choices and was ready to follow up on them. And then I stopped thinking even of that, focusing on the moment, the task at hand. We advanced, footstep by footstep, breath held. I became aware that the underground was thinning out. The silvery light that had only intermittently penetrated the canopy above now painted the ground ahead of us and the going was less soft.

And then came a burst of noise from up ahead, and where I would have jumped in shock but mere months ago, I swiftly whirled, ready to face the threat. There was sudden movement, a rustling, a shout I couldn't quite identify followed by the unmistakable sound of loosed arrows whistling and then a shout of pain.

Aya and I had dropped to a crouch, our swords drawn. Ahead of us in the undergrowth came the sound of more arrows and then my father's voice, calling, 'Show yourself, killer! Face me!' But there was no reply.

We stayed crouched. Once more the stillness of early morning asserted itself. I wanted to call ahead but stopped myself, reluctant to give away our position, wondering why there were five of us and yet somehow I felt as though we were not the hunters but the hunted.

A sound nearby caught our attention, and then my father called out softly, 'Bayek.'

'Father?'

'Are you all right?'

'Unhurt. And you?'

He appeared from within the gloom, Khensa and Neka at his back. 'I thought I got him, but there's no sign of a body,' he said as Khensa squatted with her spear held in one hand and the other at the ground, her fingers splayed and her head cocked as though listening through her fingertips. My father, with a short tilt of his chin, bade us join them.

'Good work,' he murmured and I'm sure Aya felt the same surge of pride I did. To Khensa he said, 'Is he still around?'

'I don't know,' Khensa replied with a frown that spoke of not wanting to admit being unable to track him. 'I don't know where he is – if he's even here.'

'He was here . . .' said my father. 'Of that I'm certain.' He pulled a face. 'I could have sworn one of my arrows found its mark. Whatever this means, we know one thing at least. We know our enemy's shortcomings.'

What are they? I wanted to ask, but held my tongue.

'He's also a man who knows when the odds are stacked against him,' added Khensa.

Just then a call came to us, carried by the misty early morning. *'Medjay.'* We froze, Khensa trying to pinpoint the source. *'Medjay, we will soon meet and have our day of reckoning.'*

It was followed by a scream from Bes, repeating the same word over and over again: 'Sabu,' he shrieked. 'Sabu, Sabu, Sabu.'

We crashed back through the undergrowth, sticking together this time, weapons drawn, with my father, Khensa and Neka at our head and myself and Aya behind, ready for attack, wary of traps or an ambush. Bes was in the same position we had left him. Yet again he was trembling with terror, looking up at us with big eyes repeating the name, 'Sabu, Sabu,' over and over again. Below his wide eyes he held his hands to his cheeks. 'Demon, demon, demon . . .' he chanted. I'd never seen a man so terrified. And yet . . .

'Blood,' said Khensa, pointing to his tunic.

'Are you hurt, Bes?' asked my father, kneeling to him, looking for wounds.

'No, Sabu,' he gibbered, 'the demon is hurt.'

Father stood, sighing. 'Then the demon bleeds,' he said.

PART III

48

Many Years Later

Over the years, Bion had often thought about the night of the storm. He could have ended it that night if not for Sabu's lucky shot inflicting a wound that caused him to withdraw and spend many months recovering. Were it not for his preference for close-quarters combat. For his only passable skill with the bow.

It would not have helped, he thought. The sandstorm had been the ultimate advantage in so many ways. And its aftermath meant they had been able to regroup, present a united front. There was only so much a bow could have done for him. He just hadn't planned for that – would not have, by personal inclination. Maybe. Still. But what if it had helped? Perhaps if he'd been a proficient archer then maybe he could have finished it that night, wounded or not; he could have ended his mission. Rather, perhaps if he'd been less focused on a close kill, more open to long-range plans.

Or maybe it was all the winds and the storm, and the Medjay's own skill with the arrow, superlative no matter what excuse he tried to think of. And so, he'd always end up thinking, his own, less than stellar competence in that respect had been his downfall.

It was something that Raia had always taken great pleasure in teasing him about. Raia, of course, being an expert bowman. 'It's because you like killing too much,' Raia had told him with that same knowing smile, as though he knew Bion intimately. 'You like to see life leave your victims. You like to watch it in their eyes. Up close and personal. That's your way, isn't it?'

Bion, who had always prided himself on his inscrutability, wondered at how opaque he actually was. He knew he was a monster. He'd always known. But he thought, at least, that he'd learned to hide it. To blend in, well enough at least. Then again, Raia was the one who knew him best. They'd worked together for many years. And he'd never judged. Others, thoughts Bion, would not have been so tolerant.

Either way, his strength as Raia's assassin had been his weakness out there in Elephantine that night. Compounded by the storm and his injury, which had forced him to retire from the fight, reassess, and make his base in the Red Lands, occupying the abandoned hut of a shepherd in order to recover and start again, wondering whether he would ever see home. He had healed. He had retrained himself, making up for the lost months spent recovering. He'd elevated his bow skills, practising assiduously until in that, as in every other aspect of death-dealing, he had gained the utmost proficiency.

Eventually, Bion had also resumed his investigations – and they had taken him to Thebes, where he had crossed over to the necropolis and found the correct tomb, though it now offered no sign that the Nubians had ever been in residence.

Outside he hailed an old man and crossed the burial ground to speak to him. The day was blue and bright, and over the old man's shoulder Bion could see the city, tattered and beaten by war but still retaining stature and beauty, as though the gods refused to let anything ugly taint the world that they had created.

All the ugliness was in men. Bion knew that better than anyone. He had his fair share of it, after all.

The old man knew about the Nubians. They had moved on, he said.

'Do you know where?' Bion asked.

The old man shook his head. He wasn't sure. He thought that some of them had gone south. Not all.

'They split up?'

'That they did. There was a baby born. Off they went, maybe to start a new tribe somewhere else. Who knows?'

And that was it for the Nubians. Bion had left, thinking they could have been worthy opponents but no longer interested in them. They were not the mission. His business was with the Medjay.

49

The camel rider had appeared in the distance some time after Bion. He'd watched the rider slowly materialize from the heat haze, a smear that became a figure that, in time, became a person.

His messenger. Bion had first met Sumi as a boy, years ago, when he'd been hired in order to convey news to Raia in Alexandria. He had taken Hemon's medallion as well as the added information that Bion was now in pursuit of the final Medjay.

The message had come back: *Why is this taking so long?*

Sitting in his sparse shepherd's hut, Bion had thought of Raia. He'd pictured the commander in his Alexandria home with ivy growing up the walls of its central courtyard, raging at Sumi, wondering why he could not control his errant assassin. It had been entertaining, briefly, to imagine Raia's important rage, the self-styled soldier now as helpless as the scholars he so loved to dismiss.

So Bion had dispatched Sumi, a young man by now, to remind Raia that things had been made so much more difficult all those years ago because the Medjay knew of his coming. He reminded Raia that the blame for the leak lay at his feet. It was, after all, his scholar who had informed Rashidi, who in turn had alerted the Medjay to The Order's plan. If not for that then Bion's mission would already be at an end. Raia would have other medallions to add to his collection.

Back had come the missive, Sumi cautious as he stood and repeated what he'd been told. 'Raia has requested that you return to Alexandria in order that he can . . . let me get this right . . . "Discuss strategy". He wants you to come at once.'

'Tell Raia I have a plan in place,' Bion had instructed. 'Inform him that my request for him to trust me is made in the strongest possible terms. That he will be updated shortly.'

And now the reply had arrived.

He watched Sumi approach warily, and poured water for them both. When the messenger arrived he sat cross-legged to drink and talk.

'He's got a nice house, hasn't he?' Sumi looked around him as if comparing the two vastly different life-styles. Nervous small talk. His hands were tight on the clay cup.

Bion nodded. 'Yes,' he said blankly. 'The commander was always a great believer in embracing luxury wherever he should find it.'

'And he delegates to you tasks that lie beyond his own capabilities?'

'In a manner of speaking.'

'He fears you,' Sumi blurted out, and Bion saw fear there as well. He approved. It was important, to understand when one was in the presence of Death. The young man had good instincts.

'We agreed you wouldn't ask questions,' replied Bion. 'Now, the exchange. You gave him my message, I take it?'

Sumi nodded quickly, so much so that Bion fancied hearing his brains rattling within his skull. He was all wide eyes and nervous limbs. 'I did give him the message. He was not very happy.' He rubbed his cheek, frowning in remembrance. 'I got the sense that I was lucky to make it out of there alive.' He paused, and Bion knew he was wondering whether he would make it out of this particular moment alive as well.

'Did he want to know of my whereabouts?'

'He said he knew better than to ask.' Relief, bright and honest.

'What was his dispatch in return?'

'He says it has been many years now. He says he would like to see the job complete.' Sumi sounded almost apologetic and Bion had not a single doubt that the original message had not been so carefully worded.

Of course you want to see the job complete, thought Bion. *Of course you do.*

'You didn't tell him anything else?'

The messenger shook his head. He and Bion had an arrangement: Sumi had recruited urchins, rapscallions and scamps – street children across the region – and those street children had recruited other street children, and yet more, all on the lookout for Sabu, Bayek and the girl, and each would report to a contact, who would report to other contacts, who reported to the grinning Sumi, who in turn would report to Bion.

Bion, who had learned the bow. Bion, who had recovered from an injury that might have crippled a lesser being. Bion, who now intended to finish this particular mission, regardless of what Raia truly wanted, in the end. Bion sent the boy off. He knew his patience would reap a reward. Someday.

And then one day, indeed, after even more time had passed, Sumi came to Bion again, only this time it was a visit that Bion had not been expecting, and as he watched the camel approach on the horizon, he allowed himself the hope that after all these years the Medjay had at last been found.

And so it was.

'I bring news,' said Sumi, when they once more sat drinking thick, pungent beer. 'I think you're going to be happy about this one.' He eyes flickered towards Bion's pouch, but remained respectful. Money lured him back. Money, despite the worry of death.

'Go on,' said Bion.

'I know where they are, the people you seek, the trio.'

'Really?' said Bion. 'All three of them?'

Sumi nodded definitively. 'Uh-huh. All three of them. They have made camp. Looks like they have been there a couple of months or so.'

'How do you know this?'

'They sent a message.'

Bion shook his head, almost surprised. 'No, they wouldn't be so careless as to involve another party.'

'More than one other party,' said Sumi, sipping his beer. 'The message was given to a boy who took it to another boy. It's the first one who is my contact.'

'So you know where the message was coming from, but not where it was going?'

'That's about it. But I can find out, if you want.' Sumi showed teeth and held up his fingers, scared but determined, in expectation of reward.

'I'll need you to do that,' said Bion, but he was thinking – and what he was thinking was, *This isn't right. There's something untoward here.*

He leaned forward, beckoning the messenger towards him, seeing his guest flinch a little but coming in close all the same. 'Are you sure there is nothing amiss here? Nothing you want to tell me now? I can assure you that it will be better for you in the long run if you do.'

Sumi pulled back with an earnest expression as he shook his head furiously. 'No – you pay me well. I've worked hard for you and will continue to do so.' He hesitated, then plunged on. 'You're scarier than anyone else out there. I would not deceive you.'

Bion nodded, knowing the messenger was telling the truth, and they drank the rest of the beer together in silence. A little later, Sumi went to leave and Bion gave him a purse that bulged with coins. The young man looked at it, hardly able to believe what nestled in his palm, testing its weight. When he looked up at Bion he had forgotten, for a moment, to be scared.

'You're not coming back, are you?' he said.

'If your information is correct I have no need to.'

Sumi nodded. 'Thank you,' he said.

Later, Bion packed and left his base of so many years. Finally, he was ready to complete his mission.

50

'I would like to take Aya as my wife.'

My father dropped his sword. Where a moment ago his eyes had been watchful and focused as he concentrated on teaching me how to move from a left-foot forward defensive stance into a counter-attacking formation, now they became thoughtful.

'I see.' He frowned, and I steeled myself for an argument that never came. 'Then you must do so,' he said.

We had left a camel train some days ago and set up camp on the edge of the desert. That morning I'd stepped outside mine and Aya's tent, cast a look at my father's shelter – I could hear him snoring gently inside – and then stood surveying the desert, the expanse of sand, trees on the horizon and, in the distance, the town. On the air was the briny scent of the sea and the damp smell of a morning preparing to be burned away by the day's sun. These things were just as they were every morning. The world in which I found myself was unchanged.

But as for me?

I had changed. I'd changed so much that I was

unrecognizable as the fifteen-year-old who had left Siwa all those years ago.

I was different now. I knew my path. I was training to be a Medjay.

'You still require more training.'

That was what my father always said, whenever I dared suggest that the years of his teaching might have conferred on me that status once and for all. He would never say when, only that when the time came he would know. And when he knew, then I would be the second person to know.

After that night in Elephantine, we'd said our farewells to Khensa and Neka; they would travel back to Thebes and reunite with their tribe, but in the meantime we had to stay on the move. Father, Aya and I had to keep one step ahead of the assassin who, despite his injury, continued to worry my father: this ghost, this 'demon' that seemed to shadow him.

Our first order of business was to speak to The Elder, a man named Hemon and his ward, Sabestet, and we had spent months travelling to their home in Djerty. There we'd arrived to find the homestead empty and neglected. My father had taken one look and said, 'Gods, not again.'

With the house deserted, we travelled into Djerty and there it was confirmed what we already feared: Hemon and Sabestet had been murdered.

Father had not handled the news well. Things had changed. He withdrew into himself for some time, as though seeking his own counsel, and during that period Aya and I looked after ourselves and, so far as we could, offered him support.

It took him a while, but at last he came round, and one day, early in the morning out hunting, he made his announcement: 'Your Medjay learning begins tomorrow,' he told me.

It was an acknowledgment, or as much of one as Father would give, that he had not been training me seriously before. First came a period of what he called *unlearning* – getting rid of all those bad habits I had apparently picked up. My mind had gone back to the hours Aya and I spent practising during our time in Thebes. Much of it wrong, according to my father, though not a disaster, considering we had been improvising, learning on our own.

The whole time we'd kept moving. Years of being what Aya called 'on the run'. I think I'd trained in every town and village in the region, honing my sword skills and becoming an expert with the bow, making death and defence my trade.

In addition he schooled me in the ways and history of the Medjay. Once upon a time these proud warriors, whose ranks I hoped to join, had the status of the Phylakes or the Royal Guard. They were the protectors of the people, the *meketyou*, of temples and tombs, statues and idols. They were the guardians of everyday life but also of the people, keeping at bay the outside forces that threatened us.

Just as the priestess Nitokris had told me, he reinforced the ideas that, although they had protected temples and tombs – and in the case of Siwa still did, the Medjay's power and influence had decreased over the decades. No longer were they proud and very literal sentinels, protecting brick and flesh and blood. Now diminished, they protected something more important: a conceptual way of life, an ideology. His views differed from those of the priestess in one critical aspect, however. To him, Egypt was a country upon which others imposed their own convictions. First Alexander's ideologies had come to us, and now there were other, Roman voices clamouring to be heard, and all this time our own countrymen had been happy, nay enthusiastic, to allow these changes. The great city of Alexandria, which Aya loved so dearly, had even been built in our conqueror's image.

'We did not ask for this mode of living. This way of life was imposed upon us,' my father would say. 'We are being asked to worship status and power and gold, and these things are taking the place of the old ways; they are taking the place of the gods, Bayek. But the Medjay can rise again, to restore the principles by which we used to live, in simpler, less corrupt times. We are a part of that, Bayek. You will one day be the torch-carrier for our whole creed. We will rise again, my son. Hemon envisioned a resurgence. He planned for one, and you and I are key to that. The fate of the Medjay rests upon our shoulders.'

Then, of course, there was Aya. Nothing had changed between us, and yet it was as though *everything* had changed. She did not particularly care for my father, and he felt likewise. The two of them put up with one another mainly for my benefit. He made no secret of the fact that, as far as he was concerned, she could never be a Medjay – not a true Medjay – and she betrayed no interest in the brotherhood while in his presence. Her need to learn meant she'd often quiz me at night, rarely offering her own opinions, just listening, though I could tell she had doubts. She saw how much the teachings meant to me, whatever her feelings, and whether the Medjay principles as described by my father coincided with her own. I was never certain. After all, her heart lay in Alexandria; she was firmly an adept of the learned thinking there. No doubt that also meant being a supporter of its progressive ideology.

Perhaps we should have spoken about that more.

One thing she and my father did agree upon, however, was that I should act as Aya's tutor, just as my father was tutoring me. There was learning to be acquired in the act of teaching, Aya had stated, and my father had acquiesced on the spot. Thus was fashioned the routine: in the mornings I trained with Father and in the afternoons with Aya, moving from being pupil to teacher.

These were happy times. They were for me, and I think they were for her, too, because they were the times most like our childhood in Siwa and the months we spent in Thebes, when we were most . . . together. Teaching, learning, and, when the work was done, enjoying one another. I found comfort in her arms. On her lips I tasted rapture. They were heady times, spent in love with love and the joy of discovering the warriors within us.

Like all things, of course, it had to come to an end, and in many ways – maybe all the ways – it was my fault, because at first, indeed, for many years, I felt as though Aya was happy with our life together. We were always on the move, but it was an adventure and she enjoyed it; she loved learning.

But so did I, and as my learning progressed something happened that I couldn't really help. I began to gravitate to my father. I took deep joy in finally getting glimpses of the man behind the façade. Of our familial bond finally settling in. Yet I saw what was happening between Aya and me as a result, and so I took the decision that I hoped would balance things. I decided that we should become man and wife.

His acquiescence surprised me.

The hardest part was done, for Aya would surely accept my proposal.

51

'No,' she said. She was standing opposite me, her sword arm loose, a strange parallel of what had happened that very morning with my father.

'What? Why? I talked it through with Father, and he is happy for us.' I saw her face cloud and immediately tried to correct myself, 'I mean, you know, don't you, that might have been difficult for us. But he's happy, he's proud. He wants us to be together.' She was shaking her head but I ploughed on. 'And when my education is complete, we will return to Siwa so that I can take up the mantle of *mekety* as well as be a Medjay.'

'No,' she said firmly. 'I'm sorry, Bayek, but I shan't be doing that.'

I blinked. 'We can have a house. A family. I will seek the permission of your aunt.'

She flinched away, eyes dark with distress, but I wouldn't realize the significance of that until later. For now I continued, 'My father will stand down eventually and it will be up to me to protect Siwa. I shall be its guardian, Aya, I will be helping to keep the ways of the Medjay alive . . . But the most important thing is that you and I will be together. Don't you want that? Don't you want to spend the rest of your life with me?'

She raised her head, threw back her shoulders and then slammed her sword point into the ground so that it stuck there, the sword juddering slightly. Eyes ablaze she said, 'Bayek, I don't know where to start. I really don't. The wife of Siwa's protector. Medjay wife. Did you stop to reflect on whether I truly believe in the ways of the Medjay?'

'Well, don't you?'

'Perhaps. Perhaps not. That's not my question. My question is, did you stop to think about it?'

'Well, no, but . . .'

'Of course you didn't. Of course you didn't, because he's filled your head with all these . . .' She was whirling her hands around her head as though trying to ward off a swarm of flies, '. . . *ideas* and you're not willing to question them.' She sighed explosively. 'He's holding you back, Bayek!'

I felt a flash of anger at that. She'd given me space all these years, let me work on my relationship with my father. But a part of me had wondered, all this time. It was a part I'd not been willing to acknowledge then. I was not ready now. I pushed the doubts away and pressed my case, instead.

I reached my hands towards her as though trying to bridge the gap between us, a gap that seemed to be getting wider with every passing second. 'I have *you*,' I said. 'I have you to help me question things. To learn all I can. You won't let me become complacent. He knows that too.'

She was shaking her head. 'Did you stop to think what I might want?' I felt unsteady, unmoored. The question was fair. But I was still angry, too. I'd tried to talk to her earlier in my training. I'd tried to ask her – and she'd demurred, citing respect for what I was trying to build with my father. 'Here's something else: you say you're happy to ask my aunt, but what about my mother and father in Alexandria?'

'But you haven't spoken to them in years, not since you were a little girl,' I said defensively. Inside, though, I was thinking that she was right. If it even had crossed my mind to visit Alexandria and persuade her father of my suitability as a candidate for a husband, as was the tradition, then surely I would have dismissed the idea. Oh, I had a lot to persuade him with: I was a Medjay scion, destined to become Siwa's protector, living in a well-appointed dwelling as one of the town's most respected inhabitants. I had much to offer my potential bride, I had no worries on that particular score. And yet the idea of doing that, the thought of making that journey to Alexandria, filled me with more horror than the thought of fighting any man. And part of that, I was starting to realize as we spoke, was in no little part due to my father constantly hammering into my head how important Siwa should be to me. How it should matter to me, above all else, to protect both my home town and the people of Egypt.

She knew it. She read my mind and answered her own question. 'No, you were hoping not to involve my parents, the Alexandrians, is that right? Don't they represent everything that your father worries about? His son, out in the world. A potential target for all and sundry due to his secret heritage.'

'You're a Siwan.'

It was a feeble response and I knew it.

'By birth I'm an Alexandrian. That great city was my home, and I hope that one day it will be my home again. Had you forgotten that, Bayek, son of Sabu? Had you forgotten my dream that one day I should study in the great library at Alexandria? Or did you assume I would simply abandon that plan in order to stay by your side, be left at home alone like Ahmose, your mother?'

I found myself floundering, not knowing what to say. I was aware only that this was a situation that was getting swiftly out of hand. A scene that I'd pictured heading one way was hurtling off like a startled animal in the wrong direction.

But she was also right. Many were the times I had worried about my mother, alone back home. Many where the times I'd nearly asked my father about her, only to stop before her name crossed my lips, worried I might cause even a greater rift between us.

'Did you ever stop to think when you were considering your path, that I might be considering mine?' she was saying.

'Of course,' I said, and despised the desperation I heard in my own voice, knowing how it made me sound. Then again, I couldn't let things go this way. I had to convince her.

'No you didn't,' she was saying. 'You simply saw a way to please your father.'

'"Please my father"? How? He is approving of the union, if that's what you mean.'

She reached for her sword, plucked it out of the ground then slammed it back down again. But if the movement was designed only to dissipate some of her anger, it failed, because when she spoke the fury seemed to tumble from behind her teeth.

'Your father has never liked me.'

'But you just said —'

'Gods, Bayek, can't you see? What have you been telling me all this time? What has your father been telling you? He's been telling you about the Medjay *bloodline*, hasn't he? How it needs to be continued. That's why he agrees to your request for a union. It's nothing to do with what he thinks of me. He doesn't care that I'm training, beyond my ability to protect myself and your heirs. He knows that I'm the best chance he's got of carrying on the bloodline. Right now you and he are the only true Medjay left, maybe in the whole of Egypt. He wants to grow himself another one, and he'll use anyone convenient in order to do it.'

I felt myself becoming angry. Not because of what she was saying so much as that I knew she was right. I had hoped it would not matter – after all, we loved one another.

The answer, of course, was that to Aya it mattered – it mattered an enormous amount.

I held up my hands. Tried to find words that were not placatory but mirrored what we both felt. Instead, all I could find was a question.

'Why did you never tell me you felt this way?'

That took her by surprise, and though she'd been ready to answer in anger, she hesitated, clearly troubled.

'I . . . I was foolish.' She bowed her head, took a deep breath, and offered me a pained smile. 'I wanted to give you the opportunity to get to know your father once more, and so I stepped back. But I stopped talking to you in the process.'

And that explained why she'd never answered the questions I'd asked of her, early on, as to her thoughts on my father's ideological teachings regarding the Medjay.

'It's not your fault,' she continued. 'You tried to ask me. I just . . . I did not wish to come between the two of you. I should have told you,' she said, dignified yet sorrowful.

'I don't think I gave you much room to tell me,' I murmured, reaching out. She came into my arms willingly, the both of us quiet as we reflected how we had grown closer in some ways yet drifted apart in others. We had a lot of talking to do.

'We'll speak of my proposal some other time,' I offered. 'For now, let's just try to mend things between us.' I could feel her smile against me, and felt some measure of peace steal over me. 'We'll continue training. Take our time.'

She shook her head and gently disengaged herself, stepping away from me a few paces, bracing herself.

'Bayek, we cannot. I have something to tell you.'

'What now?' I was puzzled, but no longer angry. Confused, but eager to talk, to discuss plainly as we'd failed to do so much the past few years.

'There will be no more training. I have decided to return home.'

52

I knew what she meant, of course, but even so I couldn't quite bring myself to acknowledge it, because acknowledging it made it true, and I didn't want it to be true. 'Back to the camp?' I said.

She shook her head gently. 'No, Bayek. To Siwa.'

'We will all be going back there soon, when . . .'

She sighed, a touch of exasperation returning. 'You mean when your education is complete; when your father is confident that you are fully indoctrinated, when you talk in exactly the same riddles he does. When he's finished being scared for you. Is that what you want? We all go back to Siwa when *he* decides. When *he* says so.'

'We are being hunted, don't you forget that.' I didn't understand her urgency – for it was there, easy to see now that I was looking for it.

She stared away, arms still folded, chin jutting, before replying, 'No, I won't forget it. I've never been allowed to forget it. And yet of our pursuer there is no sign. There has been no sign for years, Bayek – *years*.'

'The blink of an eye.'

She thumped a hand to her chest. 'Not to me. It hasn't been "the blink of an eye" to me because I'm not the one following my one true path, remember?'

'And that's why you're going home?'

I was so perplexed, but we were talking now. I could feel her relax too, realize that this communication was good, even if the topic was . . . difficult.

'No.'

'Well . . .' I stopped, not sure what to say. 'Why, then? Why do you want to go home?'

Had her eyes been misting up before or had I only just noticed? Either way, I saw now and the sight sent me spinning, because Aya rarely cried and seeing her do it now made me feel strangely uncomfortable – as though there was even more wrong with the world than I thought.

And, of course, I was right about that.

'My aunt Herit is ill,' she said.

This was it. This was the reason. But it took a few moments for me to process, to understand quite what she meant, and my heart went out to her because nobody knew better than me how much Aya cared for her aunt. Herit had raised her since she was small. Just a little girl. She was the only guardian Aya had ever truly known, even as she worshipped her scholarly parents from afar. While my relationship with my father was always . . . well, I suppose you'd have to say 'complicated', hers with her aunt could not be more different. Herit doted on the pretty little girl who had arrived from Alexandria. Aya had always made her proud. You only needed to look at her face when she turned it towards Aya to know, that mix of devotion and fascination. I knew because I sometimes felt it too.

For her part, Aya treated her aunt with total respect and love. If Aya occasionally had the habit of seeming to think herself above her contemporaries in Siwa, that certainly didn't extend to her aunt. I never heard her say a word against her. I never saw the slightest flicker of irritation or disdain for her aunt's homely ways. If Herit was ill then, naturally, she would be devastated. Of course she would want to go back home.

Could she, though? Was it possible when we were being hunted?

Would my father even allow it? And . . .

The realization had thumped into me late.

'Wait – how do you know? How do you know she's unwell? Oh no, you haven't . . . ?'

She nodded defiantly. 'I had to. I had to know how she was. I hoped merely to pass on news that we were well and hear the same in return. I never expected to be told that she was sick. It was the worst news imaginable.'

My head was spinning. Looming at the back of my mind was my father, and I was worried what he might say despite my resentment at even feeling that emotion. How he would react – his anger if he discovered that Aya had endangered our position by sending messages – didn't bear thinking about. But also, I shouldn't have to feel that way, should I? Regardless of my father, though, one concern remained true and valid and very much present.

'*It was dangerous*,' I exploded. 'How could you be so . . . ?' I stopped myself before I shouted some more, working to catch my breath, to deal with this properly. She took a step back as I did so, and I could see the emotions playing on her face – defiance, determination, concern for me – but in the end defiance triumphed.

'I'm going back home.' She spoke calmly, though her voice was shadowed in anger. I felt betrayed and adrift, and so very worried at the thought of the assassin finding us, and perhaps killing my father, myself, or her.

'How could you? You know how dangerous the man hunting us is!'

'You want your father to hear you?' she retorted. I wasn't keeping my voice down as much as I'd thought, it seemed.

'He'll find out anyway,' I snapped out, aggrieved.

'How? Because you'll tell him?' she snapped back.

I was dismayed and scared of his reaction, I realized. And angry at myself for the fear, and more angry at Aya as a result, because it made me wonder if she had been right about him, about what he truly wanted. That I'd doubt my father after working so hard to get closer to him unmade me. In another world, in another time, some better future, maybe Aya and I would laugh about this and she'd apologize and say she'd pushed too hard, hadn't explained well enough, and I'd say, 'No, really, I went too far, I was scared, I was being blind. It served me right,' and all would be well with the world.

But not now. Now was just the whirling sense of things spinning suddenly and horribly out of control. Of all the hopes I'd nurtured slipping away.

'I'll have to tell him.'

'Why?'

'Well, he's going to want to know why we are having to move on, for one thing.'

She pulled a face. 'Maybe there is no hunter, did you think of that?' She cast her arm around in a gesture that encompassed the hill on which we stood, our encampment below a desert on all sides of us, a town in the near distance. 'Do you see any hunters coming to get us?'

'What does that mean? Only that they're not here yet.'

'No one's coming, Bayek. That's what I mean. That's the point. Anyway, you tell Sabu if you want to. I won't be here to watch him curl his lip at me yet again. Yes, I sent the message months ago. I've had a reply. I'm leaving in the morning.'

She loved her aunt. So much. If it had been my mother, what would I have done? I took a deep breath, shoved everything aside and nodded. Regardless of the consequences, this was a choice only she could make.

'Very well.'

She looked at me, softening. 'I'm leaving in the morning, Bayek. It just means that I won't be here for a while. Not that I'll be gone for ever.'

I smiled back, reassured but tired beyond measure.

'I'll tell my father in the morning. After you've gone,' I said.

'Very well.'

53

When I woke the next morning and scrambled out of our shelter, my eyes went directly to where our horses grazed. Hers was missing. Aya was gone. Across the way, my father's shelter flapped slightly in the breeze, empty, and when I looked across to the hill where we trained each day, I saw him there, his back to me, lunging and twirling, his shirt billowing.

'Where is Aya?' he said, when I'd dressed and joined him.

He rarely referred to either of us by name. Not during our training, anyway. He seemed to consider it an act of weakness. This morning, of all mornings, it rankled.

'Is she out hunting?' he went on.

'No, she's gone.'

His head jerked. 'Gone?'

'Home,' I told him. 'She's gone home. To Siwa.'

'Why wasn't I told?'

For all that I'd wanted to take his side the previous night, the doubts had grown into self-reflection. Dawn had brought to my heart a level of critical defiance towards my father that I'd never felt, never expected to nurture. And yet there it was.

'Why do you think? You would have forbidden it.'

'I would have.'

'That's your answer.'

The focus he'd brought to training vanished, replaced by a flash of anger, and he stepped forward swinging his sword and I blocked it with my own, the clash of metal ringing like an early morning bell piercing the lazy morning. His wrist flicked and his sword came up from beneath, fast – too fast for me – and I only just managed to block in time. The move sent me slightly off balance, enough that he read my stance, adapted his own and advanced again, this time with the flat of his sword that he smacked against my temple. A little dink at the end opened a tiny cut on my face and I felt blood course down my cheek, and tasted it on my lips. He brought his left leg around, planted it and stood in a wide-legged stance with his hand on the hilt of his sword, the point of it on the ground.

I dabbed at the blood but kept my expression neutral. 'You're angry,' I said uselessly. He looked away. His chin jutted. For the first time in my entire life, I found myself critical of him for reasons that had nothing to do with me. He had struck out at me from anger, the one thing he kept training me not to do.

'You have not angered me,' he said after a pause. 'You have disappointed me. You have endangered our position here.'

'Have I really?' I found myself echoing Aya, and my anger at her was bleeding away, just as my anger at my father was solidifying. 'Do you really think we're still being hunted? This Order you speak of? Why haven't they sent armies of men against us if we're so important to them? Isn't it possible that Hemon was the real target?'

My father glared at me, nostrils flaring, gaze intense, but I went on – not with my usual hot headedness but, rather, calm and methodical. It seemed I'd learned something from Aya as well, after all. 'Did you ever think that with him dead we're no longer considered a threat? Or that perhaps the man hunting us at the Temple of Khnum has told his paymasters that we're dead in order to collect? Who knows how diligent an employee he really was? There are a thousand and one things to consider, Father. He can't still be after us.'

'He was good,' he said, almost to himself. He took one deep breath, then another. Tamping down his own anger. Listening to me, for once, finally listening. 'He was possessed of great expertise.' At that, a look came across his face, falling across it like a shadow – a look that I couldn't decipher at the time. Only later would I realize what it meant.

'And yet he has never appeared again,' I pressed.

'He was patient.'

Had we not been as well? Keeping ourselves far from Siwa, training in exile for years?

'Father, it's time for us to return to Siwa.' I was determined. Focused. I knew this was the right thing to do.

He had not moved. Deep in thought. 'Your training is not complete.'

It was more rote and habit, by now, than fact. Or so it felt to me. But I had one belief, learned from Khensa and Aya, one that had allowed me to acquire peace with that statement – there was always something new to learn. I would never truly finish training.

'It can be completed there, back in Siwa,' I answered, with complete equanimity. 'When I am back by Aya's side.'

'No, it is not seemly for those whom you protect to see you still not fully trained.'

'Then let it continue in private.' I shrugged. Barely anyone knew that father was a Medjay even, much less I. And we could easily just say I was still training as *mekety*. 'Siwa is unprotected.' I told him the other worry I'd carried all these years. 'Mother worries for us, and has been alone for too long.'

'I'm well aware of that,' he snapped, but there was no fire to his voice. 'Nevertheless, you should return to Siwa only as a fully fledged Medjay.' The protest was weak, at best. Habit and stubbornness, and not much more. I could see him, suddenly, much more clearly than ever before, and Khensa had been right, I realized. He loved me. He truly did, even though he was atrocious at telling me so, or even at showing me so. I suspected that, despite the fact he'd not mentioned her once, he missed my mother more than he could bear.

And he was so very scared of what could happen to me, once I took up the mantle of Medjay. Aya had been

285

right, in a way. He was holding me back. And in doing so, he was holding everyone back.

'Then make it so, Father. Pronounce me one.'

He looked at me, eye to eye. Truly looked at me, letting me see more than he'd ever shown before. He looked older and tired, but also, I realized, proud.

'You're close, my son. So very close. I see how much she means to you. I've been stubborn and I miss your mo—'. He cut himself off, shaking his head ruefully. 'Train. Let me think. Then perhaps we can consider returning home.'

That morning, as I trained, the sun casting its gaze upon me, I wondered. Was I training to become a Medjay or to see Aya sooner? Could it possibly be both – and that these goals were not as incompatible as my father believed? I wasn't sure yet, but I felt as though I could reach a balance in this, someday.

I trained harder than I ever had before.

54

Aya prided herself on being observant, but she also had a lot on her mind. And that's why she didn't think much of the men at the watering hole, at first.

She did notice them. But what she failed to do was instantly recognize the threat they posed. She had seen them without truly *seeing* them. She failed to register the scars and sullen expressions. She had missed the sidelong looks to her horse, the voices speaking in hushed tones, the moistened lips and calculating eyes . . .

Because, yes, she had a lot on her mind. She was feeling oddly unwell, making her worry she'd allowed herself to become dehydrated. There was also the sighing; the fact that she kept going over and over her conversation with Bayek. The regrets. So many things she should have told him over the years they'd trained, instead of keeping them bottled inside.

It was strange, she thought, that she had almost forgotten how to communicate properly with Bayek even as they'd grown closer. And she thought that if Bayek had been here by her side then he would have said to her, 'Aya, why do you sigh so much? We'll sort it out, we always do. It will be fine.' And he would have made her feel as though sighing was the very last thing she should be doing. He would have drawn her attention to something wonderful: whatever plan they had fermenting, some combat move they'd learned that morning, or even something simple like a bird wheeling in the sky — whatever it was, Bayek would have made it seem to her as though it were a miracle. How could she possibly sigh when the world around them had so many treasures to reveal? How could she sigh when they were together?

But, of course, there was no Bayek beside her, riding his horse, following the rhythm of the plain; no Bayek standing opposite with his sword raised, urging her to continue her drills; no Bayek sitting on the other side of a campfire, eating whatever they'd caught that day, between grins. And no Bayek to distract her about her concerns regarding her aunt, whom she desperately hoped would be alive, perhaps even fully recovered, when she finally arrived in Siwa.

Purely and simply, no Bayek at all. That was why she sighed.

Who knows? Maybe sighing stopped her from doing something silly like going back. Between missing Bayek and worrying about her aunt, it seemed as though anything involving a connection between two people so important to her would catch her attention: the innocent face of a child paddling in the river towards her mother. The hippo with her young. An affectionate couple kissing, an old man on a camel, kind face crinkly, laughing at a joke told to him by a younger man driving oxen.

And so she did the only thing she could do. She

travelled, riding along the route of the river, along the banks of the Nile, where she passed peasants working in the field, labourers who would occasionally stop, watch her pass and wonder where she was going, this dusty woman with braided hair and a face that seemed to speak of sadness.

Until she came to the watering hole, where she stopped, parched and grateful to rest.

She had taken to talking to her horse. It was a lovely, white-hair gelding with a beautiful temperament that she came to consider a friend. Out here in the desert, no doubt about it, her greatest friend. She'd begun training it while at the camp, and it was paying off now. The horse came to her call, never strayed far from her side. It was beautiful, and smart.

She walked it to the edge of watering hole, which had been improved with a sandstone brick border, and it followed her, a few steps behind. Surrounding the water was vegetation, all of it leaning in as though bowing in the water's presence, paying homage to the precious liquid.

Not for the first time when arriving at a watering hole, Aya had thought of the oasis at Siwa, how the breeze that seemed to come off the water acted as a respite to the oppressive heat of the desert. Just being there reminded her of home, of her destination. It reminded her of her aunt and Bayek, and that made her sigh once more.

The gelding drank as Aya took a seat on the sandstone border, dipped her hands into the water, deep below the surface where it was coolest, and then scooped handfuls of it on to her face, neck and shoulders.

To her left were the men with their narrowed stares, but she was tired from travel and keen to take the water, and she missed their sideways glances. She didn't register the fact that avaricious stares were being aimed at her horse, and disdainful ones at her.

In the distance a horseman approached. Little more than a black speck on the horizon.

She filled her waterskin, still unaware that the group seemed to have drifted closer. Nor did she notice that their murmurs had stopped, only to be replaced with a subtle, conspiratorial whispering. She was too absorbed in slaking her thirst, and trying to stay cool, letting her gelding wander off to find the shade of a nearby yew.

From around her waist she took a red scarf, dipped it in the cool water and used it on her face. For a moment or so she draped it there, feeling it mould to the contours of her face before taking it off and letting it drop wetly to the stone. A shadow fell across her.

'Hello, girl,' came a voice from behind her.

Aya distantly recognized the voice as belonging to one of the men, and instinctively knew that its tone had changed.

This was not the quiet banter he used for his friends. Not the polite and respectful tones a merchant might have used, a trader hoping to sell goods, or even a stranger in search of romance. She'd fended off her fair share of all three on her travels.

No, this was something entirely different. There was an edge to this man's voice that – at last – made her sit up and take notice, and belatedly sense *danger.*

Her tunic was belted up tight. Beneath it all was the short sword with which she had spent so many years practising. She wondered whether the men would have seen it jutting as she knelt. She casually reached now, wanting to check it was still there, and she felt her right hand twitch, thinking how best to handle this: draw the sword now, use it as a deterrent, prove herself a threat? No. They'd take that as a challenge. The only option was to await their first move and then draw.

Even so. The men had a leader, the one who had spoken, with his nose that looked as though it had once being broken and never properly set. He moved closer, repeating his introduction, 'Hey, girl.'

She stood to face him. 'What can I do for you?' she said, looking not at him but over his shoulder at the three men behind him, who hung back, looking greedily at her gelding.

Horse thieves. Gods curse them, they were horse thieves.

He lifted his arm, putting one finger of his outstretched hand to her chin, moving her face so that she was looking at him. She let him do it so that their eyes met for a second and she regarded him carefully before pulling away. 'Don't touch me again,' she warned him softly.

'Well, it's simple, isn't it?' he rasped. 'Don't raise a fuss. We take that pretty horse. And maybe that's all we do.'

Without the gelding, she would never make it back to Siwa to see her aunt.

'You can't have the horse.'

But the ringleader was already gesturing as though to say the conversation was over. 'How about you just give us what we want? Don't be so troublesome. We'll take good care of the beast.'

Aya put her hand to her chin as though pretending to consider his kind offer, but really thinking hard. Her back was to the waterhole. She knew it was deep. It was no good trying to escape there, and in any case . . .

She couldn't afford the delay.

No, she realized. She didn't want to. She had training, after all, and not just any training, but the teachings of the Medjay. This gave her options. A choice.

She wanted to fight.

'Will you?' she said. 'Or will you just sell the poor animal off like the horse thieves you are?'

His lips pulled back over dirty teeth. 'Rude.' He hand twitched towards the weapon at his side.

Keep something in reserve, she thought. *Don't show what you've got straight away.* Her sword stayed where it was, hidden beneath her robes.

'Come on, then,' she said, 'let's see, shall we? Let's see if you can take my horse from me.'

He grinned. She could smell his breath. 'Yes, let's see, shall we?'

And with that he stepped forward.

55

As he reached for Aya, she stepped back and then reversed her momentum and instead of pulling away from him thrust forward into him, at the same time grabbing his arm which she twisted, hearing with some satisfaction his scream of pain, then swivelling, pulling him round behind her and dumping him face first into the water.

A perfect move. *If only Bayek was here to see it*, she thought. She then whistled sharply – one short but piercing burst. The startled gelding bolted a few paces, as it had been trained, ears pinned down. It stopped and turned, at the ready, snapping its teeth warningly at one of the thieves as he tried to creep closer. Woe betide anyone attempting to lay on hand on it. She smiled, satisfied.

The horse thieves were not pleased.

In a second her attacker was yelling, 'Get her,' and his three companions launched themselves forward. She darted to the side, mentally calculating the odds. The rider in the distance might just turn and leave. The men were too close. It was time to show them her sword.

She turned and was about to draw her weapon but

one of her pursuers was faster than she had anticipated and was already upon her. His lips pulled back over bad teeth and he was growling with fury, and from his similarity to the first attacker she guessed that he might be the brother of the man she'd just dumped into the watering hole, in which case he was probably keen on restoring the family name. For all that was worth in a family of horse thieves.

He lurched forward, fingers like claws trying to get her, but her feet were firmly planted, centre of balance correct, and she ducked beneath those outstretched hands, using both fists to pummel his soft yielding stomach – *one, two, one, two* – and then spinning to the side. He went down winded, his breath escaping in a whoosh, just as the second man reached them and Aya, still low, pressed a hand to the sand and pivoted, sweeping out a foot that took the legs out from her next attacker.

This was it – her training in action. Not just a series of moves, but a way of thinking. She felt confident. Grounded and powerful. For the first time in her life she believed her intellect to be matched by her physical skills and dexterity. She felt strong.

The attacker went down, on his face a look of shock. Nevertheless, all she'd done was slow his progress, and even on the sand he scrabbled for her, grabbing her leg before she could rise to her feet. She kicked out. Her boot caught him in the face and he yelled and let go, allowing her to stand but checking her progress sufficiently that the next man was already upon her. She felt arms encircle her neck.

Behind them the ringleader was pulling himself from the watering hole with soaking clothes, his face twisted with fury and hatred. Thumbs pressed into her windpipe. Spittle flew in her face. She dropped, rolling on to the small of her back, bringing her legs and knees up and springing upwards in the same movement, planting her feet into the chest of her attacker and sending them both tumbling back to the ground. The action worked, his hands were released from her throat, and she quickly rabbit-punched him twice in the throat – sweet revenge – and then rolled to safety as he writhed in agony.

A second later she was back on her feet, sprinting for her gelding, hoping that a mixture of caution, disarray and good old-fashioned pain would slow them down and she could reach it in time.

And she was almost there, about to throw her leg over the flank of her horse, when the ringleader appeared at the tree with a faceful of fury, the tree at his back. From his belt he snatched a knife, cursing as the horse reared and wheeled, kicking dust up at him. The man dripped and his shoulders shook with a mixture of anger and breathlessness but even so he was enjoying the reversal, swapping the knife from hand to hand, beckoning her forward. 'Come on, girl,' he said. 'Come on.'

She risked a look behind. Two of the robbers had stood, poised, waiting to see what transpired at the tree. She turned back to the leader, aware that she still hadn't drawn her sword, but knowing that now was the time – knowing now she had to kill him. Wasn't it just what Bayek had always told her? In a situation like this, kill the leader and the rest will drift away?

Even so, she didn't want to do that, despite the fact she'd trained for it, prepared for it, and despite the fact that her enemy would quite happily kill her. Confronted with the reality of combat for the first time, she hesitated. She'd always believed she was being trained to fight, to defend herself and those she loved. She understood she was being trained to kill. The act itself was . . . something else.

'One day you may have to,' Bayek had told her, and she had hoped that day would never come, though she knew it inevitably would. And now, here it was, and the choice was simple: this was not a killing made for moral reasons, there was no revenge intended, no honour to be defended. She had to kill this man in order to survive.

She drew her sword.

It was longer and more wicked than the knife he held, and quite possibly she had spent more time practising with it.

'I know how to use this,' she warned, trying one last time to put a stop to this.

He sniggered. 'Sure you do, girl.'

Behind them, the men were ready, waiting, and who knows what they were thinking? Maybe they wanted to see their leader prevail. Maybe they wanted to see him fall on his face and suffer the shame of being beaten in combat by her, a mere woman. Maybe they were just curious to see how events unfolded.

She would kill him if she had to. That much she now knew. She had calmed herself and just as she and Bayek had discussed, she had taken all that fear and foreboding and was using it to her advantage.

'Let's see how you fight,' he said, still swapping the knife.

She took up her stance. And heard the sound a second before she saw the arrow. It cut the air past her ear and into the ringleader, hurling him backwards. For a moment she thought he'd been hit in the chest, and then realized that the arrow had pierced his robes beneath the armpit and now pinned him to the tree. He was about to wrest himself away when there came another arrow, this time on the other side, also pinning him to the tree by his tunic. Then a third – between his legs.

Aya spun, as did the other thieves, all eyes going to a man on a horse at the edge of the watering hole. He wore a shawl draped over his head, keeping out the sun, but she could see dark eyes with kohl applied. He had the look of a seasoned traveller and his ability with a bow was certainly in no doubt. He'd notched another arrow and his bow was wavering between the pinned ringleader and his three followers.

For a moment or so, nothing was said.

'You come to save her, have you?' sneered the leader, pulling feebly at his tunic.

The new arrival laughed drily. 'Any fool can see it's you I'm saving.'

For her part, Aya wasn't sure how she felt. Gratitude, relief. The day she would kill was a little further away. Was there even a tiny measure of disappointment in there somewhere? She had, after all, been prepared to do it. She had been willing to take that step.

'Now,' said the new arrival, 'it's time for you men to make your choice. Die or leave, it's up to you.'

56

The men had chosen the second option, scrambling away and leaving with their tails between their legs. As they did so, Aya was able to get a better look at the stranger. He had removed the shawl from his head and she did her best not to wince at the sight of the scars on his face. With the men fading into the heat blur she watched him dismount and perform the same rituals as she had: watering his horse, washing and drinking, seemingly at ease with her studying him.

'You're wondering whether to thank me,' he said at length. 'You're wondering whether you *need* to thank me, whether you thanking me will be an acknowledgement that you are somehow in my debt, and that maybe I will want to call in that debt.'

Well. That was an odd thing to state.

'Possibly,' she said. 'What is your name, stranger?'

'My name is Bion.'

'Bion of . . . ?'

This was not a man who betrayed his emotions, she decided. His face was still and placid when he made his reply. Was it serenity, she wondered, or something else? 'Bion of Faiyum, once upon a time. Now just Bion of the desert.'

'You've been in the army?'

'Very astute. The Royal Guard, yes, the Machairo-phoroi.'

'Which is where you got those scars? Where you learned your bowmanship?'

'Indeed.' He cupped his hands and did the same as she had, finding the cool water, drinking and then splashing it on his forearms and face.

Her scarf lay by the side of the watering hole. Seeing him use his hands on his face she handed it to him. Regardless of who this man was, it was the least she could do in return.

He took it, thanking her silently, using it as a facecloth.

'I was also one of the best bowmen in my company,' he said.

'Yet your bow looks new,' she said when he had finished wiping his face.

He sat back on his haunches. He was smiling, but it was a blank smile, she decided. Weirdly empty, even. He was winding her scarf in his hands, wringing it out, making it taut. 'You're observant,' he said.

Droplets of water fell from the scarf to the brick-work. He wrapped the ends of it around his knuckles. The moment felt odd, and Aya found herself tensing, unsure why.

Then he turned his face towards her.

57

We had moved, of course. Our new camp stood between a fast-flowing section of the river and two hillocks that shielded us from the worst of the weather. It was up on to those hillocks that we went for each morning's lessons, when I tried so hard not to think of Aya, because the thought of her would divert me from my true purpose, which was to learn and get back to her.

Only the gods knew how much I missed her, and as each day passed I became more and more frustrated that I was no nearer to seeing her. What my father thought of my mood, I couldn't say. Whatever he thought of what Aya had done he'd kept to himself, had done ever since our morning conversation. But he worked me harder than ever before, tested me unrelentingly.

Until one day it came to a head. I pulled back from an attack, took several steps back, refusing to parry. It was time to go. I was heading back to Siwa. With his approval or without. Upset at my behaviour, my father dropped his sword arm, snapping at me, 'What is it, Bayek?' I must have glanced in the direction of Siwa. For before I even spoke, he sighed explosively.

'You're not done yet. Your training is not complete. I'm trying to teach you as fast as I can, but –'

'Not complete, Father?' I snapped, sheathing my weapon. 'I've been training for years now, every single day, standing on hilltops and in the sun, a new camp, a different base, a new place, and my dedication has never wavered.'

'It is now. I can see it.'

It would never be enough training, I could see that now. And it had nothing to do with me. My father was afraid. Not for himself, no. He was afraid for me.

'I need to see Aya and my mother again.' I kept it as simple as possible, hoping he would break through his worries. Understand.

'When you are a fully fledged Medjay.'

'When will that be? Weeks? Months? *Years?*'

He indicated the cut on my face, still not entirely healed. 'When you no longer are susceptible to an attack like that.'

I scoffed. 'How many times have you told me that a Medjay's apprenticeship never really ends?' I did not tell him that Aya always believed this, had even approved when I'd told her my father had said that to me. 'Just because an opponent can inflict a cut that doesn't mean to say he could deal the fatal blow. I want to do it now, Father. I want to return to Siwa. I want to see Aya, perhaps even catch her up if I'm lucky.'

At that I straightened, shoulders back, looking at him with eyes that I knew blazed with determination and that I hoped hid the more tremulous feelings swirling within. I loved him, but also I felt sad for him.

He rolled his eyes. 'You're reckless. You're impetuous. You're driven too much by what's in here, and not enough by what's up here.' He tapped at his chest and then at his head.

I set my jaw. 'That is so, and I can try to curb it. But consider this: wasn't it my impetuousness, my recklessness, that brought me to you?'

He gave a short laugh 'But you almost destroyed my plans.'

'Your plans are to continue the way of the Medjay, to extend the bloodline, isn't that the case?'

He looked at me, neither confirming nor denying it, and I ploughed on. 'And didn't my recklessness achieve that? Aya believes that you tolerate our relationship because you see her as being our best chance of producing a child, a future Medjay to be trained at some future date, am I right? Is that why you never sent her away?'

Again there was no confirmation. No denial. Just those same neutral eyes that I had watched for so long. It struck me then that Aya had left us because what she felt for her aunt was love in its purest and most undiluted form, and though what I felt for my own father was love, too, it wasn't as unadulterated, as uncomplicated as that. It came in strange, indecipherable patterns and I was far beyond childhood. I respected him, but his approval was no longer my overriding goal in life.

I had lost something important when Aya left. Something that meant more to me than earning my father's respect, I now realized. Pure and simple. The love Aya brought into my life had gone, and that was not something I was willing to give up on.

I knew with complete certitude, then and there, that I was leaving. And if I wasn't fully trained to be a Medjay, then, well, so what? I was of the bloodline. Nobody could take that away from me. I had years of training. I had a lifetime left to train, and learn more. Maybe – just maybe – I didn't even *need* my father in order to follow this path.

And so: 'I'm going,' I told him. 'Call it impetuous or reckless if you like. Tell me I haven't yet completed my training and I may well believe you. But this,' I waved a hand at the hills, at camp, at the river and the open land beyond, 'this is not enough. I'm sorry, Father. I wish you would come with me. But I'm going either way.'

He came towards me and I found myself tensing, no idea what he intended, his eyes unreadable. But what I finally saw in them was a sorrowful understanding. A dawning respect. Somehow it had grown in the space between us, since our last argument, the morning after Aya had left.

'No, you're not ready,' he said, 'although you're not as unready as you used to be. But I recognize determination when I see it. We'll travel back to Siwa together. Perhaps we will indeed catch up with Aya, and even if we don't, you will see her when we get there. Make your peace with her. I won't interfere – neither one way nor the other.'

The next thing I knew he was pulling away, and there was a softness about him I'd never seen before. 'Here,' he said reaching to a bag that he always brought to the hill, from which he usually took a flask of water, offering me a drop if he thought I'd practised hard enough. Only now it wasn't water that he offered me but something else: a medallion, the like of which I'd never seen before. And yet at once it felt so familiar. Even the weight of it, when he reached, took my hand, and pressed it into my palm, felt just right.

'Only given to true Medjay,' he said. 'I want you to have it.'

I held it. Astonished. Years of scrabbling for approval, and now that I was beyond that need . . . 'This is yours?' I asked him. 'You want *me* to have it?'

'You have earned it. I should have given you the opportunity to earn it before. I regret my lack of faith in you. I see in you what I once saw in myself.' He sighed, slowly. 'I too often still see my little boy, instead of a grown man.'

The admission pained him. I stared at the medallion. It sat in my palm. I did indeed feel as though I'd earned it. And yet I still couldn't quite bring myself to close my fingers around it.

'What of Aya?' I asked him.

'You don't need my approval,' he said.

'But if I did?'

He sighed. 'You and she want different things, Bayek, I think you know that. Perhaps at some point you might need to make your choice between Aya and the way of the Medjay. For your sake, I hope not. Perhaps even she will choose to join our fight. Whatever happens, and for the sake of Egypt I hope you both choose wisely. But you don't have to make that choice here and now, so take the medallion you've earned. You are a Medjay now.'

I pushed it into my pouch where it nestled with the feathers I still kept there, and other little tokens of my travels.

But then, looking up and about to speak, I saw him tense, raising his head and sniffing at the same time.

His eyes widened. His mouth dropped open. The air seemed to crackle.

'He's here,' my father said.

58

Two things came at once: the sound of an arrow and my father hurling us both to the ground. We rolled, my father pushing me like a sack of grain down the opposite side of the hill. I saw red blood and realized he'd been hit, a wound in his arm, the arrow already snapped in the fall.

At the bottom of the hill he grunted, reached, grasped the snapped-off shaft, tried to pull it from his shoulder, and then stopped with an agonized growl of pain.

'He's barbed it,' he grimaced, but when he looked at me, what I saw in his eyes was something I'd seen only twice before: the night of Menna's attack on our house and the night that we'd hunted the killer in Elephantine. It was a look of excitement. This was what he had prepared for. In action, his fears and worries faded away.

'Well,' he said, 'it looks like our man has taught himself archery in the meantime. His scent hasn't changed.'

'You smelled him?'

He clapped a hand to my shoulder. 'This is why you're not quite a fully fledged Medjay, Bayek,' he grinned, clearly finding steady ground while in danger.

'Can you move?' I asked him quickly, conscious that our attacker would be trying to press home his advantage.

'I can walk, I can run and I can swing a sword.' He gestured towards our camp, the two shelters resting on supports, not exactly sanctuary. But inside them were our bows.

I hadn't yet trained myself to detect the scent of an advancing enemy on the wind, but my bowmanship had improved in leaps and bounds during my training. I was a natural, it had turned out – as good as my father, perhaps even better. Together we were more than a match for our attacker.

'Come on,' said my father, 'we need to get there before he makes his way around.'

We took off running, the shelters containing our bows and quivers like a pair of prizes before us. A peaceful scene. Four horses munching away at the grass that grew there, the soil fed and enriched by the water flowed close by where the bank fell away sharply to the river.

Now, if we could just reach our bows.

But no. What we heard as we made our dash between the foot of the hill and our camp was the sound of approaching hooves, and when I twisted my waist to look behind us I caught sight of the killer.

At last. The man who had been hunting us all these years. He sat upright, steady on his horse, holding his bow and arrow with all the balance and confidence of the best Nubian bowmen. I thought to myself that if indeed he had gained his prowess in the intervening years then he had learned it to perfection, and the thought chilled me. The idea that he might have spent all these years searching for us; that my father had been right, and that Aya had been wrong – that chilled me too.

He wore his shawl like a cowl over his head. His eyes were blackened with charcoal, a weathered face was scarred and inset with eyes that were alert and hard, and on seeing them I realized that I was used to eyes like that. I'd looked across the training area at eyes like that every day for so many years.

And then it struck me. I remembered a look I'd seen on my father's face, and suddenly I knew what it meant. All along my father had sensed that he and the killer were the same. And the reason he could say with such certainty that the killer would never give up was that he himself would never have given up. He would have left the battle, reassessed, taught himself to use a bow in order to surprise his prey, kept looking. He would have finished the job and, sure enough, here was the killer – come to finish the job.

And then I saw something else: around the killer's wrist was tied a red scarf I recognized.

It belonged to Aya.

I didn't have time to react. The killer loosed his arrow. 'Father!' I screamed and perhaps my warning was enough to save his life because he jinked quickly to the left and so instead of piercing his body, the arrow once again found his shoulder, sending him to the ground.

Gods! Now he had a second arrow in him. And as I scrambled to him I saw that his face was already draining of blood. His tunic was saturated with it, front and back. Right then it struck me that my father might have met his match, and at that thought terror coursed through me like a flooded river, washing away all my youthful arrogance and confidence, revealing only failure on the rocks.

On my knees, I saw the horseman pull his steed round close to the edge of the river, notching another arrow. I snatched my knife, bought in Zawty a lifetime away, stood and threw. My best throw, in the circumstances a great one, and it took the bowman by surprise, thudding into his shawl at his side, doing enough to unseat him so that he tumbled backwards off his horse, bow and quiver going with him.

Father had pulled himself to his knees and now stood. Offering him my hand I dragged him up with me, drew my sword and started off across the plain towards where the bowman now knelt close to our shelters. He looked up, saw me coming, my father not far behind, and then reached and yanked my knife from his side, throwing off his shawl at the same time and then standing, drawing his sword.

I saw his scars. I saw his teeth bared, his eyes cold and emotionless. Light ran along his sword blade. The river bubbled and churned behind him. The scarf that I knew so well fluttered at his wrist.

'Brave Medjay,' he said, a sneer from most people, but this man's eyes were flecked with emptiness as he spoke, as he brought his sword to bear.

Metal met metal with a sound that rang in my ears. I had dared to believe that the ferocity of my attack might put him on the back foot – even that I might take him by surprise. But no. He met the move with an ease that I might have found impressive had I not been his opponent.

'*Where is she?*' I yelled at him, surging forward again, my blade swinging, trying to remember to keep my emotions in check, knowing that to lose control risked losing the fight. 'What have you done to her?'

Beside me I registered my father arrive and saw his brow cloud with confusion. He hadn't made the connection I had; that our pursuer had been watching us for some time and that he had seen Aya leave and followed her.

But what then? Gods, what had he done to her?

'Where is she?' I repeated, no longer shouting. Let him think me weakened by concern. A perceived lack of focus would be to my advantage.

'Bayek, recover yourself,' warned my father from by my side, a common mantra from our coaching, spoken whenever my temper seemed to be getting the better of me. I didn't bother to answer. At least I was rewarded by the sight of the killer's tunic reddening, just as my father's had. The wound I'd given him would bleed a lot, and maybe if I could prolong the fight for long enough then he would weaken and tire and his superior swordsmanship be not such an advantage. Perhaps I could even dream of prevailing.

And then it was no longer just me. My father had joined the battle, surging forward to engage the killer, their swords meeting – *clash, clash, clash* – two men who were better matched in a sword fight, each of them trying to find a weak spot, some vulnerability in the other one, probing with attacks, defending then moving back into offence.

Father was tired and, like the killer, he was bleeding. The two of them had only a limited time before blood loss would send them to their knees, and then – this is where a connection between my father and me came in – I could move in to finish the job.

But the killer knew it, too, of course, battle-hardened and cool headed. And knowing he could not afford to let his opponents dictate the rhythm of the battle, he drew me into it, driving back my father with hard downward strokes. It was the kind of power another man would have needed full-blown swings to create, but the killer seemed to achieve it with small flicks of the wrist. In his other hand he held my knife, slick with his own blood, and if I came forward, trying to find a way around his defence, he used it to ward me off.

I felt frustration bubbling within me, crushed it ruthlessly. We were two, he was one. The battle should have been short and brutal and yet we could not find a way round him – his strength, his determination and undeniable skill. My father and I were protectors. The man we were fighting was a master of his own craft, a soulless killer, pure and simple.

I saw my father. I saw the effort playing out on a face that was drawn and pale. I saw the doubt in his eyes.

And then it happened. The killer opened a cut on me. As I surged forward, falling for a feint I would never fall for again, he took my lack of actual combat experience and used it as a weapon against me, probing beneath my swinging sword with the shorter knife and with a flick, opening a cut on my stomach that sent me stumbling back, one arm across myself. His sword slashed my upper arm. Another, and then another.

There came a lull, and for a moment the battle stopped and we all stood, our shoulders heaving as we caught our breath and leaked blood from our various wounds.

'Who is paying you? The Order?' asked my father of our enemy. 'We can pay you more.'

I didn't like the sound of that. It was tantamount to an admission that this opponent was too much for us. At the same time, I could see how pride could lead to a downfall, how just paying off an enemy could be practical. As long as you could be sure not to wake up with a dagger in the chest for it later on.

'I do not work for money, Medjay,' said the killer dispassionately.

'Then you work for principle. Perhaps your ideals are more closely allied to the Medjay than you think.'

'Perhaps I don't have ideals,' said the killer. His eyes flicked to me and I thought of Aya, and was about to speak when my father cut in.

'Your job is to kill me, is that it?'

'My job is to destroy the bloodline, to eradicate the Medjay.'

He admitted this easily. Confident he was near his goal. That we were done for.

'You'll never do that. You cannot kill an idea.'

'My employer begs to differ,' he surged forward, 'and your tie to the bloodline is your weakness.' I could not help but feel he had a point. And the fight resumed, swords swinging, hard and fast. My father's shirt was soaked red. Of us all he was the most badly wounded, but I could feel my own warm blood beneath my belt, and when I shifted I imagined I felt the wound part and open like a mouth on my stomach, spilling more blood which ran down my stomach, down my legs and into my boots, my toes squelching in it.

Meanwhile the fighter opposite us seemed to deal with his pain, keeping it hidden behind his eyes, refusing to let it beat him. How badly was he hurt? It was difficult to tell. He came forward relentlessly, mercilessly. This was a man who had hunted his prey for years. He was in no mood to stop. He came forward, inexorable, implacable, pitiless, and when he landed yet another blow on my father, the end seemed inevitable.

I saw him stagger – my father, whom I never believed would taste defeat. His eyes, which before had seemed to gleam with the thrill of the oncoming battle, now spanned with the knowledge of certain defeat: fear not of pain or death – though both were surely to come – but of failure. Of loss. Later I would realize that when he raised his sword again as if to mount another attack it was done with no expectation of triumph. All he could do now was try to save me.

Seeing him so weak, and thinking of Aya, what rose to the surface was a fury that eclipsed anything else I might have felt. A need for vengeance. A bone-deep hunger to inflict the same pain on this deathful ghost – to do to his world what he was doing to mine.

Father saw. Even in the depths of defeat he was able to read the situation and react, just as I made my move and lunged forward to begin an unstructured and chaotic attack that would have inevitably ended in my own death. With a grunt and a surge of strength he threw himself to one side and shoved me into the water. My arms flailed. I hit the river with a slap, went under, then surfaced, gasping for air.

The current was strong, the river unexpectedly deep. I grabbed at bulrushes to try to prevent myself being carried off but they came away in my hand. I grabbed for more, found purchase and, for the moment at least, avoided being swept away. At the same time I felt blackness coming down, as though clouding my brain, threatening to take me, the pain of my wound flaring, and I looked up to the bank to see the killer standing over my father. I saw his sword flash and my father drop to his knees then lurch to the side. I saw the killer raise his sword then slam it down, pinning my father.

And then the darkness that had been threatening to claim me closed in. My clutching fingers relaxed on the bulrushes and I was carried away, leaving behind everything I ever was.

The last thing I saw was own blood colouring the water. My last thought was for the father I had just truly begun to know.

59

Aya had no desire to return during the day, when she would be under the watchful eye of every Siwan going about their business. Thus it was no coincidence that it was dark when she came in sight of the place she had last seen what felt like a lifetime ago.

And yet, of course, nothing was different. Astride her horse, watching the old village come into view, she almost smiled at the thought of it. Everywhere else in Egypt was changing; indeed, so much of what she and Bayek had discussed was involved with those changes to their country. Siwa, though, had resisted it. Laid before her was the oasis, the moon rippling like a wafer on its surface. Rising up beyond that, the township itself: the fortress, the temples, the memories . . .

It was a place that existed in her past, represented by Bayek and her aunt Herit, and it was a place that represented a future that she now knew in her heart of hearts was not for her. She might stay for some years, still. Would have stayed with Bayek, certainly. But for ever? No.

The village was quiet and sleepy as she made her way up the path towards it. She couldn't help but cast her eyes up towards where Bayek had lived, wondering about his mother, Ahmose, and knowing that she would pay her a visit. She would see Rabiah as well. That would be an interesting encounter.

The streets were dark and quiet. The only sound was that of her horse's hooves. When she arrived at her aunt's house, her old home, her breath caught in her throat to think that she was here – that this was journey's end – and she found herself staying seated for a moment or so, trying to readjust and dealing with waves of memory and nostalgia that ran through her. The worry, too, that she might be too late to see her aunt.

Exhaustion hit her, and she felt her shoulders drop, her head nodding forward, braids hanging as she gathered strength and resolve, telling herself that she had to do this, she had to go in.

And then with a deep, decisive breath, she dismounted, took her pack from her horse, slung it over her shoulder and crossed to her front door.

There, something had changed. She sensed it right away.

The flowers, that was it. It used to be that her aunt always displayed flowers outside. In fact, the sight of Herit returning from market with a basket of fruit and flowers was so familiar to Aya that when she turned and looked down the street it was as though that figure was imprinted on the scene, even though it was dark.

But no, there were no flowers outside any more. In fact, the exterior of her aunt's home looked a little uncared for. Had it always been like that or was it just in her imagination that it was perfectly painted and adorned with vibrant blooms each day? She reached, chipped a little paint off with a nail and wondered whether it was just her memory playing tricks on her.

The other thing was the smell. Now, this definitely wasn't her memory. And neither was it a smell she associated with her childhood. It was . . .

Gods, what was it? As she went to push aside the screen and step into her old home the stench leapt at her from the interior, forcing her to put a hand over her mouth and instinctively reach for her scarf before remembering that she had given it to Bion at the waterhole.

Thoughts of that strange encounter were pushed to one side by the smell she was now confronted with, and, being careful to breathe shallowly, she advanced, cautiously and as quietly as possible. Burners flickered. Tendrils of oily smoke rose into the room. The smell was nauseating. Otherwise, the house had an air of emptiness.

She extinguished the burners, trying to match their presence with the absence of her aunt – why would burners be lit if Herit were dead? – and trying to ignore the worry gnawing away in her gut. Once she might have rushed out into the street, knocked on the nearest door and demanded to know where her Herit was. She would have looked and sounded like a panicky fool and the gossip – oh, the gossip: 'Did you see Aya, Herit's girl, came back from her travels, shouting up the place . . . ?'

But not any more. Not the Aya she was now. Instead

she went calmly back into the street, grateful to escape the almost overwhelming burning-oil inside, turned to her right and went to the house of Herit's neighbour, Nefru – her aunt's best friend.

'Hello?' she called at the door, and then reeled back. That same smell, just as pungent and, if anything, even more intense. It was almost unbearable.

'Hello?' came the reply, the Nefru she remembered. 'Come in, whoever you are.'

'Is that . . . Nefru?' called Aya. She held a hand over her nose and mouth and stepped across the threshold into Nefru's home, just as Nefru appeared in a doorway into the sleeping area. A lantern flared.

'Aya? Is that you?' Nefru was saying, moving into the room and raising the lantern so that it threw a light not just in the space but on herself as well.

And at the sight of the first familiar face she had seen in so many years, Aya almost gasped, because seeing her was like a portal to a world of childhood memories. This was Nefru, Herit's next-door neighbour: short and slightly rotund with ruddy cheeks that Aya always remembered as bulging slightly when she smiled, which was all the time, because Nefru smiled a lot. As well as being a neighbour she was Herit's best friend and the two of them – well, as far as Aya remembered, anyway – never stopped laughing. Always giggling about something.

'Can that really be you?' Nefru looked almost overcome. She had always doted on Aya and Aya loved her in return. Now as the two women faced one another, reunited by sad circumstances, the emotion caught up with them and tears divided Aya's vision as Nefru came forward and took her in her arms.

'Child, child. Herit will be . . .'

Aya grasped at hope. 'She's alive? Where is she?'

'Why, she's back there,' said Nefru indicating the sleeping area at the rear. 'I've taken her in to care for her.'

'And does she thrive?'

'She hangs on, child she hangs on. We do what we can, myself and the physician.'

'What ails her?' Aya asked Nefru.

'It's the coughing,' said Nefru. 'The physicians say the demons are in her and they're making her hack.'

Aya looked around doubtfully. 'And it's the physician who insists you have all these burners here?'

Nefru nodded solemnly. 'It will drive them out, so he says. We have them next door as well in case they're lurking there too.'

You don't any more, thought Aya, but chose not to say, instead asking, 'Can I see her?'

'You can, of course you can, child, but all in good time; she is resting at the moment. Sleeping, bless her, and she hasn't been getting much of that so I'd rather not disturb her right now. Have a peek, though. See for yourself.'

Once Aya had peered inside the other room, satisfied her aunt was just sleeping and not dead, Nefru led her to a table that took Aya by surprise. Her memory of that very same table had it much bigger when she'd last seen it, and yet here it was in reality so much smaller.

'Are you well?' asked Nefru, settling on a stool with a little wiggle and beckoning Aya to take a seat. 'Have you brought that young man of yours back with you? Do you have news of the town's protector? So many questions I have for you. How long have you been back? Have you seen anybody else? There's lots who will have questions, that much I can tell you, so you better get used to answering them.' She nudged Aya and winked. 'And make sure you get your story straight.'

The last time Aya had sat with Nefru and drunk milk she'd been an adolescent. Doing it now, she was a woman. Everything she had been through – the 'adventures', as she and Bayek used to call them – had changed her. She had gone away one person, returned as another. Yet talking to Nefru helped her locate that girl she had once been. It brought her back in touch with the curious, mischievous tomboy that Nefru remembered. And so she told Nefru her story. Rather, she told Nefru a version of her story, omitting some of the more distressing details and failing to mention the Medjay and The Order, although she told her that Bayek had remained behind, training with his father to become the town's protector.

'Can't he learn his trade here?'

Aya chewed her lip, thinking that telling Nefru they had spent years wondering if they were likely to face an assassin any time soon, of her doubts, of Sabu's insistence on not returning no matter what, was not the best

way to stop her from being worried. 'It's, er, complicated,' was the best she could offer.

Despite the dim light she could see Nefru studying
her hard. 'Have you two had a falling-out, by any
chance?' said the older woman.

Aya's head dropped. She knew she'd find it difficult
to talk about. All that time trying not to think of Bayek
on her journey, convincing herself he truly did understand, that everything would be all right once they sat
down and talked properly – she couldn't bring herself
to cry now. But then she was nodding, hoping that
would be enough to satisfy Nefru, oh, but now her bottom lip was trembling, and in the next instant she was
in Nefru's arms, curling in close for comfort. 'I miss
him, Nefru, I miss him so much.' *I'm worried for him,* was
what she truly wanted to say, *worried the killer might be
after him for real, and that I'm wrong.*

'There, there, child,' said Nefru. 'There there . . .'

After a while, Aya caught hold of her emotions and
cleared her throat, standing as she and Nefru disentan-
gled themselves. 'I'll stay next door, then, while I'm
here.' The question of how long she planned to stay
went unexamined. 'When are you expecting to see the
physician again?' she added.

'He said he will come back in a couple of days,'
replied Nefru.

'I see,' said Aya. 'In the meantime, then, we're going
to get rid of these burners.'

'Oh, child, are you sure you know what you're doing?'

'The smell is horrendous, Nefru. How can you even stand it?'

Aya shook her head, wrinkling her nose, as Nefru frowned, confused.

'But Aya – this is what the physician says will chase away what ails her.'

'Well, I'm no physician,' said Aya, 'but the smell is suffocating, and I don't see how they can be good for anyone. We're taking these burners away.'

Aya weaved slightly, dizzy still from her travels and the smell, and Nefru reached out to steady her, slowly grinning. 'Tears one minute, bossing me the next. There's no doubt about it, child, you're back. That's for certain.'

60

When Herit awoke the following morning there was another tearful reunion. Some hours later, Aya had told her the same story she had told her aunt's friend, and then dispatched Nefru for supplies (knowing full well that her news would soon be making its way through the streets of Siwa, Nefru being a lover of gossip). Just as perceptive, Herit had also discerned that things weren't right between her niece and Bayek, and for the second time, Aya found herself seeking comfort in an embrace and in her aunt's comforting reassurance that all young people were dramatic, and everything would work out well enough, given time and proper thought. The comforting familiarity of her aunt transported her back to a childhood unsullied by killers and ancient ideologies.

She preferred it here, she decided. Right now she liked the past much more than she did the present.

Shortly, Nefru arrived back and came into the room where Herit lay on a mat, tended to by Aya. Aya had taken down the hangings that covered the windows – quite how the demons were supposed to escape with those there, she wasn't sure – letting in the fresh air and doing her best to expel the last of the noxious herbal oil recommended by the physician.

'Why,' Nefru exclaimed to Herit, 'you look better already.' She turned her attention to Aya, insisting on taking her to the window to look at her in 'the proper sunlight for the first time since only the gods knew when'. Feeling slightly better, Herit had pulled herself up a little too, and for a moment Aya surrendered herself to the inspection of the two older ladies.

'Doesn't she look lovely, Herit?' crowed Nefru.

'That she does. Just like her mother . . .'

'And her aunt,' said Aya, smiling, joining in.

'Mind you . . .' said Nefru, peering more closely. Her own ruddy cheeks came so close to Aya that she could see broken veins as Nefru inspected her. 'You're looking a little bit pale, child. It's all very well you giving me and Herit advice, but you need to start taking better care of yourself by the looks of things.'

It was true. Out in the desert, Aya had been feeling ill. She brushed off Nefru's concern, but the truth was that she still felt nauseous – likely the remains of that horrible oil, she decided.

The smell, and also, she told herself, probably nerves. After all, she had depended on Nefru's expert gossip-spreading talent to soften the blow of her return to Siwa; she could walk the streets at least. But it also meant that Ahmose, Bayek's mother, would be expecting a visit, and to leave it too long before going to see her would be considered disrespectful. No doubt about it, it had to be done, and sooner rather than later. It had to be done this morning.

And so, when she had finished being inspected by Herit and Nefru, Aya left the relative safety and sanctuary of Nefru's house and took to the streets of Siwa.

Seeing Siwa bathed in sunlight did nothing to soothe her nerves, and, of course, it didn't escape her notice that people in the street were literally stopping to stare at her. Then, suddenly, standing before her was her childhood friend Hepzefa.

Perhaps it was because they'd all been so much younger when she and Bayek left, but where Nefru and Herit had seemed somehow preserved by the years, Hepzefa had grown.

Looking at him as he stood before her, grinning broadly, with his arms wide, she was reminded of Bayek. And for a second the jolt of suddenly remembering Bayek threatened to spoil the reunion. But then the two were in each other's arms, and once more Aya was fighting back tears – of joy this time.

She told her old friend the story – with promise of more detail to come. 'What news in Siwa?' she asked, and Hepzefa shrugged and laughed as though to say nothing much, and life goes on. Sennefer would want to see her, he said, and she promised to make time for both of them. But first there was the small matter of . . .

She jutted her chin up the lane towards where the house, her destination, lay like a lioness's.

'How has she been, do you know?'

'Ahmose?' said Hepzefa. 'Like always. Giving you a hard time one minute, keeping herself to herself the next. As long as the news you have to give her is good then I suppose you should be all right.'

She wasn't sure that it was.

With promises to see Hepzefa later, Aya continued on her way, treading up the path until she came to Bayek's house.

It was funny, while everywhere else in Siwa was a storehouse of memories, this was the exception. Sabu had never really approved of her and Bayek's relationship so she'd rarely come here, and even then only to give their familiar whistle, at which Bayek would usually appear. But Ahmose had never shown any animosity towards her, she reminded herself. She'd smile and wave in greeting before Bayek joined her, most times.

But, here she was, ready to do something she had never done before, and that was knock on the door of Bayek's house.

'Come in,' came the voice from inside. 'I've been wondering how long it would take.'

Aya steeled herself, went inside and there she was, Ahmose, waiting primly on a stool, her mouth set. It struck Aya that she too was preserved, like Nefru and Herit – as though time had passed her by – though her neat home was more spacious.

'You haven't brought them back, then?' she said, without offering Aya a seat. She looked her guest up and down, somehow friendly without being welcoming.

'No,' said Aya.

Ahmose digested the news, although, of course, it wasn't news. Perhaps she had needed to hear it from Aya's lips. 'How are they?' she said at last.

'They're well. The same as ever.'

Ahmose harrumphed. 'Really? That's not what I want to hear. By telling me something you *think* I want to hear you're telling me exactly what I *don't* want to hear. How about just telling me the truth?'

Aya stood, not sure what to say or how to react. She remembered Ahmose as formidable but didn't recall her being quite so forthright, and for a moment she didn't know how to reply. She was right, though, and the younger woman could do no less towards someone who had been separated from her family for so long. That realization left her at a loss for words, bereft by the enormity of it all.

Then, thankfully, the older woman broke into a smile. 'I'm sorry,' she said. 'I just hoped . . . well, you know what I hoped.' She stood, crossed the room and took Aya in a warm embrace. 'Darling Aya, you look even stronger and more beautiful than you did when you left,' she said. 'I can't tell you how good it is to see you again after all these years.'

Now came the offer of a seat – as well as the invitation to start again. 'And please don't tell me they're the same as ever.'

'They're not, Ahmose, no. Your two men have become father and son.'

It was the truth, and a good one, after all.

'He's grown up, has he?'

'He's training to be a Medjay.'

Aya was unsurprised when Ahmose showed not the slightest reaction to the word, though the look of amusement she was given did cause her to blink in confusion.

'Oh no, dear, I didn't mean Bayek . . .'

Aaah. So it was that once more, Aya told her story – this time with less of it left out.

61

Her next stop was to see Rabiah, and so she walked across the village, once more subjecting herself to the curious glances of Siwa, whispers behind hands, greetings that she fended off by saying she had important business to do as she made her way to her next port of call.

'Hello, girl,' said Rabiah when she called in.

'Don't tell me, you were expecting to me to come,' said Aya, who, despite the overall warmth of her reception, was beginning to weary of being the returning face of Siwa. 'So, what made you think I would come to see you?'

Rabiah shrugged. 'You no doubt have questions.'

Aya shook her head. 'Not really. What questions I had were all answered out there.' She jerked a thumb behind her.

'Really?'

'All right,' conceded Aya, 'perhaps there are a couple of things I'd like you to answer, like, did you ever really think that Sabu left because of Menna?'

'I didn't know,' replied Rabiah. 'I knew it was dangerous, that's all. That's all that Sabu told me.'

Aya looked carefully at her, deciding that she was

telling the truth. Or rather, not concealing anything in addition to this truth.

'So?' pressed Rabiah, 'was Sabu called away to deal with Menna?'

'No, but Bayek and I did as you suggested and met the Nubians, who were able to deal with Menna.'

At this, Rabiah, leaned back in her stall a little, tilting her head back, staring at the ceiling. Her eyes misted and she looked like a great weight had been lifted, as though relief were flooding through her. 'Then it's over.'

'As far as Menna is concerned, yes.'

'And what of the Nubians?' asked Rabiah sharply, returning her attention to Aya and then remembering her manners at the same time; shades of Ahmose. 'Here, girl, take a seat. Would you like some water? Wine?'

'I've had enough liquids for one day, thank you,' said Aya.

'So go on – the Nubians?'

Rabiah listened intently as Aya related the news of Khensa, Seti, Neka and the rest of her tribe. On hearing that the Nubians had been depleted by their war with Menna, she frowned sadly, perking up to hear about Khensa. 'There are not many like her,' she said.

'We owe her a great deal.'

'And what became of them, the Nubians?'

'We had to split up. I know they planned to leave their home in Thebes, the gods only know how much they must have wanted to do that. They'll be travelling. No doubt we will hear more of them in due course.'

'But Menna definitely wasn't the reason that Sabu left?'

'No.'

'Then what was it?' asked Rabiah carefully. 'What was the danger?'

'A threat to the Medjay,' said Aya. 'Do you know of The Order in Alexandria?'

'I have heard of them,' conceded Rabiah.

'It seems they are hunting Medjay.'

'I see,' she said.

'You haven't anything to say about that?'

Rabiah shrugged. 'What would I have to say about that?'

Aya stood up, exasperated. 'Did you know about them, Rabiah? Did you know this would happen?' she said, and as she said it, anticipating the answer, she wondered how angry she should feel at being used by Rabiah to facilitate some grander scheme.

Rabiah had been watching her carefully, then suddenly gave a short, quick laugh. 'You're like Ahmose in some ways, Aya. She's is always accusing me of knowing so much more than I do.' She waved her hand. 'As though I have tricks up my sleeve.' Aya raised an eyebrow, feeling rather united with Ahmose on that front. People thought that of Rabiah because often, Rabiah did know more than others did.

'Do you think I can see into the future?' the older

woman continued. 'If only it were so. No, sadly, I have no such gifts. Simply a desire to maintain the ways of the Medjay and the knowledge that to do so involves protecting these temples.'

'The temples are guarded.'

'Not by Medjay. This town needs its protector. It needs Sabu. It needs Bayek.'

'Well, at the moment it seems to have neither.' Aya knew she was being unnecessarily blunt, but apparently Rabiah was used to bluntness. Aya was reminded of Ahmose at this, and of her travels – and of how she had grown and changed since she'd last been in Siwa.

Rabiah nodded, conceding the point. Then added, 'But one or both will return.'

'How can you be so sure?'

'Of Sabu coming back? I'm not. But Bayek. Oh, he'll be back. He'll come because you're here.'

'I'm bait, is that what you mean?'

Rabiah threw her arms up in frustration. 'Again! How could I possibly control your presence here, child? You came of your own volition. I'm pleased that I appear to you like one of the gods, manipulating you all, but I'm really not, you know.'

'Just that it's worked out that way,' said Aya, suddenly tired. Years of being on the run had taken their toll, and what was a natural level of suspicion out there seemed suddenly unwarranted here, in small and safe Siwa.

And now she felt some vile mixture of emotions that

she couldn't quite decipher: nausea, disgust, outrage, frustration, anxiety. She found herself reeling out of Rabiah's home, dispensing with the usual courtesy and almost stumbling out into the street, the older woman calling out after in worry until Aya waved her off, pleading tiredness.

On her walk home she began to feel worse. She remembered the attack in the oasis, the point where she knew she'd kill to defend herself. Replayed that moment right before the arrows of the rider had struck home. At one point she staggered and reached to a low wall for support. Her thoughts whirled. She wondered if this feeling that events were out of her control, even here in Siwa, was the cause of the churning of her stomach, the dizziness that threatened to send her to her knees. She'd hated it when travelling with Bayek and his father, and she hated it now. She heard somebody call her name, looked over and through this division saw a figure – one she briefly thought might be the killer. But no, it was just her old friend Sennefer. She didn't have the energy to stop and speak so she smiled weakly at him but shook her head, needing to move on and hurry home.

At last she got there and almost fell inside, wanting desperately to lie down. The building was dark and she was disorientated, her limbs feathery and shaking in the aftermath of the storm of emotions that had hit her in the street, and it took her a second or so to realize that there was somebody standing in her house. The figure of a man.

'Bayek,' she said, but it wasn't Bayek. It was him – Bion – the man from the watering hole.

What was he doing here? she wondered dimly. But her stomach churned, the air smelled odd, and her vision was clouding. Air seemed to elude her, and everything was slowly turning sideways. He was moving towards her, something red in his hand. *My scarf*, she thought. *Oh good. I was missing my scarf.* And then she felt her feet go, saw the floor rush up to meet her, felt strong arms grip her. And then nothingness.

62

After the fight, as Bayek had been washed away and Sabu lay vanquished on the dirt, Bion had knelt, his shoulders heaving and his head lowered, exhausted and in pain, listening to . . .

Nothing.

Silence. Not even the shrieking of birds circling above his head. Even the blood rushing in his ears had subsided. But now the body of Sabu lay at his feet, which meant his mission would be at a close.

The killing would soon be at an end.

And he could find peace.

There was one other noise, though. It came from Sabu and was the sound of his laboured breathing. From his chest protruded Bion's sword – the killer had been taking no chances, he had pinned the Medjay to the earth like a butterfly. Blood foamed at his mouth and Sabu's eyes seemed to be drifting in and out of focus as he attempted to fix them on Bion, trying to see the face of his killer before he died.

In pain himself, Bion shifted slightly, grimacing from the wound at his side in order to look down upon him.

'Your name,' said Sabu weakly. Bion gave a short

nod as though to confer the dignity of the vanquished upon him.

'My name is Bion,' he told him. 'I am sent by The Order to kill you and your kin – sent by an Order official named Raia. Is he known to you?'

Sabu shook his head, causing himself pain. He screwed up his eyes to recover and when he opened them again his sight once more came to rest on Bion, who saw no hatred or anger there, just deep sadness to mirror his own. He wondered if Sabu wore his scars on the inside, and if he, too, were exhausted by the killing; if there was some part of Sabu that welcomed departure from this life.

'Where is he?' asked Sabu.

'Your boy? Elsewhere.'

'Dead?' managed Sabu.

The killer spread his hands. 'Who knows?'

'He's a strong boy,' smiled Sabu a little wistfully.

'You taught him well, Medjay,' said Bion, and he reached to brush a lock of hair from Sabu's eyes. 'I watched you from a distance. I saw you pass him the medallion. You felt that his education was complete, I know. You had handed him the mantle of Medjay.'

'I gave him a death sentence, did I?' said Sabu.

Bion shook his head. 'No, that had already been passed. The Order of Alexandria has decreed that the Medjay and its bloodline should be extinguished. When my work is done, only your adherents and pretenders will be calling themselves Medjay. The Order will have nothing to fear. The era of dominance will be uninterrupted.'

'And that suits you, does it?'

Bion shrugged, the very act causing him pain and making him wince. 'No, it does not suit me. I do nothing but the bidding of my masters. I kill. That is all. I have killed your friends. I have killed your master Hemon and his boy Sabestet.' He indicated the sword that pinned Sabu to the ground. 'I have dealt your death blow and shortly I shall kill your son in order to complete my task. None of this *suits* me. It is simply what I do.'

'You'll have to find him first,' said Sabu. He forced a smile. 'No easy endeavour, that.'

Bion had seen Bayek swept away by the river. But he knew more than Sabu gave him credit for. He knew that if Bayek were alive then he would be making his way to Siwa.

There was, however, no reason to tell Sabu that he knew these things. Let the man nurture his false hope as he passed to the other side; let him deliver himself into the gods with faith as his companion. He didn't tell Sabu that he had to recover the final medallion in order to take it to Raia, to make the mission complete and end the killing. He didn't tell him that because, quite simply, Sabu had more than enough to contend with. He had his final moments to live.

Instead Bion said, 'You were a fine and worthy opponent, Medjay, a great warrior. I'm sure you don't need me to tell you that. Take that to your gods. Know that you served your creed and your family and your . . .' He was about to say 'township' but stopped himself. 'You have acquitted yourself well. You are right, Medjay, I may never find your son. I may never complete my task. You may take away with you the consolation that you made my labours a great deal more exhausting than they might have been. Goodbye.' And with that, he sat back on his heels, deciding as a mark of respect to wait until Sabu passed until he tended to his own wounds.

It took the Medjay some moments to die. But when at last he did his eyelids flickered one last time, a final breath escaped in a gentle sigh and his head rolled to one side.

Bion checked the Medjay was dead and then retrieved his sword, left Sabu's body for the carrion and then dressed his own wounds before returning to his horse and setting off in the direction of Siwa.

63

How long had I drifted? I had no idea. What sort of shape was I in when the elderly couple had pulled me from the water? I had no knowledge of that either. All I knew was that I was lying on a sleeping mat and yet the floor didn't feel secure beneath me, as though it were . . . Yes, that's right, it was moving.

Moments of disorientation followed, and then a searing pain from my arm and my stomach, each painful twinge reminding me of his blade, flashing in the sun. I thought of his kohl-blackened eyes, dead; the scars on his face that seemed to glow like white worms. I thought of the red scarf and I tried to pull myself upright, only to be sent back, speared by agony that seemed to lance through me.

The thought of Aya stayed with me, anchored to the base of my skull, while I fought the dizziness that prevented my ability to think clearly and make sense of my surroundings. And then, with a delayed reaction that I was almost shameful of, I remembered my father. I saw again the vision that had followed me as I was swept, bleeding, along the river away from the scene of battle: a sword that rose, glittering almost prettily in the sunshine, and then fell, plunged downward into my father.

He had his worries about me, which he'd expressed as doubts as to my suitability as a Medjay. I knew it was fatherly concern he'd never been able to articulate, but it had also created the distance between us. One I had struggled to cross these past years. In the end, I suppose for that reason as much as any other we'd never really got to know one another as friends, but we in a fashion finally became father and son, and he had taught me to become a Medjay. We had intended to return to Siwa together, where I would eventually take up the mantle of town protector, so perhaps friendship would have developed in time. Who knows? Maybe not.

One thing was certain, I would never find out now.

Where was it, the medallion he had given me? I wasn't sure, but I knew that for now it didn't matter. Unless I was very much mistaken, I was the last Medjay.

Whatever Medjay would be, from now on, was up to me. Even with the grief haunting me, it was a grounding, sobering thought.

After some time I became aware of another presence in . . . well, I wouldn't call it a room, it was more of a space. But either way I realized I was not alone. Raising my head to peer towards the end of the sleeping mat, I could see a man who now spoke. 'Hello,' he said.

He stepped into the light and to my relief it was not my father's killer. This man was much, much older, and stood slightly stooped, the way that I suppose is usual when you make a boat your home. He wore a white tunic, and his hair was held back by a band across his forehead. Standing just to the left was a woman I correctly took to be his wife. She looked fretful and concerned, and as I watched she gave him a nudge with her elbow so that he stepped forward and introduced them as Nehi and Ana, man and wife, owners and residents of the boat in which I lay, which they used to fish and to transport goods up and down the river.

'Are you feeling better?' asked the woman. Like her husband, her voice was gentle and reassuring. It reminded me of my own mother at her most comforting, and the thought alone sent a pang of homesickness through me that was sharper and more painful than any of my wounds.

'Where am I?' I said.

And so they told me. They told me that they lived on the boat and that we were travelling north, which, of course, I knew meant home, and that they had found me in the water grievously wounded.

'You looked like you'd really been in the wars, young man,' said Nehi.

'We thought you were dead for sure,' agreed Ana.

'We tended you as best we could,' said Nehi, quickly clarifying, 'not that you owe us anything, of course, we wouldn't hear of it.'

'Then I can't thank you enough.'

Next came the question how long I had been there, and they looked at each other, pulling faces, shrugging. 'Not that long,' said Nehi. 'Only four nights.'

I tried to think. That meant that the killer, whoever he was, had four nights' head start on me. 'If you take me north with you, then I think I would stay.'

'What is there?'

'My home town. And the woman I love.' I paused, not willing to endanger them by mentioning the Medjay. 'My life.'

I hoped that these answers were not contradictory. Either way, I knew I needed to be in Siwa.

64

'I just wanted to return your scarf,' Bion had said when Aya awoke to find him standing over her. 'You fell.'

She had taken a moment or so to focus, unnerved by a man being in her house without her inviting him in, careful as any woman would be. The strange smell was gone, at least, but she remembered it nonetheless.

'Your neighbour said you'd be returning soon,' he was saying. 'She kindly suggested I wait for you here.'

By now she had got to her feet slowly, testing her steadiness, not wanting to feel at a disadvantage. 'My aunt . . .' She began.

'Yes,' he said, nodding to acknowledge the point, 'I've been speaking to Nefru.' He smiled faintly, though his eyes never changed. 'I told her about our encounter in the oasis. She's told me everything.'

Aya smiled carefully, falling back on a more serene persona, hiding her inner turmoil as thoroughly as she could.

Why? Why would she want to avoid this man's company? That was a good question and one she couldn't quite answer. After all, she knew she had nothing to fear from him. And yet, on the other hand, maybe she did, because there was something about him. Definitely something about him. Something that put her ill at ease. She could not help but wonder if the horse thieves in the oasis had perhaps found her because someone had told them she'd been there. Someone who had followed her to the oasis. And then to Siwa.

'How long was I . . . ?'

'Moments,' he said. 'I caught you and laid you down to give you water.' He indicated a beaker set upon a stool. 'You revived before it became necessary to seek further assistance from next door.'

Nothing had been disturbed, she noted, glancing casually at the beaker and the room beyond. She took another breath, as though trying to clear her senses — still no smell. Keep things normal, small and familiar, she reminded herself. Let him think her unawares. She might be wrong. But she might be right.

'Well, I'm glad you didn't go there. I wouldn't like to worry my aunt or Nefru. But wait, when did you speak to Nefru?'

'Oh, well that was when you were away, seeing . . .' He looked as though he were thinking, although to Aya it looked as though he were pretending to think, 'somebody's mother. Was it Bayek's mother?'

'Something like that,' she said cagily, and then went to move past him. He had no reason to bring up Bayek. None, save perhaps his own interests. Aya forced herself to remain calm, calculating the possibilities. He was trouble. But was he the killer? 'I ought to go next door, to check on my aunt.'

He had now stood too, and moved across, almost blocking her way. As though a coincidence. 'Do you think you should be going next door if you don't feel well? I've heard medical men say the demons of ill health can feed off one another.'

'I'm sure we'll be fine,' she said casually, manoeuvring past him in the way anyone might if facing a random stranger, not feeling threatened. 'I need to check she's all right.'

He looked uncomfortable. Had she not been already paying attention, it would have looked normal. 'In that case, perhaps I should leave.'

Yes. Yes I would prefer you to leave.

'No, no, of course not,' she said quickly. If he was trouble, if he was the killer or one of his agents, then she wanted to know where he was. She wanted him in her sights. 'Please stay. I was very grateful for your support when those men tried to attack me and you can stay as long as you like. Now, I'm going to check on my aunt. I'll be but a moment. Perhaps we can eat after that? I'm very keen to know more about you.'

A strange look flitted over his features, one she would have been sure she'd imagined had she not been looking for any clue, anything at all. 'Thank you,' was all he said.

She bobbed her head to escape her aunt's house, gulping in the air of the street outside, blinking in the sunlight that bounced off bleached stone, her eyes going to the temple as though somehow drawn there. She wished for the presence of Bayek. Right now she would have settled for the presence of his father, even. She went to her right and was about to duck into Nefru's house when she stopped herself. What if her aunt was in danger? Then again, he'd already spoken to Nefru. If he was the danger, then it was too late to stay away.

'Nefru,' she spoke softly at the door, 'are you there?'

The old woman appeared. 'You've got a guest,' she said meaningfully. Aya gently backed her into the house, away from open windows nearby, and possible listeners.

'You spoke to him.'

Nefru nodded. 'Well, he seemed nice enough. And you didn't tell me about what happened with those thieves,' she fussed gently over Aya, looking her over as though invisible injuries might suddenly come to light.

'What did he ask you?' pressed Aya.

Nefru nodded again and rolled her eyes. 'Well, he certainly was inquisitive. He wanted to know everything there was to know about you and Bayek, your aunt, Bayek's father . . .'

'Everything, then?' interrupted Aya.

'Oh yes, pretty much everything.'

And you told him, didn't you? Aya took a short breath, funnelling her frustration into as tight a ball as possible, setting it aside with all her determination.

Standing there, she felt aware of him somehow, almost as though he might be listening through the walls, even though that was a fanciful idea.

Of course, you told him everything. You have no idea.

She checked in on Herit then left. As she did so, she came upon Bion in the street, just leaving the house next door, making her jump a little. She turned her startlement into that of any woman, hand on her heart, a breathy chuckle of recognition.

'Hello,' he said with a smile. The more she looked at him, the more it felt as though he were empty. He tilted his chin, looking over her shoulder, and she turned to see Nefru turning back inside the house with a wave. 'Did you find out everything you needed to know?' he asked her. His smile was fixed and practised, in no danger of reaching his eyes.

'Yes, thank you.' She allowed herself a slight weave, the memory of her earlier anxiousness easy to recall. 'If you don't mind, I'm going to have another little lie down.' She passed a hand across her forehead. 'I'm still feeling a little weak from earlier. Perhaps we could have something to eat later on.'

'I would like that,' he said. 'In the meantime, I think I'll have a wander around the village.' He indicated upwards. 'Your temples are renowned.'

With that, they parted ways.

As she turned he leaned in towards her and she fought an impulse to flinch. 'You didn't mention either to Nefru or to your aunt that you're not feeling well, I take it?' he asked.

She shook her head but found herself puzzling on why he wanted her to stay silent, and then, as she went into her home, some instinct made her look out of the door again. Her eyes went to where Bion was walking up the street, although he was not heading towards the temple. If anything, she decided, he was going in the direction of Bayek's house.

65

I was sad to leave Nehi and Ana. Just being with them felt like being cocooned in a shawl, and not just any shawl, but one belonging to my mother. I'd got used to the night-time rhythms of the boat. During the day when I had felt better I had gone up on deck, sitting to watch the business of the Nile, enjoying again all those aspects of the river that had enchanted me when I first clapped eyes on it so many years ago, a callow youth setting out on a journey to find my father. I trained as well, subtly so, the boat an interesting challenge to my balance. Nehi and Ana taught me more than they ever realized during those times when the waves were choppy, and I struggled to maintain my footing on the wet wood.

But then the time came and I had to take my leave. I would miss them, but I was eager to get going. I bade them a fond farewell, thanked them for nursing me back to health and assured them that there would always be a place for them in Siwa, and that on arrival they should ask for me, the town protector.

'We will look forward to meeting this Aya we've heard so much about,' said Ana.

'Yes,' I said, and hoped my face did not betray my fear that Aya had fallen victim to the killer.

I traded for a horse from a local caravan at the first opportunity, spending most of my remaining coin. As I began my trek across the desert towards Siwa, my thoughts turned to the killer who wore her scarf. My thoughts were dark. They tortured me at night. Had he killed Aya?

At a settlement I asked a merchant, 'Have you been here long?'

'Day and night for over seven summers.'

'You must see most people who go through here.'

'That I do.'

'Have you seen a girl, a woman? One who would have been travelling for many days. She wears her hair in braids, scarves gathered at the belt, wrist guards, very beautiful.'

'Oh yes, I've seen a girl who looks like that. She bought bread from me.'

'She didn't happen to mention that she was on her way to Siwa?'

'That she did.'

Relief had flooded over me and I made to leave, but then something, some instinct, made me turn back. 'Can I just ask, about a second person?'

I described the killer. And then a chill ran through me when the trader told me that this man had also passed through the settlement, also on his way to Siwa. In the next moment I was on my horse, redoubling my efforts to get home.

66

Bion had returned, and now sat cross-legged on a mat on the floor, tunic stretched across his lap and a beaker of wine cradled in his hands. By his side lay a plate, on it crumbs of bread. Sitting opposite, Aya had watched him eat intently, with his head down, eating habits that were, she decided, the result of a lifetime spent either in the army or as a nomad. Only through her training with Bayek could she see the small signs of a man economical with his motions, could she spot the calluses specific to someone who wielded a sword, used a bow.

She knew very little about the scar-faced stranger who was now her guest. He seemed to have discovered everything about her, yet given away nothing in return. That in itself, though, told her so much. She was now certain he was the killer. Lying in wait for Bayek, having found her.

She crossed, picked up his plate and then poured a little more wine into his cup. Next, she dragged a stool to the opposite end of the room, wanting to put a bit of distance between them, then taking a seat and reaching for her own wine. 'So,' she said, 'what's your story? Why have you never settled?' The question of any young woman in a small town such as Siwa, intent on acquiring gossip. Nefru's habits were easy to adopt, to hide under while she watched intently.

'Who can say? Years spent in the Royal Guard, I suppose. As a young man I lived and worked in Alexandria, my job was to protect the rich and powerful.'

She perked up a little at the mention of the great city. 'My parents live there, in Alexandria,' she said, and let the happiness at the thought of them swim through the worry she'd kept hidden away, another layer of misdirection. 'I spent my very early years there before coming here to live with my aunt.'

She was thinking, *But you probably already know that.* And, indeed, he was nodding. It felt more like acknowledgement than the casual assent one might give a story heard for the first time. 'I'd like to go back there one day,' she ended. He asked no questions. Did not pursue the topic.

'Well, that is something I never want to do,' he said. 'It is a life I am more than happy to leave behind.'

'We're very different, you and I,' she said, wondering at his composure, knowing she trod a dangerous line in pointing that out.

He nodded. 'Yes, indeed we are. Except in one important respect.'

'Oh yes?' she said cautiously. 'And what respect is that?'

She didn't like the look she saw in his eyes. There it was again. It was as though there were a hollow space behind them. Nothing there.

354

'You remember that day at the watering hole, when you complimented me on my skills with a bow and pointed out that my bow looked new?'

'Yes.'

'I told a lie when I said that I was the best with a bow in my company.'

'I see,' she said. Her eyes flicked to the doorway, wondering whether she needed to make a run for it, whether she could reach the doorway before he could stop her. 'I suppose the question is why you felt the need to lie to me?'

He chewed a lip. 'I was never very good with a bow. My commander, Raia, would often mock me for my lack of bowmanship.'

'You were ashamed?'

'It was not something to be proud of as a member of the Machairophoroi.'

She felt a crawling sensation in her belly, knowing he knew she knew. Their words were knives now, and any moment blood might be drawn. Nonetheless, she kept still. If he wished to harm her, he would have done so by now.

She'd been right earlier. *Bait.*

'I think that was it,' he was saying. 'You see, I am only a recent convert to the bow. I think for that reason – embarrassment, vanity – I preferred to keep that fact secret.'

'There is no shame in that,' she told him, still wondering what point he was trying to make but also not really

355

caring. As long as he was talking, not moving, he was not trying to kill her. As long as he was talking, whoever approached might hear him and know. 'Nobody, least of all me, would have judged you on something so trivial. Your appearance at the waterhole that day was most welcome.'

'You hardly needed help from me. I could see that you were proficient in combat. I wondered then as I wonder now where you learned such skills.'

'My . . .' She paused. 'My friend, Bayek, was keen that I should be able to defend myself on my travels. It was he who taught me.'

'You put them into action magnificently. And where is he now, this Bayek?'

'You asked that same question of Nefru. You know the answer. I wonder why you ask it again of me now.'

He spread his hands as though to offer no firm reply either way. Hollow eyed, he spared her a slight smile. Tacit acknowledgement that each had divined the other's deceit. She thought she saw a glimmer of respect there, but refused to believe that it meant anything. The man killed because he could. Whatever else he might feel was unimportant. If given the chance, he would kill Bayek, then he would kill her, and probably Nefru, Herit and Ahmose just to tidy up loose ends. She would talk to him until the end of the world, if need be, to keep that from happening.

'This thing we have in common,' she reminded him, 'you were going to say . . . ?'

He nodded. 'You noticed, is what I was leading on to. You saw that my bow was new. I think I can remember that I complimented you on your observation. And that, Aya, is what we have in common. I, too, am observant.'

Her eyes remained fixed on him, though she was mentally gauging the distance between herself and the door. The weight of the stool she sat on. How quickly she might throw it at him to buy time. 'Why do I have a feeling this is going somewhere?'

'It is.'

She swallowed, steeling herself, feeling a crackle in the room. She hid the flash of hope under her fear, let the latter bubble up a bit more. He wanted to talk. She would talk until the day the sun failed to rise, if need be. 'Go on, tell me. This is what you've been leading to all along, isn't it? So tell me. What is it that you've observed that you so wish to tell me about?'

'Very well then,' he said, 'I shall.' And he fixed her with a gaze, those dark eyes seeming to pierce right through her . . .

67

I rode — faster than I had ever dared before, pushing my horse onwards, onwards, promising it water and oats and all the horsely pleasures its heart desired if she could just spirit me to Siwa in time.

Night fell, and still we thundered on, man and horse, and I spent every moment in mortal dread that my steed would lose her footing, plunge and throw us both into the dirt.

And if that happened — if we really did crash to the ground — then whose fault would it have been? Would it be the poor horse's, exhausted and foaming at the mouth, forced to gallop in the restricted vision of a dying day, but steadfast to the last even though its new owner treated it so poorly? Or would it be the fault of her rider? A man driven almost insane with a desperate need. A man on a mission?

I knew the answer to that question.

And then, at last, the moonlit water of the Siwa oasis came into view and I bullied my mare into an extra burst of speed, promising her all sorts of treasures, and . . .

She fell. Either through exhaustion or a misstep her front legs buckled, she pitched forward and we were suddenly both on the ground.

For a moment or so I lay there, groaning. Then I rolled over, checking myself for broken limbs or bleeding wounds, and to my great relief finding none. Beside me my horse scrambled to her feet and stood, head lowered but otherwise, thankfully, unharmed. I had pushed her hard, too hard, but she had rewarded me by getting me here.

She was exhausted, but I could run the rest of the way. 'Thank you, thank you,' I gasped, dragging off my pack, taking my sword and bow, slinging them across my back and beginning the journey around the oasis. Above me was the hillside of Siwa, the fortress and temples regarding me imperiously. I hit the track that led into the village, arms and legs pumping, weighed down but determined.

There was no time to ponder upon my return. My only thought was for Aya, and it was to her house that I ran. My breath was ragged, my limbs heavier than I had ever imagined possible, pounding along lanes and streets I knew so well but had never before trod with such purpose and determination.

And then, there it was: her aunt's home. I'd last seen it the night I left Siwa and arriving there now dragged me back in time, but I was in no mood to savour it. Right now, I had to think, I had to be clever – wasn't that what Father had always drummed into me? Exercise caution. Think. Plan.

I withdrew into shadows offered by homes opposite in order to get my breath back. Silently, I deposited the pack, eyes going to the frontage of Herit's home. It struck me that the house had become shabbier since I last saw it. I checked for my sword, grasped the hilt of my knife, taking strength from their presence there at my waist, and then I darted across the street. At the doorway I stopped, listening, expecting to hear what, I wasn't sure. Either way, there was no sound from within. Even so, the house looked occupied. There was a screen at the door and hangings at the window. There was no way of making my way around to the rear. I would have to enter by the front door whether I liked it or not. Taking a deep breath, I slipped inside.

Darkness. Silence.

As I cast my eye around the place I noticed something: on the table were two beakers, which I lifted to inspect. They'd recently been used. They were still wet. Still traces of – I smelled – wine. Was this Aya and her aunt, I wondered. Perhaps Herit had revived? Was it possible that the killer had not yet arrived? Or had he arrived and was biding his time? Maybe the trader I spoke to was simply mistaken?

Now my attention went to the sleeping arrangement. I knew the layout of the house. There was only one bedding area and so it was likely that Aya would be sharing it with her aunt. I stood for a moment, debating what to do. On the one hand, to be caught peeking into the chamber would be so very shameful; on the other, it could be that Aya lay on the other side of the wall: Aya, whom I had spent so many months missing. Aya for whom my heart ached.

Right. I took a deep breath, peered quickly around the side of the door and into the sleeping area.

It was empty.

I had another look. Still empty. And now any trepidation I'd felt was replaced by a new sense of foreboding. Aya was here, and yet she wasn't here. So where was she?

Something occurred to me and I hurried back out into the street, taking less care to be quiet now. Next door lived Herit's best friend, Nefru. She wasn't going to take kindly to being woken up, but then again the circumstances demanded it. Just as I was about to enter, I heard voices from within. Voices that I recognized: Nefru, Herit . . . and Aya.

And now I forgot about manners and propriety. I suppose I even forgot about thoughts of the killer and avenging my father. In fact, all I could think about when I heard that voice was her. And with a cry, Aya's name springing from my lips, I burst into Nefru's home. No, it wasn't the most elegant of entries, but I had ceased to care – all I wanted to do was see her, and the sight that greeted me was more precious to me than water, food or air. It was Aya, rising from her seat, her eyes wide and her mouth dropping open, a look of abject surprise that became something else, a reflection of my own feelings, something I can only describe as joy.

I heard their voices, Nefru saying, 'The gods, child, he's come,' and Herit agreeing. But they were mere background noise, hardly even a distraction, as Aya and I rushed together like water closing over the wake of a passing ship.

'I've missed you so much,' she was saying in between kisses. She'd taken my face in her hands and was showering me with them, accepting them in return. Behind us Nefru and Herit were cooing, making noises about 'young love' and 'wasn't it sweet' as though we were a couple of freshly minted lovebirds, children exchanging shy first pecks, rather than a couple who were on the verge of becoming man and wife, whose parting, I now realized, had been like a little death.

'I thought I would never see you again,' I breathed.

That slightly sardonic smile I knew so well had returned. 'Rabiah told me that I would definitely see you again,' she told me.

'I wish I could say the same about you,' I replied. 'I feared you dead.'

She shook her head, an odd relief colouring her voice. 'No, I'm fine. Where is your father?'

Having to break the news of my father's death brought me a fresh and piercing pain. 'He found us, Aya. The man who'd been hunting us all those years. He found us and attacked.'

'Sabu is dead?' she said, paling. 'Bayek, I'm so sorry.'

I took her and grasped her by the shoulders. 'Is he here?'

Aya had frozen. She tightened her hands into fists, falling unconsciously into a stance we'd both learned during my training. Ready to go to battle. And I knew. 'Yes,' she answered in a quiet voice.

From behind her piped up Nefru: 'This man you're talking about, Bayek. He's dangerous, is he?'

I didn't take my eyes off Aya. 'Dangerous like you would not believe, Nefru – dangerous and intent on killing me and all my kin. If he's here then I must know at once where.'

But the look in Aya's eyes told me all I needed to know. It was hardly necessary for Nefru to go on. 'What does he look like, this man?' the older woman asked, even as Aya slowly shook her head.

He was here. The knowledge was in the room just as surely as if the killer was standing there in the flesh. And in the end it took just one word from me – 'scars' – and the two older women blanched with shock.

'He's been next door,' said Aya's aunt. 'His name is Bion.'

For a crazy moment it occurred to me to ask Aya if she was all right – although she was fine – or maybe if anything else had happened. Yet no. It seemed that she was, on the outside at least, unharmed. He hadn't touched her. He was waiting for me. I was the real prey.

'Where is he now? He's not there.'

'I'm not sure,' began Aya. 'I don't . . . Bayek, I think he might have —'

But I was thinking. *The bloodline.*

'My mother,' I said suddenly, releasing Aya. Belatedly understanding why she was gearing up for combat in her aunt's home. 'Gods, my mother.'

And in the next moment I was dashing back out into the street with Aya just behind me.

'Bayek, stop!' she called. 'He won't kill her without you there!'

'We have to hurry,' I yelled at her, racing up the street.

'I know that,' she said, 'but he didn't kill me without you there, he told me he'd wait.' I nearly tripped at that, which gave her a chance to catch up. 'And you're not taking him on alone.'

I saw faces appearing at the windows and the doors of the houses around us but had neither the time nor the inclination to quieten down for their sake. 'You don't know this man like I do,' I said.

'You'd be surprised.'

'He's acquired . . .'

'Bow skills, I know. I told you I'd spoken with him.'

That took me aback, yet again. But she had told me. She used the pause to tell me, once more, 'I'm coming with you.'

And, of course, she was right. The rest didn't matter for now. My father and I, two Medjay, had fared badly against this Bion. In all of Siwa there was only one person who had trained as hard as I had over the years, and it was Aya. We had no real plan, but the two of us together, it would be enough. Suddenly it seemed clear – the very idea of setting off without her was ludicrous.

The moment passed between us. We ran side by side and, despite the situation, she was smiling. She knew that I had come to the right decision. 'Wait there,' she commanded, before dashing inside her house. A second later she was joining me, only this time she carried her sword and was buckling up her wrist guards even as we continued our ascent through the village and up towards my house.

All these years I had longed to see my mother again and now I was the one who had brought death to her door. If I was too late, could I ever forgive myself? I already knew the answer to that question as Aya and I skidded to a halt just short of my old home. There it seemed that it threw its shadow across me once again. The truth was that I had always found my family home forbidding, perhaps for the simple reason that it contained my father. Even so, it was still home; it was where I lived. Now, things were different. Now, as Aya and I pulled up and looked at one another, both of us wondering what would happen next, it looked a lot less like home to me, and more like a battleground.

During our years spent together, coaching one another, Aya and I had developed an unspoken link and we used it now, as I gestured for silence and then indicated that she should go around the back of my old home. In the meantime, I went to the front door, heart hammering.

Our door was more substantial than anything on the houses down in the village. I tried it, remembering from various youthful escapades that it squeaked, but unable to do much about it. Time was of the essence now. If Bion were here, then why would he be hanging around? The fact was, I had to go in, and I had to go in at once.

Was I rushing in unprepared, just as my father had always warned me against? Probably, although this time I wasn't alone. This time I had Aya with me.

68

I suppose that a little bit of me had hoped that once again I would burst in to find the place empty, just as I had at Herit's. Yes, I wanted to confront and stop the killer, but more, much more than that, I wanted my mother to be all right.

My old house was just as I remembered it – just as it always had been. What I'd expected to see, I don't know, but the sight that greeted me was him – Bion. Here he was, the rider, the bowman, the swordsman, the man who had killed my father and who had made it his mission to kill me as well.

Except that this was a very different assailant I came upon. The last time I'd seen him he'd been spearing my father with his sword, drenched in blood and badly wounded himself but victorious, and made into a towering figure for that reason.

Now, however, he couldn't have been more different.

He sat on a stool. His knees were apart and he seemed to be staring at his lap. At least, that's what I thought he was doing at first, until I saw the sliver of metal in his hand. It was a blade, just a small one. A dagger. His sword hung from his belt – my own was in my hand – but even so concern for my mother stopped me from rushing to press home the advantage, and I looked through the room carefully, trying to make sure she was not there.

He was aware of my presence. How could he not be? The room was empty apart from him and me, and every noise in this empty space was like a vase being dropped. But even so there was little change in his demeanour and he didn't acknowledge my arrival. There was just him, the stool, the blade and, in me, a rising sense of vengeful fury – the knowledge that I was here to make right the wrong that had been done on the banks of the River Nile.

And now he looked up, found my gaze.

'Hello, Medjay,' he said quietly.

There was a finality about his greeting that left me in no doubt as to how things were going to go.

And I knew. It was time.

I launched myself forward, crossing the room in two quick steps and slicing underhand with my sword, hoping to catch him on his unprotected left flank. But he anticipated, had already stood and drawn his own blade in one almost impossibly fast movement that belied his apparent state of mind.

Our swords clashed once, twice, and then I took a step back, rearranged my stance, watched as he did the same.

Father, I hope you are with the gods now and looking down upon me. You and Tuta both. For whatever happens now, I want you to know that I do what I do for you and for the Medjay and for my family. And if it means that I die then at least I die here, in my home, defending my loved ones.

Mother. My thoughts went to her. As if in reply, Aya appeared in the doorway behind Bion. 'She's all right, Bayek, she lives,' she cried. And there were tears of relief in her eyes.

The Order's assassin looked from me to Aya, and did I imagine it, or did his gaze soften as it alighted upon her – soften and then gain an extra layer of emotion? Somehow, I sensed something new about him this time. He was just as implacable as before, but different somehow.

Aya's sword was in her hand. When he adjusted his position to confront her, I noticed a slight awkwardness about his movement. I wondered, did it emanate from the wound I had inflicted during the battle at the Nile? Was the killer I faced now a reduced, less effective presence than he had been that day?

I caught Aya's eye, gave a signal by tapping at my side and at once could see she'd understood.

Bion saw the movement and understood, reaching his dagger hand to keep that flank protected. At the same time Aya was moving around from the side, coming at him from just outside his field of vision. She gave me a quick nod, and together we attacked, rushing him in one movement.

Our swords met. The battle began.

We didn't waste our energy talking to him or taunting him. Instinctively we knew that to be pointless.

Instead we just came at him, the wordless agreement being that we would harry him, keep picking at him, one sword strike at a time, wear him down until we found his weak spot and then we would strike, a two-headed snake.

But he was fast, and very skilled. His sword point found my shoulder. I felt warm blood rushing down my arm but thankfully no pain – not yet – and I quickly responded with first blood of my own, on his side just above where I had struck him with my knife at the river. He reared away from it and Aya caught him on his thigh. More blood ran down his leg and on to the stone below. I noticed him give a little twist of his foot whenever he adjusted his stance, checking for grip. He was good, so good.

But we were good too. And there were two of us. And while his sword strikes were as hard as I remembered, I felt more able to parry them.

'You have improved,' he said at last, after some moments of battle.

'I fight from the heart. I fight to avenge my father's death.'

But now something happened, and inwardly I cursed. At the doorway to my mother's room, she had appeared, and I saw her put a hand to her mouth to cover her gasp. It wasn't quite how I imagined breaking the news.

'And to avenge your creed. Isn't that right, Medjay?' said the killer. Cold and uncaring. Whatever I had seen before was gone.

'That too. Yes. That too.'

Clash. Clash. Metal meeting metal, a constant, never-ending dance around the room, tunics soaked through with blood, the floor slick with it.

'And if you do it – if you avenge your father, what then?' asked the killer. He formed the words around hitches in his breath, and though he maintained an implacable air I could sense him tiring. He continued: 'There will be killing and more killing. One day you'll be as tired of it as I am now. One day you will be as sickened by the sight of your own reflection. That is how other people feel, I am told.'

'The difference is that you kill for the sake of killing,' I told him. 'I wish to help build a better Egypt.' The words felt right. Solid.

His smile was sudden – twisted, sardonic. 'The trouble with all of you, The Order and the Medjay, is that you *all* think you're helping to build a better Egypt. You all think that your way is the only way. And while you're all so busy being right, the bodies pile up.'

'Drop your sword and end it then, paid assassin. I promise to make your end swift.'

Clash, clash. Both of us trying to find a way through the other's defences, Aya attacking too. She scored two quick hits, earning herself a glare, and a strike she dodged just in time. I darted back in. And so it went on.

'I cannot do that, Medjay. Much as I might like,' he said.

'You have to end the bloodline, is that it?'

Bion nodded. 'All in this room must die.'

'Not Aya,' I said.

'Even Aya.'

'Why?' I said. 'She doesn't share the bloodline.'

Bion looked at her – and it was to her that he spoke. 'You don't know?'

Her eyes flitted to me and I saw disquiet. *What did he mean?* Fear slithered in my belly.

Don't lose concentration, I thought. *That's what he wants.* And for a moment the battle was at a pause, the three of us circling one another. Over the killer's shoulder I saw the figure of my mother still in the doorway but refused to let it distract me.

'Do you know what he means?' I said to Aya without taking my eyes off Bion, my sword held ready.

'Don't let him take your attention away from the matter at hand,' she said. She had recovered her composure, seeing through his tactics.

'I won't.'

'Simply a matter of timing, nothing I was trying to avoid,' she assured me. 'I'm not keeping anything from you, Bayek.'

'She carries your baby, Medjay,' said Bion, and leapt at me.

It was true that his words had an effect, striking at me like a gut punch. I heard Aya's gasp of startlement in the background. But even so I was able to fend him off, and any advantage he hoped to gain was lost as we once more resumed our positions. I allowed myself a smile, knowing that I had gained the upper hand. Was I supposed to be weakened by a declaration that Aya was with child? Was he hoping to catch me off guard?

Either way his ploy had been a failure. The opposite: I felt stronger, more confident. Hopeful. Hopeful that he was right. That even if it had been just a ploy for now, it might be a truth later. I was fighting for more than the Medjay and my father, and I came at him with extra ferocity, Aya doing the same.

And just as I had looked at my father on the banks of the river and seen his impending defeat, I saw it now in Bion. His defence was more desperate, his moves less disciplined. His face was pale and sweat shone on his brow. He had miscalculated. What he'd always seen as weakness was strength.

But he was a soldier, a warrior, a killer with a job to do. Defeat simply wasn't in his lexicon. And that made him dangerous.

As if to give my thoughts form, he made his move. Aya had strayed a little too close, emboldened, perhaps, by the way she saw the fight proceeding and Bion threw a feint, ducking inside her, grabbing her and pulling her into him.

And in that one move, he turned the battle. Now he held Aya hostage, his knife at her throat, it was he who had the upper hand.

69

I froze. I heard the word, '*No!*' and realized it was I who had spoken it. Aya had tensed, her chin raised, the blade angled at the nape of her neck. She was angling her sword slowly – I knew the strike she was considering and ice inched its way down my spine. If she managed to drive the sword through both of them, at the right angle, she might survive. Or not. Over her shoulder his eyes regarded me, and they were cold and ruthless and spoke of bottomless pain and anguish, both given and received. Hers spoke of love and determination. And even though she didn't want to do it, she would.

I saw his arm tense, about to draw the blade across her throat. Her sword angled further, dangerously ready. My hand reached for my knife in what I already knew was a pointless and futile move, and then . . .

His eyes widened, mouth dropped open. His sword hand relaxed and in the next moment the blade clattered to the stone. Aya's joined him a moment later. I rushed forward to take Aya in my arms as the killer staggered, as Aya gasped for air, turning to look over her shoulder. I saw the knife embedded in his back – and my mother standing behind him, her arm still raised.

'Tell my husband I sent you,' she said to him, watching him vengefully as he dropped to his knees then keeled over on to his side, coming to rest on the stone, letting out a sigh that I recognized as a prelude to death.

The room settled, the danger seeming to dissipate. My mother's rage burned, fierce and bright, and I remembered the night she had killed Menna's men. Defending her family. For a moment it seemed hardly believable that the battle was over, but it was: our enemy lay vanquished at our feet. His boots kicked weakly. Words were forming. I saw him beseeching me with his eyes, and so I took my dagger, about to go to him.

'Careful, Bayek,' warned Aya, and I nodded, approaching Bion carefully and getting down to my knees. Aya came with me and we crouched to him, seeing that the end was imminent. In his eyes was acceptance of his defeat, maybe even relief it was all over. An odd curiosity, as though he were wondering what happened next. Just before he went, though, he had some final words for me, fingers drawing me near. I drew close, knife held ready. Surely he would try nothing now?

'Congratulations, Medjay,' he gasped.

'Will there be more assassins?'

Blood flowed from his mouth quite freely now. Every word was a mission. 'My employer's name is Raia. You will find him in Alexandria. He was using his hunting of the Medjay – he was using me – as a way of increasing his own standing within The Order. Only Raia knows of my existence. The scrolls that first alerted The Order to your creed's plans were discovered by his master and Raia had him killed. Do with this information what you will.'

'Does he know where I am?' I asked.

Bion's eyes travelled to Aya, kneeling by my side, to me. His mouth opened and I wondered if he might be about to apologize for the misery he had wrought, and then realized that no, it wasn't in his nature. His nature was to kill, and to die, and to take whatever demons haunted him to the beyond.

And that is what he did. Bion, the killer who had haunted us for so many years, closed his eyes, breathed his last and a great peace descended upon us all.

I stood from his body, knowing that I had performed my first duty, not just as protector of Siwa, but as a Medjay.

Epilogue

Despite everything I had once said and promised myself, some months later I found myself in Alexandria, outside the home of a man I knew only as Raia, a name passed to me from the lips of a dying assassin sent to kill me, my mother, my wife to be and the child she carried.

Aya and I had since married, and our child was now born, a beautiful baby boy we named Khemu. Nefru had been endlessly pleased at guessing Aya's condition before all of us, citing the dizziness and Aya's reaction to the smell of the physician's healing herbs, though suitably contrite that she had blurted it out to half of Siwa and our would-be killer before thinking to tell Aya herself. No day passed when we weren't delighted by Khemu: tiny hands that reached up to grasp our faces. So much love, unconditional, uncomplicated. He would grasp for my nose, pulling me to him for kisses and snuggles. On those occasions I looked at my son and wondered if my father had done the same with me. I knew he had looked at me and wanted to shield me from the world. I understood so much more.

And so my life in Siwa had begun afresh. I was now the town protector. I knew, of course, that Aya had not abandoned her dreams of one day revisiting

Alexandria, but she had chosen not to accompany me when I'd left Siwa three weeks ago. The next trip we would do for her. She wanted to meet up with her parents, introduce both myself and Khemu to them. I think, perhaps, I was even growing to look forward to it.

It took me a while, but I found Raia. His home, at least. There, I took up a position in the undergrowth opposite. His was a luxurious, well-appointed property, and I lay down to wait, knowing that when I saw him, I had a choice: either I would kill him there and then, or spend the rest of my life looking over my shoulder, wondering whether he would send more assassins after me and Aya, and now our son.

Really, it was no choice at all.

I waited for hours until, at last, he appeared. Smartly dressed, just as I imagined he would be, he led a short procession, with a woman I took to be his wife some steps behind and, following along, two daughters.

They were about the age that Aya and I had been when we first left Siwa all those years ago. I watched as the four of them approached the front of the house, wondering at his family, biding my time. Night would fall soon. Darkness would hide my approach. None would know what had happened until dawn brought awakening. I had made my choice.

My family, and all of Egypt, would be kept safe.

Acknowledgements

Very special thanks to Andrew Holmes & Ann Lemay

And also

Yves Guillemot
Alain Corre
Laurent Detoc
Geoffroy Sardin
Anouk Bachman
Aymar Azaizia
Antoine Ceszynski
Maxime Durand
Anne Toole
Elena Rapondzhieva
Jean Guesdon
Alain Mercieca
Etienne Allonier
Matthieu Bagna
Andrien Gbinigie
Cecile Russeil
The Ubisoft Legal Department
Clément Prevosto
Justine Toxé
Jillian Taylor
Elizabeth Cockeram
Caroline Lamache
Anthony Marcantonio
Victoria Linel
François Tallec
Julien Fabre
Clémence Deleuze

Cover art: Liu 'Sunsetagain' Yan

He just wanted a decent book to read ...

Not too much to ask, is it? It was in 1935 when Allen Lane, Managing Director of Bodley Head Publishers, stood on a platform at Exeter railway station looking for something good to read on his journey back to London. His choice was limited to popular magazines and poor-quality paperbacks – the same choice faced every day by the vast majority of readers, few of whom could afford hardbacks. Lane's disappointment and subsequent anger at the range of books generally available led him to found a company – and change the world.

'We believed in the existence in this country of a vast reading public for intelligent books at a low price, and staked everything on it'
Sir Allen Lane, 1902–1970, founder of Penguin Books

The quality paperback had arrived – and not just in bookshops. Lane was adamant that his Penguins should appear in chain stores and tobacconists, and should cost no more than a packet of cigarettes.

Reading habits (and cigarette prices) have changed since 1935, but Penguin still believes in publishing the best books for everybody to enjoy. We still believe that good design costs no more than bad design, and we still believe that quality books published passionately and responsibly make the world a better place.

So wherever you see the little bird – whether it's on a piece of prize-winning literary fiction or a celebrity autobiography, political tour de force or historical masterpiece, a serial-killer thriller, reference book, world classic or a piece of pure escapism – you can bet that it represents the very best that the genre has to offer.

Whatever you like to read – trust Penguin.